# ALL THE DYING CHILDREN

JAMES HALPIN

This is a work of fiction. While some real locations and long-standing institutions are mentioned, the characters involved are solely the product of the author's imagination. Any resemblance to actual events or persons, living or dead, is entirely coincidental.

For Jamie, my biggest critic and my greatest fan.

I love you always.

Three may keep a secret, if two of them are dead.
— Benjamin Franklin

There is not a crime, there is not a dodge, there
is not a trick, there is not a swindle, there is not a
vice, which does not live by secrecy.
— Joseph Pulitzer

The best way out is always through.
— Robert Frost

# PROLOGUE

When at first the children began dying, life in the rusted and worn coal country of Northeastern Pennsylvania seemed to continue on, much as it always had.

That is to say that, in many ways, it remained a land out of its time.

The region never fully recovered from the collapse of the coal industry after World War II, and the residents who remained clung tightly to tradition. On Sundays, abundant Catholics still headed in droves to towering stone cathedrals in the City of Wilkes-Barre. On warm summer evenings, churchyard bazaars fragrant with the smell of frying potato pancakes were all the rage.

Grandmothers prided themselves on their pierogies and kielbasa, and they still had the rare choice of two competing daily newspapers, the vestige of an era long since past.

Most nights, corner bars were lined with blue-collar workers — men whose grandfathers worked the mines — stopping in for a pint or two of cool amber Yuengling lager on their journeys home. Downtown shops closed early, and traffic on city streets was usually sparse by dinnertime.

On warm summer nights, neighbors would sit on the porches of their antiquated double-block homes smoking cigarettes and gossiping about whether anyone had seen the new family down the street. "They had the New York tags, heyna or no?" came the whispers, fraught with apprehension.

They had good reason to be wary. Metropolitan drug dealers had seen a business opportunity. Selling city drugs at suburban prices made for huge profits. They seized on it, with deadly results. Now the seemingly quaint existence of the people of Northeastern Pennsylvania had been marred by bathroom drug overdoses and the persistent rattle of late-night gunfire.

So it should come as no surprise that against this backdrop, nobody paid much attention at all to a teenage suicide. They mourned, to be sure. They reminisced and lamented the loss, shed tears and shook their heads at such a senseless tragedy.

But they were all so fixated upon the encroaching drug menace that all of them missed the terrible danger from within.

It took a teenage beauty sitting alone at her desk in the dark of night to shift their gaze. Kimberly Foster was an improbable harbinger, neither the first nor the last to die. The combination of her good looks and her frightful death merely ensured she was the first of the sad youths to be noticed.

# CHAPTER 1

*Thursday, March 22, 2018*
*1:37 a.m.*

The screen flickered to life, displaying the image of Kimberly Foster's sad, vacant eyes for the world to see. As Kimberly extended her arms to prop the cellphone against a book on her bedroom desk, the camera view widened to reveal her delicate features and sleek, flaxen hair. She sat back, carefully studying the phone screen to ensure she was properly framed in the shot. At this hour on a school night, most of her friends wouldn't be on Facebook to follow her live stream. But they would certainly find out about it the moment they woke up.

The room behind Kimberly was bathed in the soft glow of a nightstand lamp, revealing the typical clutter of a fifteen-year-old girl's room. On the walls, Kimberly had hung posters of Katy Perry and Imagine Dragons alongside a pilfered one-way street sign. A closet door that was left ajar revealed a closet rod overloaded with flower-print dresses, cashmere sweaters, and short checkered skirts. No fewer than two dozen pairs of shoes were lined up beneath.

On a shelf next to the closet, awards and trophies Kimberly accumulated over her short life sat on display – achievements for cheerleading, soccer, and an elementary school spelling bee.

Only the cheerleading stuck with her through the years, and Kimberly had a genuine passion for it. She was a captain of her squad at Hanover Area High School, just outside Wilkes-Barre. The other girls looked to her for leadership, and they respected her as a friend as well. When the girls got to gossiping about who was getting with whom and who needed to keep her legs closed, for God's sake, Kimberly was never among the subjects of discussion. She seemed to have a rare combination of good looks, intelligence, and kindness that made her one of the most popular girls in her class.

Which made what she was about to do all the more baffling.

Staring at the camera lens on her cellphone, Kimberly ran the top of her left index finger under her nose, sniffling as she wiped. Her eyes were glossed over and puffy, as though she had been crying – or as though she was about to. By the time she started her monologue, Facebook was showing her live stream had seven viewers.

"Hey everyone, I just wanted to say I'm sorry. I'm sorry for letting everyone down and for what I have to do tonight. I didn't want it to be like this. I just hope everyone I love knows it's not your fault. This just ..."

As she spoke, a friend posted a comment to the video.

"What's wrong?"

Kimberly barely registered the remark. A tear dripped down her cheek as she picked up the nine-millimeter Springfield pistol, the one her father kept on the top shelf of his bedroom closet. Kimberly racked the slide to the rear with a reverberating clack, chambering a round as she stared blankly at the camera.

Her last words came out softly, a suicidal poem delivered in a whispered chant: "They're watching me always. Nothing can make it stop."

Holding her death in her right hand, Kimberly raised the weapon to her temple and jerked the trigger.

In a sudden, violent burst, red mist exploded from the left side of Kimberly's head, leaving a blood stain on the wall that began to drip to the ivory carpet below. The gun was ejected from her hand as her head whipped to the side and she slumped out of her chair, landing in a pile on the floor. For a moment, there was dead silence in the room.

The first thing the Facebook viewers heard after the shot was someone, presumably Kimberly's soon-to-be grieving father Jack Foster calling out, "What was that?" Then came the sound of doors banging open throughout the house, the sound of confusion and chaos in the middle of the night. Kimberly's phone began to ring; apparently, someone who just witnessed the grisly end of her friend stupidly tried to call her, not knowing what else to do.

Then the bedroom door opened and Kimberly's mother looked in, staring uncomprehendingly at the body of her daughter and the bloody Rorschach test left on the wall, one final gift from her first-born child. A dazed moment passed and Sarah Foster ran across the floor, lifting her daughter's head and looking into unseeing eyes as she called out Kimberly's name.

For a moment, Sarah began grasping at the bloody bits of skull and brain matter staining the carpet, a desperate attempt to put the pieces back together and undo what cannot be undone. She began to wail as the other family members raced to the doorway, staring in disbelief. Another second passed before Jack composed himself enough to think to call 911. Then he saw the phone propped on the desk and the video feed on the screen. He slowly approached the phone, wondering what had just happened.

When he tapped the screen to stop the video, Facebook showed thirteen hundred and eighty-seven people were watching.

◆ ◆ ◆

Erik Daly sat at his desk in the newsroom, keeping an ear on the noon broadcast of the local news playing on a television hanging in the corner of the room. The police scanner by the window squawked to life as a dispatcher called medics to the scene of a crash on Interstate 81. There was no report of ejection or entrapment. Daly barely registered the exchange.

As the police reporter for the Wilkes-Barre Observer, he was responsible for covering mayhem — shootings, fires, crashes, and anything else that went wrong on a given day in Luzerne County. The more horrendous, or shocking, or sad the subject matter was, the better the story. Which meant that a good day for Daly was usually a pretty bad one for the people in his articles. Over the years, he'd had to learn to approach his interviews with tact, displaying the right degree of understanding while asking the prying questions he was paid to ask — on what is often the worst day of the source's life.

He had gray-blue eyes that looked sharply out from behind wire-rimmed reading glasses, combining with his sandy brown hair — always worn combed to the right — to give him a somewhat bookish look. At forty-three years old, he still had a wiry build, and the white dress shirts with rolled sleeves he wore atop black slacks always appeared a size or two big for his frame.

Sipping on a cup of black coffee, Daly peered through bloodshot eyes at the online court dockets, skimming through the overnight arrests for anything interesting. He passed over a burglary arrest from out in the sticks near Shickshinny, but stopped at a resisting arrest case from Wilkes-Barre. More likely than not, some dope fiend decided to rumble with the cops when they stopped him for stumbling around. Daly made a note to grab the complaint, thinking it would probably have some juicy details his readers would enjoy. There's news the reader needs to know and news the reader wants to know. Daly was committed to providing both.

As he moved through the docket, Daly heard the newscast turn to a story about a seventeen-year-old boy being credited as a hero for calling 911 and getting help when his grandmother fell down. Because of the boy's quick thinking, the pretty blonde reporter assured viewers, the grandmother survived and lived to tell the tale.

*For Christ's sake*, Daly thought, rubbing his temple. *Someone on the cusp of becoming a grown adult knew enough to dial three digits when his grandmother fell? Stop the presses. There should be a ticker-tape parade for this kid with the wherewithal to perform his basic civic duty.*

Daly knew and liked the reporter on the screen, but he cringed thinking about her stretching the story to fit the narrative her producer no doubt wanted. He wished television reporters would let the facts get in the way of a good story, at least every once in a while.

Daly continued running through the docket when the city editor, John Richardson, called him to editor's row, a block of cubicles in the center of the newsroom. Expecting to get drafted into chasing the "hero" story, Daly headed over, ready to take a stand. He had no intention of stretching the facts to fit a predetermined narrative, and planned to say so.

But to Daly's surprise, Richardson didn't want to talk about the television story. He glanced up and registered the bags under Daly's eyes as he waved him around the desk.

"Jesus, you look like shit," Richardson said.

"I had kind of a late night," Daly said, wishing he'd popped a couple of Advil before leaving the house. "It was a hell of a game. Utah beat St. Mary's 67-58 in overtime. My money's on Penn State and Utah for the final."

"You think the Lions can do it?" Richardson asked.

"Why not? It's been nine years since they last won the NIT. They've had plenty of rest," Daly said. "So what do you got?"

"Check this out," Richardson said.

Richardson clicked his mouse and began playing a video on LiveLeak.com. A pretty girl with tears in her eyes began talking to the camera. Together, the newsmen watched the scene play out, eyes transfixed on the gruesome fate of Kimberly Foster.

"She was a freshman at Hanover Area High School," Richardson said. "Facebook took the video down less than an hour after it happened, but someone had already posted it to LiveLeak. It's got more than 50,000 views."

"Shit," Daly said. "What do you want to do about it?"

The Wilkes-Barre Observer's policy was that suicides were generally not newsworthy. Publishing suicides would upset the families and could inspire copycats. But as is the case with most rules, there were exceptions. If the person was well-known, it would most likely be news. The same was true if the person killed herself in public. There was also a catch-all clause allowing for coverage of any suicide that editors believed had genuine news value.

So essentially the policy was that the Wilkes-Barre Observer didn't cover suicides, unless it did.

Kimberly Foster's death took place in the confines of her bedroom, which is just about the most private place in a teenage girl's life. But she also chose to broadcast it on Facebook in a video that had gone viral. Daly had to concede there wasn't much room for argument.

"I'll see what the cops have to say," Daly said.

"You good to go on this?" Richardson asked. "You look ... tired. This could be a big story."

"I'm fine," Daly said. "I'll make some calls."

Daly headed back to his desk, lifted the handset from its cradle and dialed the cellphone number for Detective Sgt. Phil Wojcik, the supervisor for Luzerne County detectives. The detectives were part of the district attorney's office, a creation of necessity in a county with seventy-six municipalities that were mostly small and poorly funded. When the local police department — if there even was one — lacked the training or manpower to investigate a major crime, the county detectives were able to step in and assist.

Wojcik had been a career state trooper before retiring into his job as a county detective. That allowed him to collect a pension on top of earning a handsome salary for doing essentially the same amount of work as before. But at fifty-three, Wojcik still had a genuine drive to be a cop. He wasn't just collecting a paycheck like a past-prime civil servant. He still had it in him to do some good in the world, and he was determined to leave his mark.

"I bet you can guess why I'm calling," Daly said when Wojcik picked up.

"The eighty-seven-year-old DOA we had in Exeter last night?" Wojcik deadpanned.

"Right. What do you know about this video?"

"Well, if you saw the video, then you probably know what you need to know," Wojcik said. "We had an apparent self-inflicted gunshot wound on a fifteen-year-old victim at a home on Lee Park Avenue."

"I did see the video. Pretty hard to watch. You got a name?" Daly asked.

"Kimberly Foster. A student at Hanover Area."

"What time was this?"

"The parents discovered her around 1:40 a.m.," Wojcik said. "She was rushed by ambulance to Geisinger and was pronounced dead upon arrival at 2:23 a.m."

"Autopsy?"

"No. It's pretty clear what happened."

"All right, thanks Phil," Daly said, hanging up the phone. He still had a few questions for Wojcik, but he wanted to post a breaking news update online first.

Daly quickly made a few other calls and then started typing, aware that the city's Other Paper — whose true name no dignified Observer reporter would dare utter — was no doubt frantically pursuing the story as well. This was a newspaper war, after all. The readers might not notice which paper had the story a few minutes before the other, but being first was a matter of professional pride for both teams.

The television news stations would certainly be on the story as well. It's said that if it bleeds, it leads. That adage has never been more true. To some extent, Daly couldn't blame the producers — images of a body draped in a white sheet bathed in blue and red flashing lights were much more enticing than talking heads debating some or another issue at a council meeting. They were interested in ratings, and for good ratings, you need good stories with compelling images.

In this case, there would be no shortage of compelling images. The question in the back of Daly's mind as he hammered on the keyboard was how much the local stations would show. No doubt the video would air repeatedly with an earnest-faced anchor warning in a grim tone that the images might be disturbing to some viewers. Of course, the anchor would really be telling everyone to immediately stop what they're doing to take a gander at some particularly sensational footage.

After about ten minutes, Daly called over to Richardson to say his update was filed. The initial version at least, he decided, wouldn't include Kimberly's name. After all, Daly would probably want to talk to her parents at some point. He decided it would be better not to anger them before he'd even had the chance to pitch an interview.

*HANOVER TWP. — A 15-year-old Hanover Area High School student fatally shot herself in the head early Thursday in a shooting that was captured on a viral video.*

*Police say the girl, who is not being identified because of the nature of the incident, shot herself after turning on her cellphone and recording her actions on Facebook Live. Facebook removed the video shortly after it was posted on the girl's timeline, but it continues to circulate on other websites.*

*The girl's parents discovered her in the bedroom of their home around 1:40 a.m. and immediately called 911, according to police. Medics rushed the girl to Geisinger Wyoming Valley Medical Center, where she was pronounced dead at 2:23 a.m.*

*The Luzerne County Coroner's Office has ruled the death a suicide and does not plan to conduct an autopsy.*

*Joseph McNamara, the superintendent of the Hanover Area School District, said grief counselors had been called in to help students cope with the loss of a classmate. He declined to comment about the student specifically, saying he wanted to respect the family's privacy.*

*"Our thoughts and prayers go out to the family,"* *McNamara said. "This is an unspeakable tragedy for the entire Hanover Area community and we will do everything we can to help those in need during this trying time."*

*Short and sweet*, Daly thought. Richardson gave it a quick read and got busy posting the story to the website while Daly gave Wojcik a call back to follow up on a few things. He started off getting some general information for a sidebar to the final story for the next day's paper — an explainer on how parents can spot depression and talk to their kids about suicide.

After a few softballs, Daly got to the real reason for his follow-up call.

"I had a few other questions about this case," Daly said. "For one thing, it seemed kind of strange for a teenage girl to use a gun. Don't most females use pills or cut themselves?"

"Usually, yes. But we do have cases of women using a firearm – especially if there have been failed attempts in the past. It's a lot harder to go wrong with a gun than a handful of pills."

"Did Kimberly have a previous attempt?"

"Not that I'm aware of, but it's still under investigation."

"Right. What about what she said at the end? That stuff about being watched and not being able to stop it?"

Wojcik hesitated, seemingly considering the best way to respond.

"We don't really know what to make of it," he said.

Daly could tell Wojcik knew more than he was saying. He decided to see if the detective would unofficially get him pointed in the right direction.

"What about off the record?" Daly asked.

"Off the record, a lot of times suicide victims will say and do things that don't make sense," Wojcik said. "I'm not saying it was the case here, but sometimes the person is under the influence and not thinking straight. Sometimes they're just so confused or scared that they can't get the words out. And that's if they even bother to leave a note or say anything at all. Unfortunately, a lot of times we just never know what caused them to snap."

"But what she said seemed like a little more than confusion. It was almost like some kind of chant. It just seemed ... out of place."

Wojcik hesitated again.

"We are off the record, correct?" Wojcik said. "I don't want this getting out there just yet."

"Sure."

"We're looking into that. It was a strange thing for her to say, and it didn't make sense. But that's not what concerns us most."

"What does?" Daly asked.

"We had a suicide last month in Kingston where a kid hanged himself in his family's garage. There wasn't any video in that case, but he left a note. It said the same exact thing."

# CHAPTER 2

*Friday, March 23, 2018*
*3:18 a.m.*

Daly awoke with a start, momentarily disoriented and confused about his surroundings. After taking a deep breath, he realized he was at home, alone in his own bed. In the corner, the fan he used for white noise to help him sleep continued to whir hypnotically.

The dream again. Always unnerving, and it always ended the same.

The dream took place in a desolate desert landscape, at a run-down motor lodge along the side of a lonely highway. For some inexplicable reason, Daly had been staying there with his wife Jessica and their three-year-old daughter Lauren.

He met his wife years earlier in college. Although it had been years since he'd last seen the inside of a church, Daly hailed from a deeply religious family. His mother insisted on a faith-based school, so Daly agreed to study journalism at King's College, a Catholic school in his hometown of Wilkes-Barre. He stumbled upon Jessica while on assignment for The Crown, the college's student newspaper.

It had been a warm spring day in May, and Daly was doing man-on-the-street interviews for a story about traveling during the upcoming Memorial Day holiday weekend. It was a story that few would read and fewer still would remember, but Daly took the assignment seriously. It just so happened that for his interview he chose the attractive woman in the short skirt who was sprawled on the lawn at Main and North streets — a place students converged, ostensibly to study, on especially spectacular spring days.

Never a ladies' man, Daly approached the encounter awkwardly, but somehow managed to make Jessica laugh and to walk away with her number. From the moment he met her, Daly loved her smile and the way she teased him. "Is this on the record?" she'd mocked during that first meeting. Daly tried hard not to blush as he smiled, finding himself infatuated with her golden locks and piercing hazel eyes. The mischievous, playful look she gave him during that first sophomoric encounter would stay with Daly forever.

Now, the look had entered his nightmare.

When it happens in the dream, Daly's in-laws are always down by the motel pool, sipping margaritas as some crackling poolside speakers broadcast Jimmy Buffett singing "Coconut Telegraph." Daly and his family are in their room when something terrible happens. Daly can never grasp exactly what it was, but when he comes to his senses he's holding a silver Smith & Wesson .38 Special revolver. The barrel is still warm to the touch, and Jessica's lifeless body is lying on the bed. A maroon puddle begins expanding out from behind her head, spreading like a tie-dye sunburst across the bright white comforter.

It's obvious the back of Jessica's head is mostly on the headboard and pillows, but still she continues to stare upward with that same playful look. Then Daly hears the sound of Lauren wailing in the corner. His hands shaking, he turns and tries explaining that everything will be okay even though it's pretty damned clear everything is not.

Daly tells Lauren to wait by the door. He looks around a moment before his gaze settles on a plastic red five-gallon can of gasoline sitting next to the door. In a panic, Daly upends the can and douses the room along with his darling wife's corpse.

Taking Lauren by the hand, Daly snaps a match to life and lets it fall gently to the floor.

As he goes to pull shut the hotel door, Daly notices another young girl standing in the corner. She's in tears and saying something he can't quite make out. She looks familiar but he can't quite place her. It comes to him after a long moment.

*That's Kelly.*

Daly feels like he wants to help her, but he can't control what's happening. He has the sense of watching himself as he pulls the door closed, muffling the sound of the crying child.

When the door latch clicks shut, Lauren stops crying and Jessica vanishes from Daly's mind. He takes Lauren down to the motel pool and joins Jessica's parents, Ed and Barbara Thompson, for a piña colada. As they sit sweating under the unrelenting desert sun, the crackling speakers blaring Jimmy Buffett are slowly drowned out by the rising, shrill sound of blaring sirens. Daly looks back toward the motel to see fire engines with flashing lights and a thick, black cloud of smoke billowing for miles into the deep blue sky.

Still, nobody seems the faintest bit concerned that Jessica is missing.

They continue sitting by the pool, watching Lauren splash in the cool, blue water, until the police come by asking if anyone had been staying in room 223. The guilt and shame overwhelm Daly as the memory surfaces of his beautiful wife lying in a pool of her own blood, looking eternally pitiful against the pure white bedspread.

Without prompting, Daly breaks down in tears and begins sobbing uncontrollably.

"I murdered my family!" he screams, holding out his wrists for the handcuffs. "I killed my family!"

Then he wakes up.

◆ ◆ ◆

Sleep was always elusive after the dream. For more than an hour, Daly lay in bed trying to drift back off until he was so worked up thinking about sleeping that he felt he would never slumber again. The sky was still dark and it was far too early for work, but Daly decided to get moving anyway. He got out of bed, hit the bathroom and padded over the hardwood floor to the kitchen to start a pot of coffee. Lauren wouldn't wake up for a few hours still, but it had been a long time since she was three years old. She could manage to get to high school on her own.

With the coffee brewing, Daly jumped in the shower, letting the hot water warm his skin in the chill of the early morning air. His waking mind had long ago learned to quickly dismiss the dream, and his thoughts turned to work.

He couldn't stop thinking about what Wojcik had said: that there was another case where a suicide victim used the same last words as Kimberly Foster. The problem was that Wojcik then got coy and wouldn't give up the kid's name. *Challenge accepted*, Daly thought. He decided to make it his mission to find out who it was and what else he could learn about the case.

Daly stepped out of the shower and dressed himself, then walked quietly into Lauren's room and looked down at her as she slept. As he watched her in peaceful slumber, he couldn't help but feel terrified by the feeling that he was losing her to womanhood. She had grown beyond his ability to protect her, and it made him feel small and useless.

He knelt down and placed a light kiss on her cheek, whispering for her to make sure to catch the bus. Then he tiptoed out of her room. Grabbing a Thermos of coffee, Daly walked out the front door into the cold morning and drove in darkness down the winding mountain road that took him from Shavertown to Wilkes-Barre.

The building and parking lot were mostly deserted when he pulled in about fifteen minutes later. A few early morning bosses were still finishing up their business with the carriers, but they paid him no attention. He swiped his electronic badge to get into the building, climbed the stairs to the newsroom, and logged onto his computer. He had a few emails about tips to check out, and knew he would have to make cop checks later, but first he wanted to start his project while the newsroom was still.

Looking around the darkened newsroom to ensure his solitude, Daly decided to get some music going. He turned up his laptop speakers and opened Amazon Music, clicking on a playlist featuring his latest obsession.

As a child of the 1980s, Daly had grown up listening to bands like Genesis and Dire Straits on MTV. One day, he heard the Ramones playing "Blitzkrieg Bop" and had his eyes opened to a whole new world. Punk rock's energy awakened an anti-authoritarian streak inside him, and bands like the Dead Kennedys and the Descendents became the gospel of a confused and rebellious teenage existence.

His aversion to authority ultimately brought him to the field of journalism. As a young student, Daly had been intrigued in his civics class to learn about the First Amendment. He marveled that the bedrock of America was a law saying the government couldn't tell him what to say or write. As he matured, the thought of exposing injustices and abuses of power — knowing the people in authority would be powerless to stop him — helped solidify his choice of careers.

Now well into middle age, Daly still had a dislike for authority, but his taste in music had shifted. When Jessica departed, Daly set aside his punk rock records and took up the blues. On its surface, the music seemed old-fashioned and tame, but something about the melancholy riffs and soulful crooning appealed to his subversive streak. Bessie Smith's mournful lamentations in "Nobody Knows You When You're Down and Out" were just what he needed on those lonely mornings after the dream.

As the opening notes of the trumpet kicked in, Daly clicked open the Observer's digital archive to begin his search. He didn't have much to go on, but he had enough that he figured the search should be pretty easy. Wojcik had said the death took place in February and that it was a kid. A search of the obituaries for the previous month returned a few hundred hits, but most of them could be dismissed at a glance based on age. Daly weeded those out and started up a list of the young deaths. Even though Wojcik had used the word "kid," Daly figured it was possible he was still talking about a young adult, so he included everyone under thirty.

When he finished, he had reduced the possible cases to only four names. And he remembered previously checking on each of them. The obits clerk was pretty good about passing along death notices for the young dead, in case a murder or fatal car crash had fallen beneath the radar. One of them was an infant whose death was ruled accidental, and another was a twenty-two-year-old cocaine dealer who had been shot at a drug house in the Heights. For the others, Daly had been told the cause and manner of death was still pending, but that they did not appear to be suspicious.

One of them deaths was a twenty-five-year-old man whose obituary said he "died suddenly" at home, which Daly knew is often a euphemism for a drug overdose. Combined with the age of the departed, Daly decided the man was probably not the one he sought. Instead, he put his money on the fourth body: Justin Gonzalez, a sixteen-year-old junior at Wyoming Valley West Senior High School. The obituary for Gonzalez said he had died "unexpectedly" on February tenth, a Saturday.

Daly printed out the obituary and ran Gonzalez's name through the archive, getting a few hits for the school honor roll, but nothing substantial. He also plugged the name into the online court record database. Juvenile criminal cases are usually confidential in Pennsylvania, so Daly didn't expect to find much, but it was always possible someone could have slipped up and put something on the public docket. No dice on Gonzalez, though – either he was clean or everything was hidden. Lastly, Daly ran the name through Facebook and found Gonzalez's page, which had been inundated with "RIPs" and other homages for a few days after his death. Since then, it had gone mostly dormant.

The profile picture featured the typical attitude and bluster of a high school kid. The kid in the picture mugged for the camera in a bathroom mirror selfie with a baseball cap turned sideways and pants that were in sore need of a belt. Daly saved the picture to his computer, knowing people have the tendency to ratchet up the privacy settings on social media pages as soon as they learn a reporter is sniffing around.

There wasn't much to go on — just a hunch based on the kid's age — but Daly decided to give it a try. He looked up the address, jumped into his car and headed over the Market Street Bridge to Kingston. After throwing the car into park outside the Gonzalez family's home, Daly stuck a slim reporter's notepad in his back pocket. If he were going to get a comment from a suspect, he would have kept it out, ready to write down whatever the person blurted out before the inevitable slam of the door. But for now, Daly just wanted to find out what the story was. If there even was a story.

Walking to the door, prepared to ask a barrage of questions about the family's late son's unexpected death, Daly wondered what the reaction might be. In such situations, some people will open right up, wanting their loved one to be remembered. Others will answer a few questions reluctantly. Others still will slam the door in a reporter's face — sometimes hurling threats to emphasize their point.

Daly rang the bell to the home, a well-maintained white and green foursquare house typical of coal country. After a moment, a woman in her early forties peeked out from behind a curtain on the front window, eyeing Daly suspiciously.

"I'm with the Observer," he said, waving a laminated press pass.

The lace curtain fluttered closed and a moment later Daly heard the clink of a door chain lock sliding open.

"Yes?" she asked through the glass of the closed storm door.

"Hi. I'm Erik Daly. I was wondering if I could talk to you about Justin."

The woman wavered ever so slightly, as though a sudden gust of wind had pushed her back on her heels. Her tired eyes watered for an instant. She glanced down the street, then met Daly's gaze.

"Why do you want to talk about that?" she asked.

"Well, I was looking into a suicide we recently had — you might have heard about the girl from Hanover Area," he said. The woman returned a slight nod. "Well, I was talking to the police about that case. There were a few strange things that we didn't put into the story, things I'm trying to look into now. The reason I'm here is that I wanted to talk about some similarities between her death and Justin's suicide."

Daly was going out on a limb here, using an old reporter's trick. He didn't really know that Justin committed suicide. But if

21

he acted like he did, the woman would either confirm or deny it.

"Suicide?" she asked, growing indignant. "My son didn't commit suicide. My son was murdered."

# CHAPTER 3

The living room of the Gonzalez home was tidy and showed some money. Sunlight from a large bay window glittered through the translucent white curtains, highlighting a large brown leather couch underneath. The couch faced a pair of reclining chairs, separated by a cherry coffee table topped with scrapbooks and family photo albums. Daly noticed that the room was bereft of a television set; apparently, this was the place Celeste Gonzalez used to entertain guests, relegating the tube to another corner of the house. Looming over the room was a large golden crucifix, displayed on a wall next to a mahogany grandfather clock that ticked away the seconds to eternity.

Celeste sat down on the edge at one end of the couch as Daly lowered himself to the other.

"So the police never announced Justin's death as a homicide," Daly began. "What makes you say that?"

"For one thing, I know my son. He was a good boy, went to church every Sunday. He made the honor roll most semesters. He had plenty of friends and didn't get picked on, at least that I know about. There's no reason he would have done that to himself."

"What exactly happened to him?" Daly asked.

"I really would rather not talk about it," she said.

"I understand. But it could really help me try to figure out what happened here," Daly said.

"I don't know," Celeste said. "I guess I can tell you. It happened the night of February ninth. My husband and I went out to see a movie that night — the Academy Awards were coming up and we wanted to see 'The Shape of Water' because it was nominated for Best Picture. We got home around 11 o'clock and when I came upstairs, Justin was in his room, messing with his laptop. I went in and gave him a kiss on the cheek and told him not to stay up too late. He was always up on the computer or playing that Xbox until all hours if I didn't stop him. He said okay and that he loved me. That was the last thing that he ever said to me: 'I love you.'"

Celeste paused as she choked up. Daly waited in silence, trying to appear understanding. He knew that with a good pause, most sources will start talking again to fill the void — sometimes saying things he wouldn't have thought to ask.

"We found him early the next morning," Celeste continued after dabbing at her eyes with a Kleenex. "My husband, Jerry, woke up around four o'clock in the morning to go to the bathroom. He checked on Justin because he could see a light shining beneath the crack of the bedroom door. He thought Justin was still up playing "Call of Duty" or something. When he opened the door, there was nobody there. Jerry looked around the house for a few minutes to make sure Justin wasn't in the den watching TV or something. When he couldn't find him, he came back up and got me.

"At first I couldn't believe it. Justin was never the kind of boy who would sneak off during the night. I asked Jerry if he was sure Justin wasn't down in the basement, but he said he was sure. As I reached for the phone on my nightstand to call the police, something outside the window caught my eye. Down in the yard, I could see a light shining in the garage. I hung up the phone and told Jerry. We went down together."

Here again, Celeste took a long pause, mustering the courage to tell a newspaper reporter about what must have been the most horrifying sight she'd ever beheld.

"He was hanging from one of the joists," she said. "There was a noose made out of a rope that had been in the garage. I can still see him, gently twisting in the air. There was an old folding chair tipped over under his feet. His eyes were still partially open. It looked like he was watching us."

"I'm so sorry," Daly said, pausing again so she could compose herself. "Was there any kind of a note left behind?"

"There was something pinned to his shirt. I don't know if you would call it a note. It was more of a memo. Or a poem or something."

"Can I see it?"

Celeste looked up, startled as if she had suddenly realized to whom she was speaking.

"I don't have it. The police took it," she said morosely.

"Do you remember what it said? Anything at all?"

"I don't remember exactly. Something about being watched. It didn't really make any sense."

"Did it end with: 'Nothing can make it stop'?"

"How did you know that?" Celeste asked suspiciously.

"The girl who killed herself, Kimberly Foster, used the same phrase. The one from Hanover Area."

"You see?" Celeste said, pointing with wide eyes. "I told you Justin didn't kill himself. How else do you explain them saying the same thing?"

"It is strange, I'll give you that. But we know for a fact that Kimberly killed herself because she recorded it. So I think it's safe to say it could be something besides murder. At this point we don't even know what the words mean or where they came from. It could be from a book or movie or something," Daly said. "That's what I'm trying to figure out. I want to know how Justin and Kimberly were connected — how they knew to use the same phrase. Are you sure they didn't know each other?"

"Not a chance. Justin didn't know anyone from Hanover Area. And we kept pretty close tabs on his Facebook page. I don't remember any Kimberly Foster on there."

"All right. Well, I'm going to help you look into this if you don't mind. Something strange is going on, and I'd like to find out what. Do you mind if I get a good number for you so I can call next time?"

After exchanging digits with Celeste, Daly got up off the couch and started walking to the front door, thanking her for talking to him at such a difficult time. As he was about to leave, he thought of something else.

"One more question: Why did you think Justin was murdered before you learned about the similarities in the last words?" he asked.

"His hands." Celeste said. "His hands were cuffed behind his back."

◆ ◆ ◆

Back in the newsroom, Daly sat down at his desk and logged back onto his computer. He clicked on the Chrome web browser and went online, intent on trying to figure out the significance of the words Kimberly Foster had last spoken — the same words that were pinned to Justin Gonzalez's shirt. He googled the phrase, expecting to get results for a song lyric or an obscure passage from a book.

Instead, he got nothing. No poems, no quotes from a movie. No indication that anyone else had ever uttered that exact combination of words before. It just didn't seem to make sense. How could two people who appeared to be complete strangers each be connected to the same esoteric phrase? *There has to be a connection*, Daly thought. *There's someone else.*

The conversation with Celeste Gonzalez still fresh in his mind, Daly decided to give Phil Wojcik another call. By the clipped answers he got, Daly could tell Wojcik was hedging, not revealing everything he knew or thought about the cases. But Wojcik was adamant that Justin Gonzalez died by his own hand.

"A lot of times, the family just doesn't want to believe it," Wojcik said. "They think their son was a good kid, not the type of person who would commit suicide. Even in blatantly obvious cases of suicide, the families are often in denial. They don't want to admit they missed the warning signs. They don't want to think that they could have intervened if they'd noticed a little sooner. Because then they would start to think it was somehow their fault."

Still skeptical, Daly asked how Wojcik knew for a fact that Justin killed himself. For one thing, Wojcik said, there was no sign of forced entry to the home or any indication that someone else had been there. The note was also in Justin's handwriting, he said. When he didn't mention the handcuffs, Daly asked the question.

"The only prints we got from the handcuffs were Justin's," Wojcik said. "We checked his computer and saw that he ordered them online himself two weeks before he died. Sometimes when people decide to hang themselves, they'll take steps to make sure they can't change their minds after they get started."

Daly ended the call and sat thinking for a minute. Two

suicides by two people who apparently didn't know each other, connected by a strange set of final words that didn't make sense. Daly decided he next needed to talk to Kimberly's family. That would probably be more difficult because her death was still so recent and so public. No doubt reporters from the Other Paper and the local TV stations had been at their doorstep already.

Daly decided to give the family the weekend to digest what had happened before he came knocking. Besides, he had some other work to get to: over on Carey Avenue, someone had been hacked with a machete overnight, and he had to cover a sentencing later in the afternoon for a drunken driver who ran down a ninety-three year old great-grandmother who had been crossing the street.

*Never a dull moment*, Daly thought.

◆ ◆ ◆

That night, Daly sat across a red and white-checkered tablecloth from Lauren at their favorite restaurant, Leopold's Pizzeria. The restaurant had burgundy mosaic-tiled walls covered with framed mirrors, black-and-white photographs, and nineteenth-century advertisements. To one side of the room, a bartender wearing a shirt and tie and a towel slung across his shoulder poured martinis behind a wide marble-topped bar lined with red and gold stools. The stools sat mostly empty for the time-being, but as the night wore on that would change.

At seventeen years old, Lauren was turning into a beautiful woman, with piercing green eyes and flowing golden hair that reminded Daly of her mother. Just like her mother, she had a fierce independent streak, and had for several weeks now been at odds with Daly over her plans for college. Lauren dreamed of going to Stanford University for pre-law. Daly knew she had the grades for it. She had always done well in school and had scored a fifteen hundred on her SAT.

Daly acknowledged she had a decent chance at being accepted, but counseled Lauren to go to Penn State instead. For one thing, he shuddered to think about how he would afford Stanford on his meager reporter's salary. His primary objection, however, was that it was on the other side of the country. Which, incidentally, was one of the things Lauren liked best about it.

Daly knew he was being selfish in trying to keep her nearby. He registered it but it didn't change how he felt. He just didn't want to be alone. Lauren could get a good education at Penn State or any one of dozens of schools that would be within driving distance for him – most of which would be considerably cheaper than Stanford.

So around they went, debating the merits of each other's visions until they decided they weren't going to come to an agreement and the conversation fell flat. Lauren poked at her salad and asked Daly how work had been.

"It was all right. I had the sentencing for Terry Fitzgerald. That vehicular homicide case," Daly said.

"How'd that go?" Lauren asked.

"He got hammered," Daly said. "He offered a half-assed apology and then started talking about how it didn't make sense that he was probably going to go to prison for such a long time when the person he killed was ninety-three and would probably have died soon anyway. I understood where he was coming from, but your sentencing hearing is not the place to wax philosophical on the justice system. The judge gave him up to twenty years in prison."

"Wow. When I become a lawyer, I'll make sure my clients keep their mouths shut," Lauren said, laughing her infectious laugh.

"That's right. If they're not sorry, just tell them to lie to the judge's face, if they know what's good for them," Daly said, taking a long sip from a Susquehanna Brewing Co. lager.

"Hey, I wanted to ask why you got up so early this morning," Lauren said after a short pause. "I thought you were supposed to be going in later."

"I was, but I couldn't sleep," Daly said. "You know how I get when I wake up in the middle of the night. I start thinking about stuff and get so worked up I can't fall back asleep. The more I think about it, the worse it gets."

"You had the dream again, didn't you?" Lauren asked.

Daly paused. He had told his daughter about having a terrible dream about her mother, but he had never discussed exactly what happened in it. Talking about it made him feel dirty and embarrassed.

"Yeah," he said.

"It wasn't your fault," Lauren said, watching her father's gaze shift to the pizza crust on his plate. Daly sat for a moment in silence before reaching for his glass.

"I know," he said, gulping down the rest of his beer.

# CHAPTER 4

As Daly stepped into the newsroom, he saw John Richardson hunched over in front of his screen scrolling through the news budget. Daly could tell he was already getting to work planning next Sunday's edition. The Sunday paper was the best-selling edition of the week and brought in the most advertising, so naturally Richardson was under the most pressure to fill it with compelling coverage — coverage that would stand out from the front page of the Other Paper.

Unfortunately, the added pressure on Richardson resulted in added pressure on the reporting staff. In the hyper-competitive environment of the newspaper war, reporters often responded by churning out lengthy reports about scheduling updates or mundane procedural explainers. Reporters and editors also often felt pressure to simply be the first with a story — even if the story was not quite ready for prime time.

As soon as Richardson motioned for Daly to come talk, Daly could tell this was going to be one such moment.

"Look, I know we need a lead Sunday story, but this isn't ready yet," Daly said. "We don't even know what we have. All we know is that two kids killed themselves and had the same last words. What would that story even say?"

"It's a mystery," Richardson agreed. "That's exactly what will make people read it. We've got a strange set of last words tying what is probably the most public suicide we've ever had to the death of another teenager a little more than a month earlier. Maybe they both read the same obscure passage or saw the same shitty B-movie last Halloween. Or maybe they both watched some kind of suicide challenge video. Hell, it could just be a coincidence. No matter what, people will want to know what happened here. We need a follow-up to try and explain why Kimberly did what she did."

"I get that, but if we do this story now all we're going to do is tip off the Other Paper so they can start chasing it too," Daly said. "I don't think anyone else knows about this angle yet. If we hold off a little longer, we can keep the exclusive for when we know exactly what's going on. I can still write it up as a mystery. But at least we'll have some answers then."

"Well, we need a Sunday story," Richardson said, looking away and shaking his head. "I'm not promising anything. Keep reporting it and see what you get. I'll see if we can find something else for the weekend. But if we come up short by Thursday, this is going to be it."

Flustered, Daly walked back to his desk. This could be a great story if told right, but now it was in danger of being revealed before its time — serving no purpose other than to tip off the competition. He put the thought out of his mind for the time being and got to work looking up Kimberly Foster's family.

A check of the White Pages website turned up a Jack and Sarah Foster listed at an address on Lee Park Avenue in Hanover Township. It was the only listing for that name on that street. *The parents*, Daly thought. He slipped a notebook in his back pocket, grabbed his coat, and headed to the door.

Daly pulled up to the house about fifteen minutes later, finding a group of cars parked out front. It appeared that the grieving family had company. It wasn't an ideal situation – Daly knew people were more likely to talk when approached alone or in small groups. A larger group increased the chances that someone would object to a reporter's prying questions. It could also embolden the subject to decline an interview the person might otherwise have gone along with. But Daly knew it wasn't a certainty. Some people prefer privacy. Others simply want their story told.

As Daly climbed the warped wooden steps to a home that was clearly over a century old, he could hear talking behind the peeling painted shingles. He rapped lightly on the door and a woman dressed in black answered, her eyes red and puffy from crying.

When their gazes met, Daly immediately knew two things. First, he recognized the woman from the video as Sarah Foster. Second, his presence on the doorstep was a mistake.

"Yes?" Sarah Foster asked.

"I'm sorry to bother you, ma'am. I'm Erik Daly with the Observer. I just wanted to see if I could talk to you about Kimberly."

Sarah's eyes narrowed, her gaze turning to steel.

"No comment," she said.

Hearing the exchange, her husband then came to the door.

"What do you want?" Jack Foster asked coldly.

"I just wanted to see if I could talk to you about your daughter," Daly said.

"Don't you have anything better to do than harass us? Get the hell off my porch before I call the cops," Jack said, slamming the door shut.

Daly turned back to his car, feeling stupid for imposing. He climbed into the driver's seat and sat staring blankly at the wheel for a long minute wondering how to proceed. He needed to talk to the Fosters to learn more about the cryptic message Kimberly had left. They obviously didn't want to cooperate. But they also almost certainly didn't know about Justin Gonzalez and the identical words he left as his parting message to the world. Daly wasn't much of a gambler, but he would be willing to bet that Jack and Sarah Foster would be very much interested in that information. He decided to give them a few more days to digest the tragedy and let things settle before he returned. When he did, he would be ready.

◆ ◆ ◆

Daly pulled back into a parking space outside the Observer and found himself hoping it would be a quiet afternoon on the police beat. He had thought of another loose end he wanted to check out. Celeste Gonzalez had told him Justin didn't know Kimberly — but how did she really know for sure? She said she kept tabs on his Facebook account, but that didn't mean she knew everyone her son friended. Daly knew most kids have hundreds of friends on Facebook, and it was highly unlikely Celeste knew them all. Daly climbed the steps to the newsroom planning to find out for sure whether there was any connection between the pair. Trust, but verify, as the saying went.

Logging on to Facebook, Daly went to Justin's profile first. Luckily his friends list was open to the public. Luckier still, Daly saw he had only two-hundred and three friends on the list. Daly opened another tab and went to Kimberly's page, seeing she had six-hundred and fifty-seven friends. It was a lot to go through, but Daly nevertheless breathed a sigh of relief. Cross-referencing two-hundred and three names against that would take a little while, but it could have been much worse.

He started by printing out Justin's friends list and then searching through Kimberly's list on the website to find any matches. It was monotonous, but pretty quick going. After searching through one-hundred seventy-six names, Daly had gotten three matching names, but he'd quickly realized they were different people with the same names. Then Daly keyed in the one-hundred seventy-seventh name and got a hit.

Daly circled the name on his list and then finished going through it, confirming that David Kowalski had been the only mutual Facebook friend of Kimberly Foster and Justin Gonzalez. Judging from the sweatshirt he wore in his cover photo, Kowalski was a student at Nanticoke Area High School. He also had an affinity for dirt bikes, all-terrain vehicles and monster trucks, as demonstrated by a series of images of mud-spattered vehicles and the motto listed on his introduction, which announced to the world that David Kowalski "like(s) it dirty."

Much of the rest of the page was private, so Daly wasn't able to see most of David's status updates or pictures. But one of the images stopped him cold. The photo, which had been uploaded the previous summer, was a group shot of a bunch of kids who appeared to be at camp. David was in the middle, smiling with his arms around Kimberly and Justin.

Daly snapped a photo of the page and image just in case anyone decided to remove it, then sent the picture to Celeste Gonzalez in a text message. As soon as it showed as sent, Daly dialed her number.

"Celeste? Hi, it's Erik from the Observer. I just texted you a picture. Did you get it?"

"Hang on," she said, fumbling with the phone on the other end. "Yes, it just came through. Oh my goodness ..."

"Do you know who that is with Justin?"

"I recognize the girl from the news. I don't know who the other boy is. I've never seen him before."

"His name is David Kowalski. Do you know the name?"

"No, I don't think I ever heard Justin mention him."

"Do you know how Justin knew Kimberly? Before it sounded like you were sure they didn't know each other."

"Yes, well I never met her. She never came around here. This picture looks like it was taken last summer. Justin spent a week at Camp Summit Lake out near Ricketts Glen State Park last July."

"How did he like it?"

"He loved it. It's a Christian summer camp. I think he had a great time bonding with other kids of faith," Celeste said.

"Okay. Thanks again, Celeste. I'm going to try and figure out who this other kid is. I'll let you know what I find out."

They ended the call and Daly grabbed his coat, planning an excursion southbound on the Sans Souci Parkway to Nanticoke. It wasn't much to go on, and Daly realized that the camp connection meant his two victims could have had dozens of mutual acquaintances from that summer.

But right now he decided to focus on David Kowalski: the only person with his arms wrapped around them both.

◆ ◆ ◆

The sloped streets of Nanticoke were lined with old coal-miners' homes, bunched tightly together amid the scattered corner bars and churches. The people were mostly hard-working blue-collar types, descendants of coal miners who bored the anthracite from the bedrock below their very homes. The collapse of the mining industry in Northeastern Pennsylvania brought hard times, not just for Nanticoke, but for the region overall. Now the mines that once helped fuel the country and sustain local families produced acidic water that poisoned area waterways. The homes on the surface were weathered and wilting, many resting atop crumbling foundations.

The home of David Kowalski was no exception. As Daly pulled into a spot a few doors down on Noble Street, he found an old, drooping structure with peeling paint and rusting furniture on a cluttered front porch. In stark contrast to the dilapidated state of the dreary home, a cherry red 1957 Ford Thunderbird sat shining at the top of the driveway, spotless and glistening in the sun.

Normally when Daly went to the home of someone who might be a suspect, he'd have a photographer staked out across the street, ready to snap a picture with a telephoto lens the instant someone opened the front door. Daly decided to hold off on the paparazzi for the time being, as to not spook Kowalski. At this point, he wasn't even certain there had been a crime to make Kowalski a suspect.

When Daly began ascending the three steps leading to the front porch, he glanced at his watch and saw it was still early enough that David's parents probably wouldn't be home yet — assuming they worked. That could also go in his favor – a parent standing behind David as a reporter asked him questions about two dead kids might get nervous and put a damper on the whole thing.

Daly pushed the button for the doorbell but didn't hear a bell inside. *Probably out of service*, he thought. He opened the storm door and knocked, closing the exterior door and stepping back just enough so he wouldn't be perceived as a threat. A minute later he heard some rustling inside, followed by the sound of giggling. David Kowalski pulled open the door and gazed out at Daly, his hair mussed and a grinning girl leaning on his shoulder.

A tall, thin kid with dark brown hair, David wore a cockeyed camouflage ball cap and a Harley Davidson tee-shirt. After eyeing Daly for a moment, he turned and smirked at the brunette using him for support.

Apparently, Daly had been right about the parents not being home.

"Hi, I'm Erik Daly with the Observer. Are you David Kowalski?" Daly asked, trying to sound casual.

"What do you want?" David said.

"I'm looking into a few deaths we've had in the area. Have you heard about Kimberly Foster?"

"Everybody knows about Kim," David said in his best no-shit-Sherlock tone.

"Well, the last thing she said on the video was pretty similar to something another boy said last month before he killed himself. It was an unusual thing to say and it didn't really make sense. I'm trying to figure out what it meant."

"Yeah?" David said, sounding bored. His mind was obviously on something much closer in space and time than the dead kids.

"The other kid was Justin Gonzalez. I saw on Facebook that you're friends with both of them. You're the only one who was friends with both of them."

As the words came out, Daly watched David carefully, looking for any sign of fear or recognition. But if David felt any of those things, he didn't show it. He looked back evenly at Daly, waiting for the next question. *Probably waiting for the chance to cut off the interview and get back to the task at hand*, Daly thought.

"How did you know them?" Daly asked.

"I met Kim and Justin at camp last summer. We hung out that week, did some archery and swimming, stuff like that. But I haven't seen either one of them since last summer. After camp ended, we friended each other on Facebook and hung out once or twice. But you know how it is."

"Did they seem depressed at all?"

"Like I said, I only ever hung out with them in person for a few weeks last summer. But they both seemed like normal kids. Kim was a cheerleader and seemed to be pretty popular. Honestly, I think me and Justin both gravitated to her, if you know what I mean. But he seemed like a cool dude too."

"Do you know why they would have said the same thing at the end? Does it mean anything to you?"

"Not really. I mean, what Kim said about being watched and not being able to stop it seemed kind of familiar. I can't put my finger on it. I can't be sure, but it seems like something I heard somewhere before."

# CHAPTER 5

The passage of fourteen years had done nothing to reduce the terror the dream brought to Daly. Every time, Daly woke up in a sweaty panic, the air in his bedroom seeming to suffocate him like he's trapped in a sauna. A moment after sitting up in bed, Daly's eyes would adjust to the darkened room and he would hear the constant whirring of his fan as he slowly remembered it was just a dream. Then, almost without fail, he would reach across his bed and feel the empty, cool sheets where Jessica once slept and be reminded of the vast void in his life.

Most nights when the dream came, Daly knew there was little chance of getting back to sleep. By the time his heart rate dropped and he assured himself of where he was, he was wide awake. Looking at the clock, Daly took solace in knowing he wouldn't have to get up for work for about six hours. He got out of bed and crept to the kitchen through the dark house, not wanting to turn on the hallway light and risk waking Lauren.

Down in the kitchen, Daly pulled open the refrigerator and looked inside, squinting in the cold, bright light. With another glance at the clock on the oven, Daly pulled out a bottle of Yuengling Lager. He popped the cap off with a satisfying hiss, dropped it on the kitchen table and sat down. As Daly tipped back the bottle, sipping the amber, rich liquid, he kicked his feet up onto the chair next to him. He decided to put on some music and called out to his Amazon Echo to play Muddy Waters singing "Louisiana Blues." As Waters sang the opening lines of his melancholy ballad, Daly took another sip of beer and started to let his mind wander. Jessica was on his mind tonight, as she always was after the unnerving dream. The dream made him feel ugly, and afterward he often felt the need to remember Jessica the way she was. He felt he needed to honor her memory.

And to apologize.

This night, Daly thought back to the first date they had after their awkward meeting on the King's College lawn. Daly had called Jessica up to ask her out to dinner, and surprised her when he pulled up to a sushi restaurant. After discovering that Jessica hated fish, Daly tried to recover by taking her to a downtown coffee shop. The place was low-key, bathed in blue lights, and had a guy playing a mediocre version of "Big Yellow Taxi" on a worn acoustic guitar. As they sipped their overpriced coffees, they started getting to know each other. With her disarming smile, Jessica teased Daly and asked if he wanted to be the next Dan Rather. Daly returned the gesture, asking if she wanted to save the world with a degree in psychology.

Jessica Thompson, he learned, was a native of Montrose who had descended from a long line of coal miners. Her ancestors had bored the earth with blackened hands, scratching and blasting prized anthracite away from the bedrock that held it in its clutches for eons. The men of the Thompson family rarely saw the sun; by the time they emerged from the subterranean labyrinth covered in sweat, blood, and coal dust, the daylight had often turned to a gray dusk.

When mining collapsed in the region, the Thompsons, like many others, had struggled to find a new livelihood. Jessica's grandfather had turned to farming, scraping together what savings he could to buy an ailing dairy farm with a dilapidated barn and sickly cows and try to start over. It was a hard life, with early mornings and work that lasted all day, seven days a week. But he fixed up the barn and eventually got the cows producing milk. Jessica's father had followed suit and took over the farm when his father could no longer manage it. Jessica, however, envisioned herself as something of a modern-day woman and decided she wanted to take the first opportunity she could to get out of the farmer's life. Wading through cow shit at five o'clock in the morning was not her idea of the good life.

She knew she wanted something more, but it wasn't until she was a freshman in high school that she found out what it was. The exact date her life changed was May 8, 1992. It was a Friday in springtime, a warm and inviting day after a long and brutal winter. Jessica and her older brother Kevin got off the bus that afternoon and rushed to the barn to get their chores done. Jessica had it in mind to go down the street to play with her friend Molly. Kevin, who by then was a high school senior, was hoping to borrow their father's pickup and go to town to shoot some pool with the boys.

After feeding the cows and getting the barn tidied up, they went home and washed up for dinner. Ed Thompson, usually a gruff man, had been in good spirits that evening — perhaps he felt a tinge of carnality himself because of the change in seasons. Whatever the reason, he didn't much question Kevin's request to borrow the Ford F-150, and he agreed to let Jessica go to Molly's until dark. Stuffing the final few bites of a pork chop into his mouth, Kevin said thanks and gave his mother Barbara a peck on the cheek. Then he grabbed the keys and ran out the door, leaving the torn screen door to slam home.

It was the last time Jessica ever saw her brother run anywhere. When the house phone rang a little after midnight, the police told Ed that there had been an accident. A drunk driver had swerved across state Route 167 and hit the F-150 head-on.

The family rushed down to Moses Taylor Hospital in Scranton and found Kevin unconscious. The only sound in the room had been the steady bleating of a heart monitor and the rush of air coming from a machine that was doing the breathing for Kevin. Jessica remembered thinking her brother — the person she had admired since childhood — looked so frail. Most of his skin had been covered in white bandages that were tinged with blood. His once-handsome face was bruised and bloodied, and tubes and wires protruded from his mouth and arms as if he were the subject of some horrific scientific experiment.

The doctors were quick to reassure the family that it might not be as bad as it looked. Kevin had shattered most of the bones in his body and had severe internal bleeding, but he wasn't paralyzed. There was still a chance of a full recovery.

When Kevin finally awoke a week later, it was apparent that would never happen. Kevin had been a smart kid who did well in school and who was always quick with a comeback. But the morning that he opened his eyes and looked to his mother without comprehension, he hadn't been able to utter a word. The doctors' talk shifted from hope of a full recovery to talk about speech therapy and physical rehabilitation. Best case scenario, they said, Kevin might be able to walk again one day — with the help of a walker. He would probably be able to hold a conversation at the level of a second-grader.

Kevin's transformation from an exuberant teenager who talked about joining the U.S. Navy to an incoherent invalid who would forever need help with the bathroom was too much for Ed

Thompson. His long workdays got longer as he disappeared into the barn for long stretches. Ed pretended to do work that had never before existed, and Barbara pretended she didn't notice the pint bottles of Jim Beam when she emptied the trash.

Jessica and Barbara did whatever they could to help Kevin's recovery. They rejoiced every time he picked something up by himself and every time he spoke a re-learned word. It was exhausting work, both mentally and physically. They continually had to keep at bay the thought that maybe Kevin was as far along as he would ever get. Disabled or not, this person was still the Kevin they loved.

It was during this period that Jessica realized what she wanted to do with her life. She wanted to get out of the farmer's life, sure, but she also wanted to do something meaningful for others. A degree in psychology, she decided, would let her work with people in need and help them overcome their obstacles. She could provide therapy and coaching to people like Kevin, and hopefully, she could have an impact on their lives.

Daly had sipped his black coffee and took in the story, feeling a little ashamed at having teased Jessica, even if it was in jest. She wasn't out to save the world. She just wanted to save her brother.

◆ ◆ ◆

After knocking back his third beer inside a half-hour, Daly decided it would be dangerous to have another and went back to bed. He drifted off still thinking about the lavender scent Jessica's luxurious, golden hair had during that first date. When he woke up again, it was already light outside and he could hear Lauren rattling around in the kitchen, getting ready for school. Daly shaved and brushed his teeth, then went to the kitchen to get a cup of coffee.

"Good morning," Lauren said. "Couldn't sleep?"

"How'd you know?"

"I saw some bottles in the recycling. And you got up later than usual this morning," Lauren said. "Plus, I heard some music playing at two o'clock in the morning."

"Nothing gets past you," Daly smiled. "Sorry, I didn't mean to wake you."

"It's okay. I went right back to sleep. Did you have the dream again?"

"Yeah," Daly said, embarrassed.

Lauren walked over to where Daly was standing by the coffee pot at the counter and wrapped her arms around him. She squeezed gently for a few seconds before talking.

"I really miss her too. But it's been fourteen years. You need to stop blaming yourself. What happened wasn't your fault, no matter how much you think it was."

"I know that," Daly said, his eyes welling up. "But I can't control my dreams. It keeps coming back, no matter how hard I try to get past it."

"Maybe you should see a therapist. It might help."

"I don't need a therapist," Daly said. "I just need a cup of coffee."

Driving to work, Daly tried to put the dream and the conversation out of his mind. It was a familiar pattern, and he understood Lauren's concerns. But he also didn't think therapy could do anything for him — because he knew why the dream kept returning. For years, everyone around Daly, including Lauren, had been telling him that what happened wasn't his fault. The problem was, he simply didn't believe them.

After arriving at the newsroom, Daly logged onto his computer and made a round of cop checks. Once he assured himself that everything was relatively quiet, he started on his top priority:

checking out David Kowalski. Their brief meeting the day before left Daly wanting to know more. He didn't know how David fit into whatever was going on, but right now he was the only person Daly knew who connected the two victims. Not only was he Daly's only lead, but Kowalski had also admitted that he heard the last words somewhere before. This kid knew more than he was saying, and Daly wanted to know why.

Court records didn't return any hits for David, but Daly expected that. After all, he was still a juvenile. Daly also ran David's name in the newspaper archives but didn't find anything useful. There were a couple of obituaries he was named in, and he had been photographed at one point as an attendee of the Cherry Blossom Festival at Kirby Park. Daly noted that he didn't come across any honor roll listings during his search.

Hitting a dead end on a criminal history, Daly turned to figuring out how he could learn more about David. He needed to talk to someone about him, but it couldn't be anyone who was too close. A friend of David's couldn't be trusted to be honest or objective. Daly needed to find someone who knew David well enough to give an informed opinion, but not someone who was close enough to put a spin on the negatives.

He found his answer when searching David's name through Facebook and seeing him tagged in a picture taken the previous weekend. David was one of about a dozen kids memorialized in the image, which was obviously taken at a house party. A few of the kids held cigarettes, and almost all of them held red Solo cups raised outward and upward as they cheered at the camera. Daly shook his head, amazed that kids would have so little sense as to allow themselves to be photographed at an underage drinking party. Not only that, but some of them had posted the proof online for the world to see.

After a little more investigation, Daly figured out a senior named Kristen Bartkowski had hosted the party. Apparently, her parents had been out of town for the weekend, so she took advantage of the opportunity by inviting over a few dozen of her closest friends. *That could be good news*, Daly thought. If the parents haven't heard about the party yet, it could be leverage to get Kristen to talk.

Daly couldn't be sure how closely Kristen knew David, but from her Facebook page, it didn't appear it was very well. For one thing, they only appeared to have a few mutual Facebook friends. Plus, Daly had not seen a single picture of Kristen and David together at the party. He figured good friends would probably have been together enough to have been photographed in their drunken haze.

Daly started to look up Kristen's address, planning to swing by just after school and catch her before her parents got home. But as he began checking the White Pages for a listing, he heard a call on the police scanner about a house fire in Exeter. The initial report had someone possibly being trapped inside. Daly decided instead of going the opposite direction to Nanticoke, he would just message Kristen on Facebook.

"Kristen, I'm a reporter for the Observer working on a story about some suicides we've had in the area. I was wondering if I could talk to you about David Kowalski. His name came up and I'm trying to get some background on him."

After hitting enter to send the message, Daly closed out of Facebook and ran the address from the fire through Google Maps. He got his bearings, grabbed his jacket and headed for the door.

◆ ◆ ◆

The fire took up more of Daly's time than he would have

liked. The report of someone being trapped had ratcheted up the urgency of the call, but when Daly got on the scene nobody would say anything about what happened. A gruff policeman with a big gut had herded Daly and the other reporters down the street. They could see smoke rising above the rooftops and little else. The burning building was obscured behind neighboring homes, and everyone with knowledge of what was happening was more than a block away.

Daly got on his iPhone, tapping at the screen with fingers that felt brittle in the chilly air of an early spring afternoon. He put together a few sentences based on what he saw – smoke billowing into the sky, the road closures in the area – and emailed it to the editors on the city desk. He also attached a photo he had taken with his cellphone before he'd been pushed back a block.

For the next hour, Daly waited for an update with the other reporters and photographers. At first, they went around knocking on doors to try and learn more about the fire and who lived in the home. But the media quickly exhausted the limited supply of residents who were at home on a Tuesday afternoon, having learned very little from their efforts. One old woman thought it might have been a house used by junkies to cook up methamphetamine. Another resident, a balding man in his mid-40s who smelled of Milwaukee's Best even though lunchtime had scarcely passed, informed the reporters that the house was vacant.

Unsure of what to believe, the reporters wrote the neighbors off. Perhaps they were both right.

Having run through the available sources, the members of the media huddled together in a circle, telling tales and jokes about past stories they'd covered together. When the fire chief finally made an appearance for the media well over an hour later, he revealed that the initial report had been wrong. There were no injuries and the only damage was to the affected structure, which was a vacant home.

The reporters dutifully took down the information and then packed up, disappointed to have wasted so much time on something that would warrant only a brief mention in the paper or on the six o'clock news. Daly jumped back into his car, cranking up the heat to restore the circulation to his fingertips. He banged out a few more sentences on his iPhone and sent the update to the city desk before realizing he had a new Facebook message.

"How did you find me?" was all Kristen had written.

She was clearly reluctant to talk, but she had responded. That was a good sign. If Daly played his cards right, he might get her to open up. He decided he would try and set her at ease by promising her anonymity. After all, she didn't appear to be a major source for his story; he was just trying to get a feel for who David Kowalski was.

"I saw on Facebook that he was at your party last weekend. I was trying to look him up because I'm looking into the death of Kimberly Foster up in Hanover Area. I don't need to use your name for this. I'm just trying to get some background information."

Daly hit send on the message and waited a few seconds until a check mark appeared, indicating Kirsten had seen it. When a response wasn't forthcoming, Daly put his phone back in his pants pocket and threw the car in gear. After making his way back out to U.S. Route 11, Daly crossed the Susquehanna River at the Eighth Street Bridge and then continued south to Wilkes-Barre on River Road. When he got back to the newsroom, he hung his coat on the back of his chair and sat down, waking his computer from its sleep. First thing, he clicked a link to Facebook to see if

Kristen had written back yet. He got a slight rush of excitement when he saw the small red dot showing he had a new message.

"I don't want my name used," Kristen wrote. "But yeah, David came to the party. I hardly know him, but he came with a group of guys my friend Katie invited. The whole time he was here he just sat in the corner, drinking. I kind of wished he hadn't come. He seemed like a total creep."

# CHAPTER 6

*Wednesday, March 28, 2018*
*10:23 a.m.*

The conversation with Kristen left Daly with one thought: he needed to find out more about David Kowalski. During their exchange of messages on Facebook, Daly had gotten Kristen's phone number. When he called to talk a little more in depth about the party, Daly learned that David was something of a dark horse in the school — the kind of kid who cracked jokes in class and sneaked smokes in passing. His parents were divorced and David was living with his father, who spent more time down at the corner bar than with his son. David's primary after-school activity was detention, as far as Kristen could tell.

He had not been invited to the party but had shown up with some kids who were members of a stoner clique who, because of their access to drugs, were able to transcend the traditional group boundaries and party with everyone from the jocks to the drop-outs. While everyone else at the party had been drinking and getting wild, David had been downing beers alone and off to the side, seeming awkward and out of place. He hardly spoke the entire time he was there, according to Kristen.

Kristen didn't think David had ever done anything violent, but after the conversation, Daly definitely wanted to learn more about him and how he connected to Kimberly and Justin. Daly decided to go to where the three apparently met, at Camp Summit

Lake, and see if anyone there knew them. He jumped onto the Cross Valley Expressway and sped across the sprawling Wyoming Valley toward the snow-capped peaks of the Back Mountain. To the east, stark white windmills projected from the mountain tops into the bluebird sky. Down below, a few logs swirled in the muddy waters of the Susquehanna River.

It took Daly nearly an hour to reach the entrance to the camp, which was down a rutted dirt road that was getting perilously close to being reclaimed by the encroaching mountain laurel bushes. As his car bounced down the muddy potholes in the road, Daly considered for the first time that it was unlikely anyone would be at a camp on a chilly morning so early in the springtime. As he pulled down the single-lane path that led to the camp office, Daly passed under a wooden sign with "Camp Summit Lake" displayed in raised cedar letters. A few more minutes bouncing down the dirt path that passed for a road found Daly pulling up to the camp office, a small log cabin that looked clean and well-maintained. Out front, a carved wooden black bear stood on its hind legs, ready to greet anyone who happened across the threshold. A couple of split-log benches lined the front wall of the cabin, which was situated between a rock-lined fire pit and a series of cabins to the rear where campers spent their nights in warmer weather.

To Daly's relief, the camp office's chimney was blowing out smoke.

Daly threw his car in park, cut the ignition and went over to knock on the cabin door. After a few seconds passed, he heard someone inside call for him to come in.

He pushed open a heavy oak door and a small bell jingled overhead as the door creaked open. Closest to the door, the office had several racks of shelves set up for merchandise and amenities unprepared campers might need. The shelves were mostly bare now, aside from a few tee-shirts and sweatshirts embroidered with the camp logo. At the far end of the room, there was a counter with a cash register and a door leading to what appeared to be a manager's office. Behind the counter, a man of about twenty-five was watching Daly with a bored expression as he stretched strips of brown rawhide across a pair of old snowshoes.

"Can I help you?" he asked. Daly could see his interest was focused on a small television showing the Philadelphia Flyers playing the Montreal Canadiens.

"I'm with the Observer. I'm working on a story about some deaths we've had recently and I was trying to get some information. Some of the people involved came here for a week last summer."

"Who were they?" the guy asked, his interest piqued.

"Kimberly Foster and Justin Gonzalez. Did you know them?"

"Justin died too?" the guy asked in disbelief. Daly gave him a moment to take in the news.

"Yeah, he died in his garage last month. Apparently, it was a suicide too," Daly said.

"Man, I can't believe it. They were really good kids."

"How did you know them?"

"My parents own this place, so I help out. During the summers, I usually work as a camp counselor. I help supervise the campers and do other odd jobs."

The counselor told Daly that Kimberly and Justin had not known each other before camp, but they became quick friends during their week there. On the second day of their week-long sojourn, Kimberly had twisted her ankle during a hike. She hadn't been able to walk back out on her own. Justin wouldn't leave her side and waited with her in the woods until the counselors could get an ATV to carry her out. After that, the two had been almost inseparable. Together they had ridden on horseback through the shadowy pine woods encircling the camp. Justin helped Kimberly hook her worm when the campers dipped their fishing lines into the murky green-brown waters of Summit Lake, as she feigned disgust. They had sat together at the evening campfires, toasting marshmallows and giggling as they whispered secrets in the dark.

"It happens with just about every camp we host," said the counselor, who introduced himself as Scott Taylor. "Classic summer romance. They fall for each other and exchange numbers at the end. Usually, it doesn't go much past that."

"What about with Kimberly and Justin?"

"I don't know about them. I didn't really hear from them after camp ended."

"Did anything ever seem wrong with them? I know it's been a while since you saw them, but I'm just trying to figure out why they might have done it."

"No, like I said, they were good kids. Seemed happy. I never would have thought they'd do something like that."

Now that Daly had gotten a little bit of background on the victims, he decided to move on to the real reason for his visit.

"What about David Kowalski? Do you remember him at all?"

"Did he die too?" Scott asked, startled.

"No, he's okay. I just came across a picture of him with Kimberly and Justin. I wanted to know how he fits in."

"David Kowalski," Scott said with a smirk, shaking his head. "Where do I begin? He was your typical problem child. Apparently he had a long history of trouble at school. He had a therapist – I think it was ordered by a judge because of some trouble he was in. I heard he tied a few M-80s to the tail of his neighbors' cat and blew it up. When the family came home, they found their cat inside out in the driveway. Anyway, the therapist recommended he come here as a way to get away from his problems at home. The first day he was here, we caught him smoking pot down by the lake. We confiscated the drugs but let him stay, since it was supposed to be part of his therapy."

"How did he do the rest of the time?"

"That was the only real incident we had with him. We usually keep the kids on a pretty short leash, so they're not really free to wander off and get into trouble."

"Got it. How about his relationship with Kimberly and Justin? How did he get involved with them?"

"I mean, I think it was just the same way all the kids got to know each other. They weren't especially close, but they were friendly. It wouldn't surprise me for them to be in a picture together. A lot of the kids take selfies together while they're here."

"Okay," Daly said, disappointed. David's background had certainly piqued his interest, but if he wasn't even very close to Kimberly and Justin, then it was all for nothing. "Anything else you can think of?"

"Not really. Well, there was one other thing I remember about David. He was telling everyone about some new app he found. It was some sort of a white noise app he was using because it gets really quiet in the cabins at night. I guess it helped him sleep. I only remember it because that was one of the only times we've had a bunch of campers plugged into headphones at night."

"What was the app?"

"I'm not sure. Slumber or Somber, something like that. No, Soma. That was it. Soma."

"Well, thanks again for your time," Daly said, passing Scott a business card. "If you think of anything else, give me a call at that number."

A burst of cool air hit Daly as he opened the door to the office and returned to his car. David Kowalski's background was certainly questionable, but all Daly had to tie him to the victims was a selfie and a tenuous connection for a week at summer camp eight months earlier. Daly jumped into the driver's seat and sat for a minute, thinking. Then he pulled out his iPhone and went to the App Store, keying in the word "Soma."

The first hit was for a messaging service, but the next result was for a free white-noise app. He clicked the icon and downloaded the app. Upon opening it, Daly wasn't very impressed. In contrast to other white noise apps that have a variety of sounds – waterfalls, waves lapping on a beach or wind blowing through mountain treetops – Soma appeared to have just one sound. Daly clicked play and listened for a few minutes to the soft rushing sound of static. It sounded like the static in just about any other white-noise app. He clicked it off and tossed his phone to the passenger seat, then threw the car in reverse.

# CHAPTER 7

*Thursday, March 29, 2018*
*8:55 a.m.*

Richardson's deadline was looming, threatening to reveal to the world what Daly had discovered without providing any answers in return. So far, he had little more information than when he started – still no smoking gun to connect Kimberly and Justin and to explain why two seemingly normal kids would have killed themselves. Naming David as an involved party at this stage was out of the question. As far as Daly could tell, he was just a mutual acquaintance who had some dirt in his past. Even raising the possibility of a connection between the deaths would be questionable at this point. The shared last words would suggest, at best, a shared interest or inspiration. At worst, it opened the door to the possibility that someone provoked their suicides. Celeste Gonzalez already refused to believe her son killed himself. Running a story suggesting he might not have — without evidence to back up the theory — would tear her apart.

Daly sipped a cup of black coffee as he sat at his cluttered desk, surrounded by leaning towers of discarded newspapers, court documents and press releases. As he logged onto his computer for the day to begin making police checks, he decided he would try to talk Richardson out of running a story for the weekend. There were still too many loose ends, and he had a feeling the story could be better with more time. But first, he would need to make another run at talking to Kimberly Foster's family. It had been a few days since he last reached out to them, and while they were no doubt still grieving, they had some time to process the loss. By now they might be more inclined to talk. At the very least, Daly thought he needed to make them aware of what he knew and the possibility that it could become a story in the very near future. He didn't want them to find out about it in the paper.

On his way out of the newsroom, Daly walked passed the newsroom mailboxes and noticed a letter in his inbox. He reached in and picked up the letter, which was in a plain white envelope. It was addressed to him but did not have a return address. The words were handwritten in block letters.

He slid a finger under the flap and pulled out a handwritten letter, also in block writing.

"MR. DALY: YOU KNOW WHAT HAPPENED TO THE CURIOUS CAT, DON'T YOU? BE VERY CAREFUL."

Daly dropped the note to a desk next to the mailboxes and took a step back. A chill came over him, sending an icy tingle up his spine. The most disturbing part of the message wasn't in the text of the letter itself. It was reading his home address scribbled as a postscript at the bottom.

As Daly tried to process what he had just read, his thoughts were interrupted by the squawk of the police scanner and a dispatcher's clipped voice. There was a teenage girl on the Market Street Bridge, reported as a possible jumper. Daly picked up his coffee and took another sip as he listened, trying to decide whether to get over to the Susquehanna River. He figured it could just be a kid who stopped to look at the water as she was walking past. Even if the kid was a jumper, there was a fair chance she would back down without taking the plunge. In either case, it wouldn't be news.

But the next dispatch that came across told Daly it was definitely a story. Multiple callers were reporting the kid had hit the water. She plunged beneath the icy, murky waters churning beneath the towering bridge and vanished. Daly grabbed his coat and ran out the door, walking the few blocks to the water's edge.

When he got to the bridge, he saw a few police cars stopped on the east side, the officers staring intently downstream in hopes of spotting the victim. Sirens blared between the buildings of the city as firefighters raced to the next crossing, an old dilapidated railroad bridge where they hoped to catch the girl coming downstream.

Daly walked up behind the policemen looking down to the river and used his iPhone to snap a photo from behind, with the river in the background. Then he started typing a web update to send back to the city desk. After sending back a few sentences saying police were responding to a report of a jumper on the bridge, he decided to go back and grab his car to head downstream. If the girl was going to be rescued, it wasn't going to happen anywhere near the Market Street Bridge.

◆ ◆ ◆

The body didn't turn up at the next crossing. Firefighters took to the water, combing the shorelines between the expanses in small motor boats for hours before conceding that the kid was gone. The cold, murky waters of the Susquehanna River ensured that rescuers couldn't see much of anything below the surface, and the swift current had likely carried the body miles downstream. When the river was ready to surrender its victim, the fish-eaten body would resurface, bloated and rotting.

Daly waited to land a brief interview with the on-scene

commander and then headed back to the newsroom, where he saw the paper's city government reporter, Joe Reed, had sent him a Facebook link. More precisely, Joe had sent the link to Daly and their editor, John Richardson. The link took Daly to the page of an Emma Nguyen, a sixteen-year-old junior at Coughlin High School in Wilkes-Barre. The profile picture showed a smiling girl with glasses and long black hair, her tongue poked out and eyebrows raised.

Her cover photo showed her wide-eyed and screaming on a roller coaster next to a boy who was similarly excited. The page contained selfies Emma had taken while dolled up in front of a mirror, her backside prominently on display. She had pictures with her friends at the Wyoming Valley Mall, trying to solve a corn maze, and of her kissing the boy from the roller coaster on the cheek while he wore an exaggerated look of surprise. One of her recent status updates contained a Graphics Interchange Format file detailing the various types of bitchface one could assume, if so inclined.

It was normal teenage kid stuff. Except for the most recent post. As Daly read the morbid post, the number of "wow" and "sad" reactions below ticked upward steadily.

"Are you OK?!" one of Emma's friends wrote.

"Call me!" wrote another.

It was apparent to Daly that this was a suicide note, and that the body that would wash up downriver in Bloomsburg or Sunbury later in the spring would be that of Emma Nguyen. The note started off with an apology, as many of them do. Emma went on to explain how hard things had been on her. She had big plans to go to State College and study at Penn State, where she wanted to take the first steps to begin a career as a doctor. Then she got pregnant and that aspiration ground to a thorough halt.

Emma figured she probably wouldn't even be able to finish high school, let alone get all the way through medical school. And forget telling her parents about it. They would absolutely kill her.

Instead, Emma decided to do the job herself. Toward the bottom of the note, the tone changed considerably, and Emma's writing became less coherent. Daly knew what was coming even before he got to it. There on the page before him – for the whole world to see – were the same last words he'd seen before.

Verbatim.

"They're watching me always. Nothing can make it stop."

Any thought of putting off the story was now gone. Now the exact passage that Kimberly Foster had used in her very public video had been written in another suicide note on a public Facebook page.

While Emma's post would most likely not go viral like Kimberly's video did, the Other Paper would surely see it. And someone over there was also certain to make the connection between the girls' cryptic last words. He'd barely finished reading Emma's suicide note when he noticed Richardson hovering over his desk, a sparkle of excitement gleaming in his eyes.

"Did you see that email?" he asked.

"Yeah. I'll plan on filing something for tomorrow to make the connection between the three cases. I figure it's out there already now. If we don't report it, someone else will."

"Right," Richardson said. "Why don't you go back to Kowalski and see what he says about it. See if he knew Emma and if he knows anything about what's going on. We'll need to be careful with this. We don't want to make him look like a suspect unless he gives something up. Let's see what he says and we'll decide whether to mention him or not."

Daly turned back to his computer and scrolled through

Emma's Facebook friends list, searching for David Kowalski or any other names that might stand out. She had a pretty extensive list – more than eight hundred people – but David was not among them. Next, Daly grabbed his cellphone and put in a call to Celeste Gonzalez, informing her about the latest death and Emma's final statement to the world. Daly could hear a slight gasp on the other end of the phone as he relayed the information. He knew that now nothing would ever convince Celeste Gonzalez that her son took his own life. He asked her if the name Emma Nguyen sounded familiar, and texted her a picture he snapped from her Facebook page. Celeste was adamant she had never seen or heard about the girl.

Thanking her for her time, Daly ended the call and set out to pay David Kowalski another visit.

◆ ◆ ◆

The second meeting with David Kowalski was less cordial than the first. Again, Daly had waited until school was out and David was likely to be home alone, and again he found him there without a parent in sight.

"What do you want?" David asked coldly after swinging the front door open.

"I got your note," Daly said, squinting.

Kowalski was the only potential suspect Daly had contacted since the case began, so he felt confident the note had been his. Accusing him was a gamble, but Daly figured if Kowalski had nothing to do with it he wouldn't understand the comment anyway.

"What note?" Kowalski stared back evenly, betraying nothing.

Daly watched Kowalski hard for a long minute, trying to gauge the response. He didn't know this kid well, but he appeared to be genuinely confused. Daly decided to change directions.

"There was a suicide this morning. A girl jumped from the Market Street Bridge and is presumed dead," Daly said.

"So?" David asked, clearly annoyed at being disturbed for a second time.

"She left a note on Facebook. She used the same phrase that Kimberly and Justin did. Word for word," Daly paused to let the information sink in, closely watching David's reaction. David just stared back, unblinking. He either had no idea what Daly was implying or he had one hell of a poker face.

"Did you know Emma Nguyen?" Daly continued.

"No, I don't think so. Where did she go?"

"Coughlin High."

"I don't know anyone at Coughlin."

Daly pulled out his cellphone and punched in the password, pulling up Emma's Facebook photo.

"Are you sure you never saw her before?" he asked.

David looked at the picture and shook his head, returning to meet Daly's gaze. "I don't know her," he said.

"Do you have any idea why these three would have said the same thing? You said before you thought you'd heard it before."

"I'm not sure. I thought maybe it sounded familiar. I know Kim was into poetry and stuff like that. She was into some pretty weird stuff when we were at camp. Maybe she got it from there."

"What kind of weird stuff?" Daly asked.

"I don't remember exactly. I know there was one about some rich guy everyone idolized. He killed himself. Maybe he was the inspiration," Kowalski snickered.

It sounded familiar, and Daly thought for a moment, trying to recall a poem he'd read years ago. Then it came to him, the iconic work by Edwin Arlington Robinson:

> *So on we worked, and waited for the light,*
> *And went without the meat, and cursed the bread;*
> *And Richard Cory, one calm summer night,*
> *Went home and put a bullet through his head.*

"Was it 'Richard Cory'?" Daly asked.

"That might have been it. It was a while ago."

"But if Kim got the phrase from a poem, how would the others have known to use it?"

"I'm sure I don't have to tell you that Justin was all about that. He was doing everything he could to hook up with Kim. It was kind of pathetic if you ask me. But it wouldn't surprise me if he started getting into poetry so he could get into something else, if you catch my drift."

"And Emma?" Daly asked, again seeking some sign of recognition or acknowledgment.

He got nothing.

"You're the reporter," David shot back. "Why don't you find out?"

# CHAPTER 8

The newsroom was humming, a soft murmur of reporters' telephoned questions being answered by the sound of fingers feverishly tapping keyboards to transcribe quotes for news stories. Above, a muted flat-screen television was tuned to CNN as one host after another recapped the same story of the day, always over a "Breaking News" banner — no matter how long the story had been regurgitated. A printer whirred as it methodically spat out pages, collating and piling up copies of the news budget for the afternoon budget meeting, in which the editors would decide where to run stories in the next day's edition.

After leaving Kowalski's house feeling somewhat defeated, Daly knew that the kid's name wouldn't even appear in the same newspaper as the story about the deaths. David Kowalski was either an innocent kid or a master manipulator, but the result for Daly's story would be the same. A quick conversation with John Richardson confirmed as much.

But now Daly waited to learn the answer to a different question altogether: whether he was doing a story at all. After he had returned to the newsroom, Daly put in a call to Phil Wojcik to verify the victim's identity. After all, he wasn't about to base a story about a fatality on a teenage kid's Facebook page.

Wojcik confirmed the suspected victim was Emma Nguyen,

age sixteen, who had last been seen leaving home on her way to school that morning. The body had not been recovered and the search was indefinitely suspended. Most likely someone would find it downriver in the coming days or weeks.

Daly then asked again about the Facebook message and the apocalyptic last words the three victims shared.

"My editor wants to run a story connecting the three victims with their last words. There's three cases now, so it seems like way more than a coincidence."

"I thought I told you about that off the record," Wojcik bristled.

It was true that the information Wojcik gave off the record was the reason Daly was able to connect Justin to the others, but Daly had since independently verified the information with Celeste Gonzalez. To Daly's thinking, there was no violation of the off-the-record agreement because he didn't plan to attribute the information to Wojcik at all. As Daly explained his thought process to Wojcik, the detective grew increasingly irritated.

"I gave that to you with the understanding you wouldn't use it. If you run this story now, it could really fuck us," Wojcik said.

"So you are looking for a suspect?" Daly asked.

"It's an ongoing investigation," Wojcik replied coldly.

"Look, I'm just trying to figure out the lay of the land. If there's a reason you want us to hold the story, I need to know it so I can explain it to my editors."

"Why should I tell you anything? I gave you something off the record and now you're trying to screw me over by printing it."

Getting off-the-record information to guide a reporter's questions and verify the facts through other sources is a big reason why reporters agree to go off the record in the first place, but Daly decided to let it go for now.

"Look, if you tell me — off the record — why you don't want us to print the story, I'll see what we can do. Right now, my editor is planning on a story for A1 tomorrow."

Begrudgingly, Wojcik explained that he didn't want a story because detectives were looking into the connection between the deaths. They didn't know that there was someone behind the scenes coaxing the victims into suicide, but they were looking into the possibility. The last words and the connection at camp – at least between Kimberly and Justin – was enough to warrant a closer look.

"I can't tell you what to publish, but if you guys do a story now suggesting there could be a connection, it would really screw our investigation," Wojcik said. "We don't have a suspect, but if there is one he would disappear."

Afterward, Daly dutifully went to Richardson to convey the detective's concerns. There were a few variables to consider here, not the least of which was that Wojcik was a good source. When the bodies fell, or the handcuffs snapped shut, Wojcik was usually good for some inside information that wasn't in the court documents. At the very least he was usually good for a heads-up about when the perp would be making an appearance for an after-hours arraignment. Crossing him on a case like this could put Daly on his bad side, and that could mean preferential treatment for the guys at the Other Paper across town.

And, of course, the editors would also have to consider the merits of Wojcik's argument, which was sound. If someone out there was urging teens to end their lives in dramatic fashion, the Observer certainly didn't want to be responsible for tipping him off and allowing him to slip away. The last thing the editors would want would be the district attorney on the television news declaring that county detectives would have caught a serial child killer but for coverage in the Wilkes-Barre Observer that tipped him off and allowed him to escape.

Then again, the editors also had to consider the public's need to know. The parents of the Wyoming Valley were, at the moment, entirely ignorant of the possibility their children could be in danger. Without knowing that someone might be manipulating kids into suicide, parents would have no idea to keep closer tabs on their children. Daly felt the newspaper had an obligation to warn them, even if the police objected. Like the police, he couldn't say for sure that someone was behind the suicides.

But it was certainly starting to feel that way.

As he waited for the editors to make a decision, Daly ran Emma's name through the archive. Emma Nguyen, daughter of Plains Township residents Vu and Linh Nguyen, had been in a spelling bee a few years back, but Daly didn't see much else on her.

He decided to reach out to the Nguyens. Ordinarily, he would go in person for such an encounter, but it was getting late and he had a date to meet up with Lauren for dinner. He also suspected the Nguyens would have little interest in talking to a reporter just then. He dialed the digits but got no answer. He left a brief message, saying he was writing a story and wanted to talk about Emma. Then he clicked the phone down into his cradle.

When the budget meeting broke up, the editors filed out of the glass-enclosed meeting room and headed to their desks to start reading copy. Richardson veered over to Daly's desk on his way to the editors' pod to deliver the verdict.

"We're going with it, but we don't want to overstate the case," Richardson said. "We feel that the information is out there already, so people will probably start making the connection on their own. And parents need to know that there's a possibility someone could be out there encouraging kids to commit suicide. That information could save someone's life. It would be irresponsible not to print it. But we also don't want to start a panic. Let's do a straight news lead about the jumper and get into the possibility of a connection further down. Make sure you're careful not to suggest there's a definite connection."

"What about the investigation?" Daly asked, seeking an official response to the obvious question Wojcik would ask.

"We don't want to make a suspect go underground, but we think the risk to public safety outweighs that possibility. Besides, if someone is responsible for this, he's probably already hiding. That's why the police are trained to track down the bad guys."

Daly put in a call to Wojcik to deliver the decision, a professional courtesy that would hopefully soften the blow. Wojcik wasn't happy about it, but he thanked Daly for letting him know. He agreed to answer a few questions on the record for the story before Daly ended the call. Then Daly got to work, typing intently on the keyboard as he cranked out copy for the next day's edition.

> *WILKES-BARRE – A teenage girl jumped from the Market Street Bridge into the cold waters of the Susquehanna River on Thursday morning and is presumed dead, according to police.*
>
> *The girl, identified by the Luzerne County Coroner's Office as 16-year-old Emma Nguyen, was reported to have jumped from the bridge shortly after 9 a.m., after passers-by had seen her loitering in the area, said Capt. John Miller, of the Wilkes-Barre Fire Department.*
>
> *Firefighters rushed boats to the river downstream at the Black Diamond Bridge and searched for several*

*hours, but were unable to locate the girl, he said.*

*"Crews conducted an extensive search of the river, but were hampered by snow melt," Miller said at the scene. "The river is muddier and moving faster than normal."*

*Nguyen was a junior at Coughlin High School who made the honor roll last semester and who was active in the student council. Prior to jumping into the river Thursday morning, she left a post on her Facebook page apologizing and saying her plans to go to college and medical school had been ruined because she was pregnant.*

*The note ended with a strange phrase – a phrase police say they have heard before.*

*"They're watching me always. Nothing can make it stop," Nguyen wrote.*

*The words are identical to the last words spoken by 15-year-old Hanover Area High School student Kimberly Foster, who fatally shot herself last week in a Facebook Live video that went viral.*

*The Wilkes-Barre Observer has also learned a similar phrase was used by Justin Gonzalez, a 16-year-old Wyoming Valley West Senior High School student who police say hanged himself in his family's garage in Kingston on Feb. 10.*

*Gonzalez's mother, Celeste Gonzalez, says she doesn't believe her son, a devout Christian, would have committed suicide.*

*"My Justin was a loving, caring boy who would never want to hurt those he loved," Celeste Gonzalez said in a recent interview. "He was making plans to go back to*

*summer camp at the end of the school year. Why would he do that if he was going to end it all?"*

*Celeste Gonzalez also noted that Justin's hands were handcuffed behind his back. She maintains that is proof he didn't kill himself.*

*But Luzerne County Detective Phil Wojcik said the only prints on the handcuffs belonged to Justin, and that there was no evidence that anyone else was present when he died. Victims will sometimes restrain themselves to prevent them from turning back, he said.*

*However, Wojcik said detectives were looking into the similarities in the final words of the three teenage victims. While there is no indication anyone else was involved, police are trying to understand where the phrase came from, he said.*

*"It is a strange coincidence for three people who died relatively close together to use the same phrase," Wojcik said. "We're just doing our due diligence."*

# CHAPTER 9

*Thursday, March 29, 2018*
*5:40 p.m.*

Sitting across from Lauren at Leopold's Pizzeria, Daly was struck by how close she was to becoming an independent woman. He was rightly worried about losing her. So far she'd been occupied with the high school marching band and her friends, and hadn't had any serious boyfriends. There had been some flirtations, of course, and a boy or two had come by the house over the years to do homework, but Lauren never seemed to keep the same one around long. Daly knew that one day – probably sooner than later – she would meet someone, or leave for Stanford, or just move to her own place across the Valley. His little girl would be gone.

As they shared the house specialty – a Stromboli stuffed with meat, cheese and peppers – Daly told Lauren about his day and the story. He skipped over the threatening letter he'd received that morning. Getting hate mail went with the job, and he didn't want Lauren to worry unnecessarily.

"What if the guy gets away with it because of your story?" she asked.

"We don't even know if there is a guy," Daly said. "Besides, don't the parents have a right to know if someone is out there trying to kill their kids?"

"I guess so. But it seems kind of wrong to print the story if the police think it could help a bad guy," she said.

"Well, we don't work for the police. We work for the readers — the public. Sometimes we have to do things the police don't like or agree with, but I think we both usually have people's best interests in mind."

Daly decided to change gears, so he asked Lauren about her day. It seemed Lauren was being unusually coy. When she said everything had been fine, Daly pressed for more details and learned her friend Mackenzie was also thinking about going away to college.

As Daly nodded and raised a bottle of Yuengling to his lips, Lauren went on to reveal that someone had asked her to the senior prom.

*Talk about burying the lede*, Daly thought.

"Who is he?" he asked.

"Kevin Fitzgerald," Lauren said, suddenly keenly interested in her plate.

"Fitzgerald," Daly said, mulling the name. "The same Kevin Fitzgerald whose father is now in prison?"

"Come on dad, he's a nice guy," Lauren said. "Kevin is, anyway."

A few years back, Daly had covered the story. The Fitzgerald family lived in an exclusive section of Dallas Township, one of the most expensive areas around. Bob Fitzgerald owned a heating and plumbing business and had done quite well for himself. Low-budget ads that ran between the local news broadcasts told viewers to "call Bob for the job" when their furnace quit. Over the years the business had amassed a small fleet of trucks and technicians to serve the region.

The empire came crashing down on New Year's Day in 2014. Bob had spent the day drinking, so by the time he began arguing with his wife Leslie that evening, his slurred words were belched out in a haze of foul-smelling gin. Bob accused Leslie of cheating on him, which to Daly's understanding was probably true. Leslie told Bob she couldn't take his drinking and his mood swings anymore. She demanded a divorce, so Bob ended the relationship on the spot with a shot from a forty-five-caliber Glock. Little Kevin Fitzgerald, then only twelve, came to the door of his parents' bedroom just in time to see the blood spatter exploding onto the wall from the second shot, which his father sent through his own head.

But as Daly had seen before, oftentimes that second shot is the harder one to make. Maybe the killer is shaking with rage or fear, or maybe he simply lacks the commitment to do the job right. Whatever the reason, over the years Daly often had to qualify that the murder-suicides he covered had been, in fact, attempted. But the attempt was always on that second shot.

Bob Fitzgerald went down, but he wasn't out. After a few months in the hospital, the doctors had fixed him well enough to stand trial for murder. Now, he would almost certainly never again see the outside of a prison.

The little boy who witnessed that atrocity — the child who ran into the room screaming as the blood from his parents soaked through his white tee-shirt — was now about to take Daly's daughter to the formal dance of the season for the seniors of Dallas High School.

"I'm not sure how I feel about that," Daly said.

"You should feel happy for me," Lauren replied.

"I know. I'm happy someone asked you to the prom," he said. "I just don't know how I like it being Kevin Fitzgerald."

"You can't blame him for what his father did. He's a really good guy. I think you'll like him."

"All right. Why don't you bring him by the house sometime so

74

I can meet him?"

Aside from his concern about a murderer's son taking his daughter out, Daly was also worried about how that meeting would go over. He had covered the murder, after all, and had aired Kevin's parents' dirty laundry out for the world to see. Some people understand a reporter is just doing his job. Others take it personally.

"I'll try to be good," Daly added.

"Thank you. Just give him a chance," Lauren said. "Aren't you always the one telling me not to judge people based on appearances?"

"You're right. And I will," Daly said, wiping his mouth and dropping the napkin on his plate. "You about done? I want to get going. Penn State is playing Utah tonight in the NIT."

"Ugh ... I hate basketball," Lauren grumbled.

"But you love me," Daly said with a smile.

◆ ◆ ◆

The sound of shattering glass tore Daly from his sleep. He looked to his nightstand. Three empty beer bottles sat next to a clock that showed it was just after 1:30 a.m. The Nittany Lions had won the championship and Daly had celebrated accordingly. He had only the vaguest recollection of bringing a few beers to his bedroom for a nightcap. There was no recollection of how or when he went to sleep.

Disoriented and startled, Daly looked around his bedroom, wondering what he had just heard. Everything seemed to be in place. In the corner, the fan continued its monotonous whirring. The unused sheets on the other side of the bed were still cool to the touch. Daly began wondering if the sound had been a dream.

Not the recurring nightmare, but some perhaps some other dream that had startled him out of sleep.

He was abruptly jarred from his thoughts by the high-pitched shrieking of a smoke detector in the hallway, its blaring alarm cutting through the nighttime silence like a razor. Daly jumped out of bed and opened his door to find a wall of black smoke that rushed at him, obscuring everything but the faint orange glow of fiery death downstairs in the living room. Immediately, Daly's mind went to Lauren, who had been sleeping in her room down the black hallway. He had to get her out.

"Lauren!" he screamed.

Daly began feeling his way down the corridor, his eyes stinging and his lungs burning from the billowing smoke that had invaded the home. He screamed for his daughter once more and tried holding his breath as he made his way to her room. His lungs, full of smoke and poison, raged in his chest and his mind began feel woozy and lightheaded as he reached Lauren's door. He crouched low to the floor as he turned the knob and pushed his way in, quickly slamming the door behind him. Gasping for fresh air, Daly wiped at his tear-soaked eyes and tried scanning the room.

"Lauren!" he yelled as he ran to her bedside. "Get up!"

He put his hand on the blanket to shake her. Lauren wasn't there.

In a panic, Daly ran to the closet in hopes Lauren had taken shelter there. It too was empty. His daughter was missing and thick black clouds of smoke and red-orange tendrils of flame were quickly overrunning the house. Daly didn't know what to do.

Desperate to find his baby, Daly ran back to the bedroom door, opening it to find the wall of black smoke had extended from floor to ceiling and grown so thick he could no longer see the glow of the flames downstairs. Determined not to leave Lauren to a terrible death, Daly screamed and began feeling his way back through the hallway.

The smoke seared his eyes like hot coals, producing a torrent of tears that left him blind. Blistering heat from a blaze he could not see raged against his skin, scalding his bare feet on the hardwood floor and his hands each time Daly groped the walls to get his bearings. The lungful of air he gulped in Lauren's room had lost its usefulness. Daly knew he needed to breathe again if he were going to continue searching the house. But taking a breath of the scorching black poison that filled the hallway would undoubtedly destroy his lungs and lead to a fit of coughing. As Daly gasped for air, he would suck in more and more of the noxious fumes. Then he would lose consciousness where he stood, falling in a pile to the hard floor to wait for the racing fire to claim his life.

He couldn't think it. He didn't want to think it. Standing in the hallway, Daly began to fill with impotent rage at the realization.

He could not save her.

As he turned back to Lauren's room, the tears streaming down his cheeks were no longer the result of the smoke alone.

Once back inside, Daly slammed the door shut behind him, gasping for breath as he tried to figure out his next move. It was unthinkable to leave his daughter inside a burning building. He would rather die than leave her alone. But he would certainly die if he tried going downstairs. The living room had transformed into a blistering inferno, with raging red flames spreading across the blackening walls like a cancer. Daly realized that even if he made it to the bottom of the stairs, he would be trapped between the searing flames and the deadly smoke.

The only thing he could do was hope Lauren had escaped.

Daly wiped his eyes with the back of his hand and looked across the room, assessing his situation. A gray, fog-like haze was beginning to fill Lauren's room, and the air was taking on the bitter, charred smell of the fire. But for now, Daly was still able to breathe it. He took another breath and ran over to the window, fumbling with the lock in the dark.

He managed to unlatch the lock and raised the window, but then was unable to find the release to open the storm window behind it. He groped around in the growing haze before finding the tabs at the bottom of the pane. They stuck as he tried to release their grasp on the window frame.

Squeezing his fingertips with all his effort, Daly pulled the left tab free — but the right one would not budge.

A trickle of black smoke that had been wafting underneath the bedroom door had intensified to a torrent, and clouds of smoke had begun spewing through a heating vent as well. As he took a breath and tasted the acrid smoke, Daly began a coughing fit he knew he needed to control. He swallowed hard to stifle the cough and lifted his tee-shirt over his mouth in a futile effort to filter the smoky air.

He had seconds left before the door would collapse under the heat of the fire and the room would became his grave. The time for struggling with the window tabs had passed.

Daly turned from the window, seeking something he could use to break it. He seized the case from Lauren's clarinet off a nearby chair on which it had been perched. Holding the case by one end, he punched it through the storm window, sending glass shattering down to the ground below like glistening drizzle. He ran the case around the perimeter of the frame, knocking loose the remaining shards of glass, then stuck his head out the window and dipped below the torrent of billowing smoke. After taking a deep breath, he ducked back inside and pulled the chair against the wall. Daly climbed on top of it and put his hands on the window sill so he could stick his legs out and go feet first.

As he lowered his legs out the window, Daly could feel tiny shards of glass slicing deep into his palms and fingers like razor blades. He tried to ignore the pain as he worked to lower himself as far down as possible. When his arms were fully extended, Daly looked down, seeing the trash cans on the lawn against the house — directly beneath him.

Daly put his bare toes on the side of the house and tried to push out as he released his grip. His body plummeted to the ground, twisting slightly backward and away from the garbage cans before landing with a dull thud on the hard turf. The impact knocked the breath out of his lungs, leaving him gasping and sucking for air that would not flow. A jolt of pain shot through his right ankle like an arrow, and his right wrist began throbbing. When Daly reached down to feel the damage to his ankle, he realized his palms were wet with oozing red blood.

All of it barely registered in his mind. The only thing that mattered at the moment was his daughter.

"Lauren!" Daly shrieked into the night after his breath finally returned.

The house was quickly becoming engulfed in flames, and menacing dark smoke poured out of the windows as it drifted peacefully upward, melding with the black night sky. Daly pulled himself up and began hobbling around the house, desperately looking for a sign that Lauren had escaped.

"Lauren!" he screamed, his shrill voice echoing through the quiet neighborhood.

As he continued limping around the perimeter, he realized

he hadn't grabbed his cellphone off his nightstand. With no way to call for help, Daly began yelling into the night in hopes a neighbor would hear and make the call.

After his second circuit around the flaming house, Daly collapsed to the ground, defeated. There was no sign of Lauren, and intense flames had burst out every window and were already beginning to claim the roof. If she was inside, she was gone.

Tears streamed down his face as he knelt on the ground, watching his life go up in smoke. After Jessica died, Lauren was all Daly had left. It was Lauren who made him keep going in the aftermath. When Daly began hitting the Scotch every night, it was Lauren who made him realize that he needed to be there for her. It was Lauren who gave Daly the strength to slow the boozing, even if it meant being tormented by the dream. And it was Lauren who gave Daly the strength he needed to get through the trial.

She had been his anchor. And now she was gone.

Daly fell over to his side, weeping in the damp grass, sweat coming to his brow because of the intense heat from the fire.

"Lauren!" he called out again.

Suddenly, he heard a shuffling sound behind him. He turned and saw Lauren running toward him from the house next door.

"Daddy!" she yelled.

Daly jumped up, oblivious to the pain in his ankle, and hobbled over to meet her. He wrapped his arms around her neck and squeezed tightly, smelling the flowery scent of her hair against his face.

"I thought I lost you," Daly said through tears. "How did you get out?"

"I couldn't sleep so I went down to the den to watch TV," she said. "The next thing I knew, I heard glass breaking. When I came out to the kitchen, I could see the living room was on fire. I couldn't get through so I yelled for you and then went to Mr. Fischer's house to get help. He called 911."

In the distance, Daly could hear the sirens of fire engines cutting through the nighttime silence. The faint sound grew louder by the second, reaching its crescendo when the red flashing lights of the engines turned the corner and came to a jarring stop in front of the house.

It was clear they were too late. The fire had engulfed nearly every room, and the ones that were not burning were filled with smoke. Soon they would be drenched in water from the fire hoses as well. They might be able to salvage some of their things, but almost all their worldly possessions were gone.

None of that mattered to Daly. Lauren was okay, and he would live to write another day.

The bigger concern for Daly was why he heard the sound of breaking glass just before the fire broke out. It seemed someone had set the house on fire in the middle of the night with Daly and his daughter asleep inside. Finding out who was responsible had just become Daly's top priority.

# CHAPTER 10

*Friday, March 30, 2018*
*7:14 a.m.*

The Luzerne County detectives' office sits in a nondescript corner of the courthouse basement, with little more than a small placard acknowledging its existence. Inside, about a dozen veteran investigators work in cluttered cubicles to assist local police departments with serious criminal investigations. This morning, Daly sat at a desk at one of them, surrounded by stacks of paperwork and case files. A few pictures of Phil Wojcik's kids were taped to a shelf over the computer monitor, over which two Philadelphia Phillies bobbleheads stood guard. As he waited for Wojcik to get finished in another room, Daly sipped a cup of coffee and ran through the night's events in his head.

Someone wanted him dead. A state police fire marshal who visited Daly's home overnight confirmed the crashing sound had been someone throwing a Molotov cocktail through the bay window in the living room at the front of the house. The gasoline inside the bottle sprayed like napalm across the room after the bottle shattered, covering the couches, carpet and a Lazy Boy with liquid fire. Within seconds, the blaze began releasing a deadly torrent of smoke, and the intense flames spread along the drywall like milk slowly expanding from an overturned carton.

They had been lucky to escape, the fire marshal told them. Lucky or not, Lauren had been scared senseless by the fire. After finding her father outside the burning building, Lauren began crying and shaking uncontrollably. Daly tried not to think about what would have happened if they hadn't heard the shattering window or the screaming smoke detector. While Daly was able to push those thoughts out of his mind, Lauren continued struggling through them.

An ambulance had taken them both to Geisinger Wyoming Valley Medical Center for treatment. Daly needed a few stitches where the glass had sliced his palms, but fortunately he had only sprained his right ankle and wrist. He was cleared for release a few hours after arriving. The doctors, however, wanted to keep Lauren a while longer for observation because of her panic attack.

After he was convinced Lauren had calmed down – and with the assurance that police would post a guard outside her door – Daly had agreed to go to the courthouse to talk to detectives about what happened and who might have done it.

Investigators had been canvassing the neighborhood throughout the night, trying to find someone with surveillance equipment that might have recorded the fire bomber coming or going. These days, someone is always watching. It was just a question of whether the police would be able to find the right angle and make the connection between passer-by and crime scene.

As Wojcik walked back to meet Daly at the cubicle, he gave Daly a slight shake of his head. So far, they hadn't found any footage that would help. Daly had expected as much. His neighborhood was suburban, and the street lights were spotty. Even if a camera had recorded something, chances were it would be a grainy black-and-white recording filmed by infrared LED lighting.

"Nothing yet?" Daly asked.

"No. But we're still looking. It's a pretty quiet area at one o'clock in the morning. Anyone out and about then will stick out. I need to talk about who you think it might have been. Is there anyone you can think of who would want to hurt you?"

Daly pursed his lips and thought for a moment, the shaking of his head increasing momentum at each pass.

"I can't think of anyone. Lauren and I pretty much keep to ourselves. And she's pretty popular at school. I can't imagine anyone would have wanted to hurt her."

"What about debt? Do you owe anyone money? Or any relationship problems?"

"No, nothing like that. I don't get out too much since my wife died."

Wojcik nodded, duly giving a moment of silence for the departed before continuing. He didn't have to ask what had happened. He had been the lead investigator.

"What about at work? Any complaints about a story?" Wojcik continued.

"I'm a crime reporter. Everyone I write about hates me," Daly said.

"Fair enough. But has there been anything specific?"

"Actually, yes. I got a letter at the newsroom yesterday. It was handwritten in block letters. It said, 'You know what happened to the curious cat, don't you?' And it warned me to be careful."

"Who sent it?" Wojcik asked.

"There was no return address. But it kind of freaked me out because it did have my home address at the bottom."

"Do you still have it?" Wojcik asked, keenly interested.

"Yeah, it should still be at the newsroom."

"Great. I'll have someone stop by to collect it for testing," Wojcik said. "Any idea why someone would have threatened you?"

"The main thing I've been working on lately is the suicide cluster," Daly said. "But you said they were unrelated."

"I said they appear to be unrelated but that we're looking into it."

Daly paused a moment, catching a slight twinkle in the detective's eye. Wojcik knew or suspected something he hadn't revealed. And from his terse answer, it didn't seem like he planned to. But knowing that detectives were seriously considering the possibility of someone behind the scenes — someone who was pulling strings and playing with the lives of young kids — sent a chill down Daly's spine.

"If you're telling me you think someone's behind it, that changes things. Then there's someone who would want to stop me from writing about the cases."

"And who do you think that could be?" Wojcik asked.

"You tell me. It sounds like you have a suspect. That would be a good place to start."

"I'm not saying we have a suspect. I'm just asking who you've been talking to about this story."

"Probably the most interesting person is a kid from Nanticoke, David Kowalski," Daly said. "I've been looking at him, asking some questions about the deaths. I found him on Facebook. He went to camp with Kim Foster and Justin Gonzalez last summer. He seemed like he didn't really fit in with the two of them, and from what I heard he's done some bad things. I've heard him described as a 'creep.' Kind of a problem child, apparently."

"Is that all?"

"Well, no," Daly said. "I was thinking that I first approached David on Monday, and then I got the letter yesterday morning. I went back and spoke to David a second time yesterday afternoon. Then my house got attacked last night."

"Uh-huh," Wojcik said calmly, showing no recognition of David Kowalski's name. "And who else have you contacted about this story?"

"Not too many others," Daly said. "I talked to a counselor at Camp Summit Lake — where Kimberly, Justin and David met —

but he didn't seem to be too attached. Obviously, I also spoke to the families. Tried to, anyway. Celeste Gonzalez was willing to talk. I left a message for Emma Nguyen's family before I filed my story yesterday, but they never called back. Kim Foster's parents were pretty upset when I showed up at their house. Her father threatened to call the cops and told me to get the hell off the porch. And I'm sure they weren't too happy to see her name in the paper again. But I don't think they would be that pissed about it. Not enough to blow up my house, anyway."

At this, Wojcik grunted and slightly nodded his head. Was it agreement? Or something else? Daly tried to read the look but wasn't sure what to make of it.

"The only one that makes sense is David Kowalski," Daly said, growing irritated. "He's the only clear connection between Kim and Justin, and I was at his door asking questions right before someone torched my house. Who else could it be?"

"Calm down," Wojcik said. "We're going to find out who did it. But it wasn't Kowalski."

"How do you know that?" Daly asked, surprised.

"Well," Wojcik said, pausing to carefully choose his words. "He's a juvenile, so I can't say very much. This is off the record — completely off the record — but last night some vehicles were vandalized near Luzerne County Community College. Let's just say David Kowalski was accounted for at the time of the fire."

Like a wisp of smoke, Daly's prime suspect vanished into thin air.

◆ ◆ ◆

When he was finished at the courthouse, Daly walked out in a light drizzle that was forming cool pools in the cracks and the dips in the sidewalk. The morning air had a chill to it, the kind of cold, wet day that brings a miserable, unshakable chill worse than any wintertime deep freeze. He wanted to get right back to Lauren and see how she was doing, but in his panic after the fire, he had jumped into the ambulance and left his car at home. Or, what used to be home, he reminded himself. Wojcik had brought him to the courthouse, and after the interview, he offered to bring Daly home to pick up his car.

They drove along the winding hills of state Route 309 to the Back Mountain in silence, watching the morning mist shrouding the trees like a phantom aura. When they reached Shavertown, Wojcik turned off the main highway onto Daly's street, then slowed down to a crawl as he neared the burnt husk of what used to be Daly's house.

Thin trails of white smoke still twisted up past the dripping wet two by fours that made up the ruined frame of the structure. The back wall of the house still appeared mostly intact – the kitchen and den on the first floor and Lauren's bedroom above them looked from the outside to be blacked by smoke but untouched by the flames. However, the front of the home, where the fire began, was gaping obscenely open. All of Daly's possessions were blackened and sopped in cold, ashy water. His living room – the back wall and the melted and charred remains of some of the furniture, at least – was on display for the world to see.

He tried to ignore the devastation for the moment and to focus on getting back to his baby girl.

"Listen, I know you have a job to do, but so do we," Wojcik said as Daly lifted the door handle to get out of the car. "It would be best if you didn't write about what happened, or about what we're thinking about what happened. The fire marshal was talking to you about this as the victim of a crime, not as a reporter."

"I want you to catch whoever did this," Daly said. "I want to

catch whoever did this. But I also know my editor is going to
need a story about the fire. I won't be able to write it because it's
my house. But what if I just give them a straight-forward story
about my escape? No mention of the possible link to my article."

"It would be best if you also left out the firebomb. Nobody
knows yet that we know that's what it was. We don't want the
suspect to think we're on to him. It would be best if you just said
you woke up hearing the smoke detector going off," Wojcik said.
"The cause is still under investigation."

"That's fair," Daly said, nodding. "All right. Well, thanks for
the ride."

"I'll be in touch," Wojcik said.

Daly stepped out into the growing morning light as the black
cruiser slid off down the road, its engine cutting through the still
morning air. He turned and looked at his house once more, then
turned his attention to his car. It was still in the driveway and
appeared intact, but the paint on the hood and front side had
been warped by the fire's intense heat, and it was covered by a
thick layer of paste-like ash and water.

Surveying the damage in shock and disbelief, Daly slowly
became aware someone was approaching him from the side. He
looked over and saw his neighbor, Scott Fischer, the man who
helped Lauren during the fire.

"Been a hell of a night," Fischer said, shaking his head in
disbelief. "How's Lauren doing?"

"I think she's okay. She was shaken up, but I think she was just
in shock. I'm about to go to the hospital and check on her," Daly
said.

"Do you guys need a place to stay? I've got a couple of couches
in the basement you could sleep on if you need them."

"No, thanks. I think we'll be all right. But do you still have the spare set of keys I left with you when we went to San Francisco last year?"

"Sure do. Come on in. They're in my desk drawer," Fischer said.

"Thanks," Daly said. "And one more thing. I need to use your phone."

◆ ◆ ◆

The sun had begun to break through the misty trees along the highway as Daly descended into the valley from the Back Mountain. Below, he could see the awakening communities stretched across the valley floor, the outlines of the homes broken up by white church spires and the muddy waters of the Susquehanna River.

At this hour, nobody would be in the newsroom, so Daly had used his neighbor's phone to call Richardson's cellphone. The editor answered after a half-dozen rings, sounding as though he were still not awake. He immediately perked up when Daly told him what happened. After giving the basic details, Daly asked if he could take a few hours off to get Lauren settled somewhere and make some calls to his insurance carrier. Richardson said he was glad everyone was okay and told Daly to take the day. Daly could tell he wanted to ask about getting the story but was holding back in a show of respect.

"I'll give Joe Reed a call this afternoon," Daly said, volunteering to talk to a reporter to ease the awkwardness. "I should have a new phone by then."

Hopping onto Interstate 81, Daly made his way up to the hospital and slid the ailing car into a spot near the emergency department entrance. He walked through the automatic sliding glass doors and went up to an attendant sitting behind bullet-proof glass at the welcome booth. Looking around, he saw bored families stretched out on couches in the lounge, their droopy eyes transfixed on a flat-screen television broadcasting the unceasing smiles of the "Today" show cast as they bantered and giggled on a cold street in New York City.

The nurse at the counter, dressed in purple scrubs with a flower-patterned shirt, peered up behind her glasses with vague interest.

"I'm trying to find my daughter. Lauren Daly," he said.

After tapping on a keyboard for a few minutes, the nurse asked for Daly's identification and then buzzed him in. Daly made his way down the hospital corridor, past rows of gurneys and patients connected to tubes and wires until he came to the door where his daughter was supposed to be. As promised, a uniformed cop was stationed outside the doorway. After clearing the sentry, Daly entered and found Lauren sitting on the edge of her bed, pulling a sweater over the long-sleeved shirt she wore.

"Daddy!" she said, running the few steps to close the distance.

"Hey, baby girl," Daly said. "How are you?"

"I'm fine. The doctor said I just had a panic attack. What happened really freaked me out."

"Me too," Daly said, nodding. For the first time, he felt a pang of guilt. It occurred to him that if the firebombing was because of his work, he would have been at least partially to blame for getting his daughter killed. And then ...

"Do they know who did it?" Lauren asked, interrupting Daly's train of thought.

"Not yet. But they're working on it. They'll get him."

"Him?" Lauren asked, her eyes gleaming.

"Or her," Daly conceded with a smile. Even now, she wasn't

about to give him a pass on a sexist remark, however benign.

"What are we going to do? Do you think we could stay at Uncle Rob's for a while?" Lauren asked.

"No, I think we should get a hotel room, at least for the time being. They say the fire was definitely arson, so either it was vandals causing trouble or someone who knew we were there. We need to lay low until we know which."

"What about Great Wolf Lodge?" Lauren proposed. "I've been wanting to go to the water park there forever."

"Yeah right. I'm a journalist, not an oil baron. And I'm not driving forty-five minutes every morning to get you to school."

"So where?" Lauren asked.

"Somewhere quiet and out of sight. I was thinking the Mountain Motor Lodge," Daly said, stifling a smile as his daughter's face became the picture of disgust. "It's close to school, after all."

"That place is straight out of a horror movie," Lauren said.

"I promise no one is going to ax murder us there."

"If anyone from school sees me going there, they might as well."

# CHAPTER 11

*Friday, March 30, 2018*
*4:08 p.m.*

The Mountain Motor Lodge sat along Tunkhannock Highway, nestled between tall oak and pine trees along a desolate curve in the road, at least a quarter mile from its nearest neighbor. The motel consisted of ten rooms in a line, doors and windows looking out over a vast gravel parking lot toward the highway. At night, the peeling paint on the walls assumed a tinge of blue as neon lights announced vacancy — always vacancy — at the establishment. At one time, the motor lodge had served travelers commuting along the highway, but that legitimate business had mostly evaporated. Now the motel served mostly to accommodate illicit trysts between lovers who couldn't take their partners home. More often than not, the guests now parked their cars in the rear lot.

In room eight, Daly and Lauren were getting settled into their new accommodations. The hotel was certainly a far cry from the watery resort Lauren had hoped for, but despite its dated decor and worn exterior the motel rooms were kept clean and neat. And though the owners prided themselves on a priest-like confidentiality when it came to who was sharing rooms with whom, they did not tolerate parties or drugs. Daly was sure it would be a safe place for Lauren to stay.

The room came with two twin beds, and Lauren promptly

laid claim to the one closest to the window. She dropped the two handfuls of shopping bags that she had accumulated at the Wyoming Valley Mall onto the faded and frayed flower-print comforter and sat down next to them. The loss of just about everything they owned was a tough pill to swallow, but Lauren was learning there could be an upside. She now had every reason to get new clothes at the mall — and Daly couldn't say no.

The day at the mall had taken their minds off the terror of the fire and the depressing reality that they had no home. Daly had watched with a smile as Lauren put on her own fashion show, trying on a seemingly endless combination of jeans, skirts, and sweaters. Lauren rolled her eyes in boredom as Daly haggled with the sales representative about getting a replacement cellphone, and then spent the next forty-five minutes talking to Joe Reed and then an insurance agent about the fire. They laughed over ice cream at the food court, and on a whim, they'd decided to catch a movie at the downtown theater – a comedy, they agreed.

It had been the first time in a long time they spent a full day together, laughing and talking. Life was always so busy that they often forgot to make time for each other. It had taken a fire that destroyed everything and nearly claimed their lives for them to realize what they had been missing.

Content after a day spent together, they decided to lay low for the night. For dinner, Daly ordered a pizza with the works to the room and Lauren clicked the remote to turn on the antiquated tube television resting on top of a faded and scratched dresser.

◆ ◆ ◆

The dream had changed.

Ed and Barbara Thompson were still down by the motel pool

sipping cocktails, and music was coming from the same crackling speakers, but this time it was "Redemption Song" by Bob Marley. Daly was with Jessica and Lauren in their motel room, but Lauren the little girl had been replaced by Lauren the seventeen-year-old high school senior. Something was wrong, but Daly couldn't tell what.

His head pounding, Daly made his way to the bathroom and threw some cold water on his face. As he stepped out into the bedroom, the towel in his hand disappeared.

In its place was the .38 Special. A slight wisp of white smoke still drifted up from the barrel. Suddenly, terror gripped Daly. Something terrible had happened, something that he already regretted and could never take back.

When he raised his gaze to the bed, he saw the white comforter had turned crimson. Jessica was laying back with the same playful expression she always had in the dream. But to Daly's everlasting horror, Lauren was laying motionless right beside her.

The room was eerily silent.

*Where is Kelly?* Daly wondered.

This time, there was no can of gasoline sitting inside the doorway. Instead on the desk sat a box of Hornady .38 Special hollow-point rounds. Looking at the bullets lying on the desktop, Daly decided there would be no visit to the pool this time. Daly pushed his thumb on the cylinder release and dumped the spent casings, sending them tumbling silently to the carpeted floor.

One by one, Daly slid fresh rounds into the cylinder, feeling each one find home with a satisfying click. With six more shots loaded up, Daly slapped the cylinder back into the revolver and sat down on the edge of the bed, between Lauren and Jessica. Their blood soaked into the seat of his pants, but he barely registered the warm liquid against his skin.

He cried.

Between hysterical sobs and gasps for breath, Daly muttered in disbelief, "I murdered my family!" Then he clicked the hammer back and put the revolver's barrel to his temple. As he tried to build up the nerve to pull the trigger, Daly's face contorted into a horrifying grimace, tears streaming down his cheeks with his teeth clenched tight.

The last thing he heard was a thunderous bang.

◆ ◆ ◆

In the darkness of the hotel room, Lauren could hear her father's breathing intensifying and his sheets rustling as he tossed. The movement grew more frantic, and soon Daly was muttering the nonsensical ramblings of a man talking in his sleep. Lauren sat up in her bed, wondering whether to wake him. As she listened to her father's restlessness, she thought she could make something out, and what she heard sent a chill down her spine.

"I murdered my family," Daly whispered.

Lauren grew uneasy. Of course, it was just a dream, but it was an unsettling thing to hear from her father.

She rose out of bed and crept to her father's bedside, placing a hand gently on his shoulder and shaking softly.

"Daddy," she whispered. "Daddy, you're having a bad dream. It's just a dream."

In his bed, Daly continued to twist, muttering. His head was damp with perspiration, and his fingers were clenched into tight fists. Lauren tried to rouse him once more.

"Daddy," she said more forcefully, shaking him a little harder. "Wake up."

Daly's eyes shot open, scanning the dark room with a wild

look. After a second, his gaze came to rest on Lauren. He stared, uncomprehending, for a moment before realizing where he was. Then he sat up and wrapped both arms around his daughter, squeezing her tight around the shoulders.

"Hey, baby girl," he said. "I'm sorry, did I wake you?"

"It's okay," she said. "It sounded like you were having a pretty bad dream."

"Yeah, it was my nightmare again," Daly said, letting go of Lauren and swinging his legs to the side of the bed. He began rubbing his temples. "I'm sorry you had to hear that."

"What happened?" Lauren asked. "In the dream."

"It's just a scary dream I have. That's all."

"You said you murdered your family," Lauren said, raising her eyebrows. "I want to know what happened."

In the darkness, Daly exhaled and looked at his daughter. She knew a little bit about the dream, but Daly had kept the most disturbing parts to himself. As far as Lauren knew, the dream was simply about her mother's death. Until now, she had heard no hint that Daly was the person who caused it. From the imploring look in Lauren's eyes, Daly could tell he wasn't going to simply wave off her questions this time. If he had spoken in his sleep before, Lauren hadn't heard it. This time, she knew there was more to the story.

Clearing his throat, Daly began to describe the dream – the original dream – and how he found Jessica dead on the bed with a gun in his hand. He described the fire and the insane nonchalance of everyone around him when his wife had so clearly been murdered.

He left out the new twist where he killed Lauren and then himself. It was just a dream, something beyond his ability to control or navigate, but Daly felt it would be too hard for Lauren to take. How could a daughter ever look at her father the same way again after he told her he had dreamed about murdering her?

When he was done with the abridged version, Daly hung his head and began rubbing his eyes. Lauren slid closer to him on the bed, wrapping an arm around his shoulder and squeezing. They sat together in silence for a moment, neither one knowing what to say next. Then Lauren told her father what she always did after the dream.

"It wasn't your fault," she said.

It was a familiar refrain that Daly had heard often before. Friends, police, a counselor and even Daly's father-in-law had at times tried to comfort him with those words, which Daly knew made sense. He hadn't put a gun to Jessica's head, nor had he pulled the trigger.

He didn't do it.

It was logical, accurate, and reasonable. But no matter how many times he told himself, it never seemed to set his mind at ease.

The dream always returned.

# CHAPTER 12

The newsroom was still quiet even at mid-morning the day after Easter. Occasionally, the scanner in the corner of the room squawked to life and dispatchers directed police and firefighters to minor calls. Around the holidays, it seemed, even the criminals liked to take a break. For a crime beat reporter pulling holiday duty at the Observer, coverage was guaranteed to consist of the same feel-good narrative that gets repeated every year. Only the names and dates changed.

The newsroom flat screen was tuned to CNN, with a muted anchor still covering a breaking story that no one seemed to care much about. At the editor's desk, John Richardson had his legs crossed as he thumbed through a copy of the Other Paper to see if there was anything that needed chasing. As Daly walked past, Richardson dog-eared a corner of the paper and lowered it, raising an eyebrow.

"I wasn't expecting you here today," he said.

"I know. But I've got Lauren in a safe place and we're just waiting on the insurance before we can move on a new house. I need something to do besides sitting at the hotel," Daly said.

"All right. I can't say we don't need the help," Richardson said. Cutbacks had made times harder for everyone at the paper. *More with less*, he thought. *Always more with less.*

"I want to go to Emma Nguyen's house and see if her parents will talk," Daly said. "Then I need to make another run at Kim Foster's parents."

Richardson folded the paper in half and dropped it to his desk with a dull thud.

"I don't know if that's such a great idea," he said.

"Why not?"

"Well, we don't know who firebombed your house, but we do know that it happened in the middle of you asking questions about this case. It might be better for you to hold off," Richardson said.

"I'm not going to be intimidated," Daly said. "We can't just fold over and stop writing about it."

"That's not what I'm saying," Richardson said. "You're too close to the case. If the attack does turn out to be related to the kids' deaths, that makes you a victim along with the kids. You're going to be conflicted out."

That possibility hadn't yet dawned on Daly. He'd been focused on trying to find out who attacked his house, and whether it was related to his stories. Now he felt a burning rage surge through his veins at the thought that whoever was pulling the strings behind the scenes had also just stolen his story.

"Hold on," Daly said. "We don't know who started the fire — or why. I've written thousands of stories here. It could be connected to any one of them. You can't pull me off the story just based on speculation."

Richardson turned to the television, shaking his head. Daly was a strong reporter and this was a big story. Daly had also done the leg work to get the Observer out front of a story that other media outlets were only beginning to pick up. By rights, the story was his, and Richardson didn't want to strip it from him if he didn't have to.

"Okay, look," Richardson said. "You can keep working the story – for now. Get with the families and see if you can develop any other connections between these kids. But listen: If it comes back that the fire is in any way connected to this case, you're off the story. We can't have the appearance of a conflict of interest in our coverage, especially with the other outlets starting to pick it up."

Daly went to his desk and put down his Styrofoam coffee cup, clicking the mouse to wake his computer. He pulled up Google Chrome and looked up Vu and Linh Nguyen in the White Pages. The address came back to a small side street off the main strip in a well-maintained part of Plains. Daly gulped down his coffee, grabbed his coat and hit the door.

◆ ◆ ◆

The Nguyens lived in a brown foursquare-style house with white trim that sat a stone's toss from the road, a narrow strip of yellowing grass doing its best to pass for a front lawn. The paint on the house appeared fresh and the hedge that ran along the front porch was trimmed neatly. Daly noticed there was a single vehicle in the driveway, a Toyota Camry, and was thankful he wouldn't be trying to approach an entire family with his prying questions. He climbed the steps to the door and pushed the bell, listening as chimes jingled inside. A Pembroke Welsh Corgi began yapping to announce his presence.

Trying to appear casual, Daly looked down the street until he noticed the flutter of a curtain at the window and the vague outline of a person behind it. The figure hesitated a moment, apparently sizing Daly up, before moving toward the door.

"Who is it?" a woman's voice called from inside.

"I'm Erik Daly. I'm a reporter with the Observer."

For a moment, there was only silence. Then Daly heard the scraping metal sound of a lock being unfastened. The door opened up to reveal an attractive Asian woman in her mid-forties wearing her jet-black hair pulled back in a bun. She wore a white sweater and blue jeans and had piercing brown eyes that looked tired and sad. If she had been crying, there was no hint of it in her face now.

"What do you want?" she asked.

"I'm working on a story about Emma. Was she your daughter?" Daly asked.

"Yes. But I don't want to talk about it," the woman said, turning her shoulder.

"Hold on," Daly implored. "Please."

The woman stopped in her tracks and turned her head back to Daly, giving him a moment to make his case. Daly noted that she didn't turn her shoulders back toward him.

"What I'm working on, it's not only about your daughter," Daly said. "We've had a bunch of teenage suicides recently. Some of them left the same message that Emma did in her Facebook post, and the police think there could be a connection."

Daly felt a little dirty at having to play up that angle. It was true, sure, and this woman probably already knew about it. But Daly knew that grieving parents are often loathe to believe their children would have made a choice that led to their own deaths. It's easier to believe someone else pushed her to take that fatal shot of heroin, or that a bully goaded her into suicide, or that someone must have dared her into getting behind the wheel while drunk, than it is to believe that years of lecturing had simply failed. Years of life lessons imparted a few words at a time, in teachable moments and during punishments, were not enough to save their child from her own free will.

As a parent, Daly understood all this, yet he was reluctant to play on it. Whatever grief this woman was feeling would not go away if she put the blame for Emma's death on someone else. All that would accomplish would be to add hate to her grief.

Reservations aside, Daly needed to get this woman talking. There was clearly a connection between the victims, and Emma's family was one of only three in the world that might hold the answer. It wasn't just a matter of getting the story – although, Daly conceded, that wouldn't hurt. No, the cold facts were that kids were dying, and without finding out why, it was highly likely that they would continue to be snuffed out like flames fluttering in a window's draft.

"They told me they were looking into her note," the woman said. "They said they don't know if it's related."

"That's true, they're looking into it. But I think they're pretty sure the cases are related," Daly said, noticing a flash of interest in the woman's eyes. "Did you hear about the reporter whose house caught fire over the weekend? It was me. And the fire wasn't an accident."

Linh Nguyen was sold. She introduced herself as Emma's mother and invited Daly inside. The living room of the home was small and furnished with white leather couches that dominated the room. Drew Carey was smiling out from a flat-screen television sitting opposite the couches as a contestant spun the wheel on "The Price is Right." The starchy smell of steaming rice drifted from the kitchen. Daly could tell the game show had simply been background noise. A woman who only just recently became painfully aware that she was a little more alone in the world had wanted some company in her lonely house.

They sat down on the oversized couches and Daly told Linh Nguyen what he knew about the previous deaths — and what happened to his house. For her, he gave the unabridged version. He wanted Linh to be honest and forthcoming with him, so he gave her everything he knew about the firebombing.

Once he'd established a rapport, Daly began to ask about Emma. He learned she was just a few weeks shy of turning seventeen, and that the family had hoped for her to go to Penn State and then on to medical school. Of the family's three children, Emma was the oldest. She had been considered the smart one. From an early age, she got started playing chess with her father, and she gravitated toward projects like the school science fair rather than sports and music. When the other kids in her class began vaping in the school bathrooms or hanging out at the mall, she remained focused on her studies.

Even her boyfriend, Steve – the boy from Emma's Facebook profile, Daly learned – was a clean-cut kid whom Emma's family liked. He too did well in school and played baseball on the school's varsity team. When he graduated, he also wanted to go to Penn State, although probably that had more to do with Emma's plans than anything he wanted to study.

"Did you know Emma was pregnant?" Daly asked.

"No. She never told us," Linh said.

"She seemed to think your family wouldn't take the news well," Daly said.

"My husband is pretty conservative about such things," Linh said, keenly interested in her hands in her lap. "He would not have been pleased. But we loved Emma, and nothing would have changed that. She could have told us. She should have told us."

Daly continued probing, searching for the elusive connection that had escaped him thus far. As far as Linh knew, Emma didn't know David Kowalski, nor did she know Justin Gonzalez or Kimberly Foster. She didn't attend church and had never been to Camp Summit Lake. She had no bad influences to speak of, and, aside from dating a boy who could use some contraceptive training, she seemed to have good judgment.

But after some questioning, Linh began to reveal some wrinkles in the glossy picture she'd painted of her daughter's life. Emma was a good girl, to be sure, but she had been getting into arguments at home. Some of them grew quite heated. In the fall before her death, Emma had skipped school to go to Knoebels Amusement Resort with Steve. This was where the picture of the two of them on a roller coaster came from, Daly learned.

The next day, the school had contacted Linh asking for a note to excuse the absence. Emma had been caught. When Linh and Vu Nguyen confronted her about it at the dinner table that evening, Emma had blown up. She began screaming that her parents couldn't tell her how to live her life, and defied them to try. After a minute of hearing his daughter shrieking her non-compliance in his face, Vu had lost his cool as well. He stood up, sending his chair tumbling backward to the ground with a clatter and yelled for Emma to get to her room.

"Leave your phone on the table!" he shouted.

Emma slammed the phone onto the wooden surface and screamed the quintessential retort of a teenager who has been cornered without a witty comeback.

"I hate you!" she blared, storming out of the room.

Later that night, lying in bed next to her husband, Linh had expressed worry about the increasingly heated arguments Emma was having with them. She wondered if someone was bullying Emma at school. *What about drugs?* She wondered.

Vu dismissed it. They kept tabs on Emma's social media

accounts, and nothing online indicated Emma was getting picked on at school. Her grades were as high as ever.

No, Vu was certain it was just a phase. Emma was being a naturally rebellious teen.

"Don't worry about it," he whispered into Linh's ear, turning away from her and closing his eyes. "She'll be fine."

But Linh couldn't stop worrying about it. She was up half that night, her mind racing and heart beating as she wondered what was making her little girl — the child who had been so sweet and loving — turn into an argumentative and hostile being. Hormones alone couldn't account for it, she ultimately decided.

The next night, after a stone-faced appearance at dinner at which Emma uttered fewer than a dozen words, Linh broached the subject again. This time, however, she was prepared. She had talked to some of her friends at the coffee shop earlier in the day, and they suggested Emma get some counseling. Talking about feelings is a good way for teenagers to vent, they told her. Sometimes it's more comfortable for a kid to tell a stranger about their problems than their own parents.

Vu grunted as he listened. He didn't put a lot of stock in such things. To his way of thinking, all this talk these days about people's feelings and trying not to offend anyone was making people soft.

"How much is this going to cost?" Vu asked.

Despite Vu's reservations, Linh prevailed. He could see from the look in his wife's eyes that she needed it, and he figured the family could afford it. Hell, if the sessions earned him some peace and quiet around the house, it would be money well spent.

Emma first went to see Dr. Marvin Radcliffe at his office in Kingston on Nov. 14, 2017. When asked, Vu would never admit there had been an immediate change in his eldest daughter's behavior. That would be conceding too much. But a few weeks after the sessions began, Vu had to admit that the change in Emma's behavior was stark. The arguments had ended and an unsteady truce had melted away into familiar laughter at the dinner table. Emma seemed to have come to grips with whatever it was that had been bothering her, and she had become the smiling, fun, playful teenager that had disappeared from family life just weeks earlier.

Vu never was sure what exactly had gone wrong with his daughter, or what she spoke about behind closed doors with Dr. Radcliffe that made her come around. To some degree, it bothered him not to know the cause of his daughter's grief. But again, he chalked it up to normal teenage hormones. And whatever it was, he figured it didn't really matter.

The important thing was his daughter was back.

# CHAPTER 13

*Tuesday, April 3, 2018*
*1:52 p.m.*

The car pulled into a spot in front of the aging house on Lee Park Avenue in Hanover Township. The sun glinted off the car's glass and chrome as the door creaked open. Daly's black Doc Martens hit the pavement, each step crunching grit beneath his heel.

Daly had walked away from his conversation with Linh Nguyen feeling lost. Any last hope he had that David Kowalski might have been involved in the deaths evaporated when Linh insisted Emma had not known him. Not only that, but Emma had never been to Camp Summit Lake, the only other connection Daly had between the victims. Either he had missed something or he was chasing a phantom that didn't exist.

When he'd arrived at the newsroom, he decided it was about time he paid another visit to the Foster home. Jack Foster made it clear last time that Daly wasn't welcome, but that had been very shortly after Kim's death. Since then, nearly two weeks had passed and by now their raging emotions would have had some time to settle.

As a precaution, Daly had run the idea past John Richardson. He wanted to make sure he was covered if the Fosters called back to the newsroom complaining that Daly was harassing them. Richardson had given the green light with a warning to back off as soon as he saw a hint of resistance.

As Daly approached the stairs to the run-down house, he saw with relief that the cluster of cars that had been present the first time was gone. At the top of the steps he reached for the doorbell, then realized the button was missing. All that remained was a gaping hole surrounded by the black smudges of unchecked grime. Daly opened the screen door and tapped on the wooden door behind it.

A moment later he heard some rustling behind the door followed by the sound of the knob turning. Jack Foster pulled open the door and looked at Daly for a moment without recognition. Then, remembering their earlier meeting, his brow folded into a scowl and his demeanor turned gruff.

"What do you want?" he asked.

"Mr. Foster, I apologize for bothering you again. You probably heard that there was another suicide a few days ago. The police have reason to believe it could be connected to the others. I was wondering if I could talk to you about Kim. We're trying to figure out if she knew the other kids."

"Just leave us alone. We don't want Kim's name in the paper. We don't want her to be remembered that way. She was a beautiful person, not some suicidal psycho like you're trying to make her out to be."

"That's not our intention, Mr. Foster. We're just trying to figure out what happened," Daly said.

"You're just trying to sell papers," Jack said.

"That's not true. Someone threw a firebomb through my window the other night. My daughter and I could have been killed. Now I might not even be able to write this story. But I need to find out what's going on. I need to know who tried to kill my daughter. You might be able to help me. And you might save some other parents from the grief you're feeling now."

Jack Foster paused, clearly surprised by the speech. He was still reluctant to talk, but he believed Daly was trying to help. And what Daly was saying struck a chord in him — a father's hungering for action. If someone really did make his baby kill herself, he would want to find out who it was.

He would want revenge.

"Come in," Jack said. "But everything we say in here is off the record, agreed?"

Daly's excitement at being granted an interview evaporated instantly. But he agreed to Jack's terms. He needed to know what Jack knew, and even if he couldn't write about it, Kim's story could help point him in the right direction.

They sat down on a dingy flower-print couch in a living room cluttered with old issues of Field and Stream and fishing tackle. The head of a twelve-point buck was mounted on a brown-paneled wall opposite the television, surrounded by a pair of mounted largemouth bass. The centerpiece of a pressed-board coffee table was a large crystal ashtray, bulging with crushed Marlboro butts. The room smelled of stale smoke and cat urine.

Daly guessed that Kimberly hadn't brought her cheerleading friends around too often.

As they began talking, Jack cracked open a Keystone Light beer from a mini fridge that doubled as an end table.

"I don't really know how I can help you," Jack said. "You already know Kim was friends with Justin. But as far as I can tell, she never met this other girl."

"Did she have any enemies? Anyone who might have wanted to hurt her? Daly asked.

"Not at all. Kim was a very sweet girl. The other girls on her cheer squad respected her, and she was pretty popular, as far as I could tell."

As Daly listened, he wondered how much Jack really knew about the social dynamics at play when his daughter left the house. She seemed happy. She seemed to have a lot of friends. But how many high school girls would want to let on otherwise?

Daly learned that Jack worked nights at a warehouse up near Pittston, and so he didn't generally see much of his family except on the weekends. Kim's mother, Sarah, worked at a hair salon in Wilkes-Barre to help support Kim and her younger brother, Derek. Kim had been big into cheerleading since she was in elementary school, and she practiced with her squad regularly. Kim was the squad leader, and the other girls looked up to her, according to her father.

Aside from that, she was a pretty typical teenager who liked hanging out at the mall, texting her friends and listening to music. She listened to both Katy Perry and Taylor Swift, feud be damned. She watched "Dancing with the Stars." She was basically just a regular kid, Jack said.

"I heard she was also into poetry," Daly said.

"Yeah, she had an English teacher last year who was big into poetry," Jack said. "Some of the parents got upset about it because he was assigning them some pretty dark stuff – stuff about people drinking and dying and whatnot. I guess some of the parents didn't think it was appropriate for high school."

"What about you?" Daly asked.

"I thought some of it was kind of out there, but as far as I could tell it was the classics. I don't know much about it, but if the experts say it's classic, then I guess it's got to be pretty good."

"Was Kim writing any poetry?" Daly asked.

"She was dabbling in it, I guess you could say," Jack said. "She never showed it to me, though. She said it was private, so I let it be."

"What about what she said ... at the end of the video?" Daly asked, hoping the question wouldn't turn Jack off. "It was a strange thing to say. Do you know where she heard it?"

Jack sat motionless for a moment, then raised the can of Keystone Light to his lips and took a long pull. When he spoke, his voice cracked and he cleared his throat.

"No," Jack said. "I never heard that before."

"What about that teacher? Do you remember his name?" Daly asked.

"I'm not sure. It's probably up in her room somewhere," Jack said, putting the can down on the table next to the mound of cigarette butts. "Come on, let's take a look."

Daly followed Jack into a hallway leading toward the kitchen in the back of the house. The walls were crowded with old family photos in cheap gleaming metal frames. Pictures of Kim smiling in her cheerleading uniform. Pictures of her as a toddler playing with her baby brother. Pictures of Kim with her grandparents.

In one shot, Kim beamed and held a fishing pole while her grandfather hoisted a smallmouth bass in front of her. Daly remarked how happy she looked. Jack nodded in agreement, then noted her grandparents had passed shortly after the picture had been taken.

Daly wondered if Jack realized how close his hallway was to becoming a shrine to the dead.

At the end of the hallway, a staircase branched off, leading to the second story of the house. They climbed the stairs in silence, their footsteps muted by the matted brown shag carpet.

Kim's room was the first room on the right at the top of the stairs. The door, adorned with a pilfered stop sign, was shut. It could not have been an accident. The shut door was a symbol, a barrier preserving what was left of the family's dearly departed

111

daughter nearly two weeks after her untimely demise. In two more weeks' time, the door would still be shut. Everything had changed for the family. There would be no more cheerleading practices, or awkward boyfriend introductions, no more bathroom-time fights with her brother or conversations over dinner. The Foster family had been forever changed by the nine-millimeter lead mushroom that tore through Kim's brain. But in an upside-down world where a lone gunshot in the night turned out to be not a nightmare but a life sentence, the Fosters were determined to hold onto the memory of the little girl they loved.

Jack turned the door handle and pushed open the door to reveal a bedroom that was no longer a bedroom. The bed still sat where it always had, and Kim's desk was right where it belonged. The posters of Katy Perry still hung on the walls and Kim's trophies continued to sparkle on the shelf next to the shoe collection in her closet. But the ginger steps Jack took entering the room and his voice, transformed into a hushed whisper, belied the new purpose of this room. No person would ever rest her head on the pillow again. It was no longer a bedroom. It was a sanctum.

As Daly glanced about the room, he saw Kim's blood had been cleaned from the wall and the carpet. But everything else appeared to have been untouched since the time the infamous video was recorded.

Jack walked over to the desk and slid open a drawer to begin rifling through school papers and documents — pages no one would ever need again. Daly stood by the door, self-consciously trying his best not to seem intrusive. After a few minutes of awkward silence, Jack put his head forward and squinted slightly, reading a sheet of paper in his hands more closely.

"I think I found it. Mr. Gillespie," Jack said, looking up from the paper. "He taught her English class for a few months last year. That's when she started getting interested in poetry."

"Why only a few months?" Daly asked.

"Oh, he was a sub. Her regular teacher had a baby," Jack said.

Daly nodded, taking in the information. A substitute teacher could move between districts, but if he'd only known Kim for a few months the year before it didn't seem like a promising lead.

"And she hadn't been in contact with him since then?" Daly asked.

"Not that I know of," Jack said. "She's been writing poetry, but I don't think she's spoken to him."

"Would you mind if I took a look at her work?"

Jack hesitated. These were poems his daughter had written in private. She hadn't even wanted her own father to read them. Now a newspaper reporter was asking to peer into her innermost thoughts. Her soul.

On the other hand, her journal could contain a clue about her last words. For the past twelve days, Jack had thought of little else besides figuring out why his baby did the unthinkable. And who might have put her up to it.

"I'll tell you what," Jack said. "I'll read through her journal. If I see anything remotely resembling what she said, I'll let you know."

"Fair enough. I appreciate it," Daly said, racking his mind for any other questions to ask. "Is there anything else you can think of?"

He ended every interview the same way. Over the years, he'd learned that often just asking what he forgot to ask about could produce solid information.

"Not really," Jack said. "She seemed like a happy girl. Everyone liked her. Dr. Radcliffe said she seemed to be doing good."

"Dr. Marvin Radcliffe?" Daly asked, stunned to hear the name of a prominent Kingston psychiatrist twice in as many days.

"Yeah, she had been going there for a few months," Jack said. "For a while, she was having some image problems, I guess you could say. Her mother was worried because she wasn't eating. She said she thought she was turning into an anorexic."

"Did the therapy help?" Daly asked.

"I'd say so. Kim started eating dinner with us again. Like I said, she seemed happy."

Daly thanked Jack for his time and offered his condolences for the family's loss. Before leaving, he repeated his promise that he would not publish anything about their conversation without Jack's permission. He walked back to his car like a man in a dream, lost in his thoughts as he processed what he'd just heard.

By their families' accounts, both girls had been happy, well-adjusted kids. Not the kind of kids one would expect to be in therapy.

And yet, both of them were going to the same psychiatrist. *Was it a coincidence?* The longer Daly was in the business, the less he believed in such things. Where there was smoke, there was usually fire. And Dr. Radcliffe's appearance in the case was setting off alarm bells in Daly's mind.

The first thing he needed to do was get back with Celeste Gonzalez. Daly needed to know if Justin had been another happy, well-adjusted kid under the care of Dr. Marvin Radcliffe.

# CHAPTER 14

*Tuesday, April 3, 2018*
*3:34 p.m.*

Daly pulled off Lee Park Avenue and began heading back to Kingston. His initial thought was to call Celeste Gonzalez to ask her about whether Justin had been in therapy, but he decided against that. He wanted to see the look on her face when he mentioned Dr. Radcliffe's name. He wanted to be able to read her.

Crossing the Market Street Bridge, Daly made his way along the wide, tree-lined thoroughfare, driving past the banks and law offices and restaurants until he reached Rutter Avenue. He pulled up in front of the Gonzalez home and was relieved to see Celeste's car was in the driveway.

Celeste answered the door after the first knock.

"Hi, Erik. How are you?" she asked.

"I'm fine, thanks. I wanted to talk to you about something. Could I come in for a minute?" Daly asked.

"Of course," Celeste said, holding open the door for him to pass.

Inside, she offered him a cup of tea that Daly declined. Then they sat on the brown leather couch in the front sitting room. Daly glanced up at the large crucifix hanging on the wall, a reminder to all who passed through these walls the Gonzalezes were God-fearing Christians. Celeste wore a hopeful expression

115

on her face, one that said she was still in denial about Justin's death and that she was wishful Daly would have something to contradict the police. She was looking to him for answers, and Daly began to doubt his decision to come in person, as though he had some big news to reveal. All he'd discovered was a tenuous connection between two kids, and here he was barging into a grieving mother's house as though he'd discovered the Rosetta Stone.

"I wanted to ask about Justin," Daly began, hesitantly. "I was just over at Kim Foster's house. Her father agreed to talk to me about her. I found out she had been seeing the same psychiatrist that Emma Nguyen was. Dr. Marvin Radcliffe."

Celeste slowly began shaking her head as she thought.

"No, I'm sorry," she said. "I don't think I know a Dr. Radcliffe."

Daly slumped his shoulders, dejected. Emma and Kimberly lived miles apart and went to different schools. For them to both know Dr. Radcliffe had seemed like too big a coincidence to be accidental. But if Justin wasn't seeing him, maybe Dr. Radcliffe wasn't the link. Maybe Daly had only what he did when he began: nothing.

"Is there anything else you can think of?" Daly asked, pleading. "I don't know where else to go from here. Did anything else unusual happen before Justin died?"

Celeste took a slow sip of her milky English breakfast tea and stared a few moments too long at the coffee table before speaking. When she did, she put her cup down unsteadily, the tinkling of chattering china momentarily filling the thick silence that had engulfed the sitting room.

"I don't want any of this to get printed," Celeste said flatly. "Do you understand?"

For the next half-hour, Daly's heart sank as he learned about the short and sad life of Justin Gonzalez. Justin, it seemed, had been a good boy who served on the church choir and had a love for God. But he also had a love for other boys. From a young age, Justin had seemed very "sensitive," as his mother put it. Most of his friends had been girls, but he didn't seem to have any attraction to them.

When Justin was fourteen, he'd had a male friend sleep over. The boys were supposed to be upstairs in Justin's room playing video games, but when Celeste went up that night to ask if they wanted a snack, it appeared they were playing something of a different kind. As the door opened up, Celeste had caught a glimpse of hurried movement between the two boys. They quickly separated, and though they were still dressed, Celeste couldn't help but think something had been going on.

Something wrong.

Something unchristian.

Her cheeks flushing with embarrassment, Celeste had whispered a hurried apology and quickly pulled her head from the doorway.

She left the door open.

At her bedside, she went to her knees and offered a silent prayer for her son, hoping that what she thought she had seen had been a mistake. Maybe they had just been horsing around. Maybe Justin had just been reaching for something.

But the thought of having a gay son consumed Celeste. A few weeks later, she built up the nerve to ask him about it. She could tell Justin was embarrassed by the questions and was hesitant to answer. He didn't know how his father would react.

But at heart, he was a good Christian boy. He couldn't lie to his own mother. He told her the truth and Celeste broke down in tears.

After service on the following Sunday, Celeste had pulled the priest aside and confided in him her son's deepest secret. Justin had stood meekly at her side, eyes fixed to the floor, as he listened to his mother describe him as being possessed by the devil. The priest agreed to take Justin under his counsel and try to reform him. Celeste didn't exactly say so, but it was pretty clear to Daly she wanted Justin to pray the gay away, as the saying goes.

For a while, Celeste thought it was working. Justin was more interested in what she considered straight activities like sports, and he stopped hanging out with the boy from the sleepover. Of course, Justin never learned to be straight. He merely learned to better hide being gay from his family.

Life went on normally for a while after Justin's counseling. Justin hid his true feelings. Celeste pretended her son wasn't gay. In Celeste's mind, anyway, everyone was happy. But then came the day she decided, on a whim, to check Justin's Facebook page. He hadn't done anything in particular to warrant a search, but Celeste liked to check in every once in a while, just in case.

Justin had gone to school as usual, and the moment he stepped onto the bus Celeste had gone to the den and logged onto the family computer. After opening the browser and navigating to Facebook, Celeste began going down Justin's timeline. Memes, videos of people falling down, selfies snapped in front of the bathroom mirror. It was routine stuff. After reading his posts from the past few weeks, she went to close out the window. But before she did, it occurred to her to check the messages. She clicked the message icon and started down the list. Justin didn't have too many new messages – he preferred texting and Tweeting – so it was easy for Celeste to pick out a thread toward the top of the list.

As she read the exchange, a nervous frown crept across her

face. She brought her hand to her mouth to cover the chasm that opened when her jaw gave out. She felt sick. Justin had been chatting with a man, a grown man. Celeste crossed herself as she read the foul exchange, stopping after a few messages to pinch her eyes and clear her throat.

She sat in stunned silence for a few minutes before slowly sliding the cursor up the screen and closing the browser. The churning in her stomach gave way to anger as she thought about how her son – her own son – had been lying to her face for months. Every week he'd assured her his talks with the priest were helping his urges. He promised he wasn't feeling attracted to boys anymore.

Now, betrayal. Justin had been lying, feeding her lines. *That will not stand*, Celeste thought.

And that man. That predator lurking behind a screen name, willing to talk to her precious sixteen-year-old son like he was some sort of a whore. A grown man who enjoyed preying on children, a man who probably jerked off every time he read her baby's words.

Celeste seethed.

When Justin came home from school that afternoon, Celeste was sitting in the front sitting room motionless, staring ahead at the wall. Justin looked at her with a nervous smile and asked if everything was all right when it clearly was not.

No, everything was not all right, she said. Not by a long shot. She told Justin what she'd found and demanded he explain himself. Justin knew there was nothing he could say. He was caught. He was caught and his mother knew it and now she would punish him.

"I want to help you," Celeste had said.

Justin's eyebrows raised up, tentatively. What was this?

Sympathy? Not scorn?

"Who is that man you've been talking to?" Celeste asked.

"He's just a guy I know," Justin said. "It's no big deal."

"You know him? In person?" Celeste asked. A chill surged through her body.

Justin assured her nothing had happened. They chatted online sometimes, but they'd never done anything. He looked his mother in the eyes and promised. He begged her not to call the police. He vowed to change.

Celeste had been reluctant. She knew how Justin really felt, and she knew it would be hard for him to deny his desires. But she could also see the pleading look in her son's eyes, a look that said calling the police would be apocalyptic for Justin. Criminal charges would mean public court hearings. Sex charges would mean media attention. Regardless, other kids in Justin's class would almost certainly find out about it. He would be outed. More than that, he would be outed as a gay snitch whose mother had to step in and save her little baby.

That phone call would have been social suicide for Justin.

So Celeste promised she wouldn't intervene. But she vowed to be vigilant. She had stood over Justin's shoulder as he unfriended the creature on Facebook, and blocked him from making future contact. She warned Justin she would be checking, and she didn't want to see any more. No more dirty talk with grown men. No more flirtation with boys in general, for that matter.

Justin promised, and for Celeste the matter was a done deal.

But Daly wasn't so sure.

"This guy on Facebook, how do you know he never contacted Justin again?" he asked.

"I guess I don't for sure. But we put monitoring software on Justin's cellphone so we could keep tabs on what he was doing.

We never got an alert about that guy again."

"Do you know who he was?" Daly asked. "The guy Justin was talking to?"

"Vincent Gillespie," Celeste said. "Justin had him as a substitute a few times."

The melancholy that overcame Daly at hearing Justin's gloomy coming-of-age story vanished in an instant. As he walked down the sidewalk to his car, his step regained a slight bounce. Vincent Gillespie knew Kimberly Foster and Justin Gonzalez, and apparently pretty well at that. If Daly could connect Gillespie to Emma Nguyen, he could have another viable lead. But for this part of his investigation, Daly decided to skip meeting back up with Linh Nguyen, at least for the time being. It was time, he decided, to meet Steve the boyfriend.

◆ ◆ ◆

Tracking down Steve was much easier than Daly had anticipated — all he had to do was call Linh Nguyen and explain he was trying to get a more complete picture of Emma's life and wanted to talk to other people who knew her. Linh had been more than happy to give up Steve Granger's cellphone number.

Steve picked up after the third ring, sounding wary and guarded about answering a call from a number he didn't recognize. Daly identified himself and in the same breath threw out Linh Nguyen's name. Emma's mother was on board with this project, and he wanted to make damned sure Steve the boyfriend knew it. At the mention of Linh's name, Steve seemed to let down his guard a bit. He agreed to talk.

It turned out some of Daly's initial information had been a bit off. Steve wasn't as much a boyfriend as an ex-boyfriend. The two had split up about three weeks before Emma died.

The timing of the split could not have been a coincidence. Emma had only recently learned she was pregnant and probably had only been with child for a few weeks when she died.

"Why did you two break up?" Daly asked.

"You probably know she was pregnant," Steve said. "I wasn't going to deal with that."

The blunt answer startled Daly. He suspected Steve had broken things off because of the baby, but he didn't expect him to freely admit it. Lots of young men get scared off by the thought of responsibility and domestication. Most of them have enough vanity to at least pretend the baby wasn't the reason for the split.

"Didn't you feel bad leaving her like that?" Daly asked, trying to bury the resentment in his voice.

"I thought about her as much as she thought about me," Steve said. "It wasn't my baby."

It was an answer Daly hadn't expected. He began to feel guilty for judging. Apparently Steve wasn't some deadbeat who left a young girl's life in ruins after he had his fun. He was just a kid who had been hurt by the girl he cared about, reacting the way most men would.

Assuming, of course, that the story were true.

"I'm sorry," Daly said, still skeptical. "How did you find out?"

"How? We never did it. It couldn't have been mine," Steve said.

Daly learned that Steve and Emma had begun dating about eight months earlier. Through the years, they had been aware of each other at school, but it wasn't until the previous fall when they really got to know each other. They had been paired up as partners in their chemistry class and hit it off right away. Steve had recently ended another relationship, what he described as a summer fling. He liked the way Emma sometimes rolled her eyes and smiled at him when the teacher made bad science puns. She liked how Steve got her jokes and the way he smiled back at her. One day at the end of class, Steve had asked her out to the movies. She said yes, and they had been an item since.

But after the new year, things were different. They were still science partners, but Emma seemed to have cooled to Steve. It was like a giant chasm had opened between them, and Steve couldn't see across it. When they kissed, Emma broke away first. She wasn't smiling the same way at his corny jokes. Her hand easily lost its grip in his.

Eventually, Emma stopped coming over Steve's place after school. She always had an excuse – she wasn't feeling well, or she had to help her mother with something at home – but to Steve, it was clear that something had changed. The relationship had undergone a shift and the chemistry that once existed had vanished.

Steve hadn't known what the problem was. As far as he could tell, he hadn't changed. He still cared for Emma and wanted things to work out. He tried small gestures to win her back. Emma started finding flowers in her locker. Love notes were slipped into her textbooks. She always smiled and hugged Steve to show her thanks, but the gesture was perfunctory. There was no feeling behind it.

Then one day in early March, Emma had asked Steve to walk her home from school. He should have seen it coming. Something was obviously broken with the relationship. It had been raining outside – hardly an ideal day for the long walk to Emma's house in Plains. But Steve said he had been clueless about the relationship's steady decay until that afternoon.

As they made their way up Main Street, Emma confided that

she was pregnant. At first, he didn't know what to say. He was a high school junior who just learned his girlfriend was pregnant. And there was no way the child could be his. The emotions ran through him in quick succession: surprise, disbelief, jealousy, anger.

"Please don't be mad at me," Emma had said, tears streaming down her cheeks. "I didn't mean for this to happen."

But how could he not be angry? Standing on the corner of Main and North streets, Steve had spoken the last words he would ever exchange with Emma Nguyen. When he stormed off, a look of rage masked the tears that were building up in his eyes. Emma stood on the corner, sobbing alone in the cool afternoon drizzle.

"Did you ever find out whose baby it was?" Daly asked.

"She told me whose it was that day," Steve said. "It was a substitute teacher she had for English. Mr. Gillespie."

# CHAPTER 15

*Wednesday, April 4, 2018*
*11:43 a.m.*

This was the day. All through the night, Daly had tossed and turned. There had been no danger of the dream returning. There had been no chance of finding sleep. For two weeks, he had been chasing a phantom, an unknown malevolent force that may not have even existed. Now, after countless miles spent driving back and forth across the Wyoming Valley, Daly felt he was finally close.

On paper, Vincent Gillespie seemed normal. Online court records showed Gillespie was twenty-eight years old and lived in Pittston. He had a few speeding tickets a few years back, but no criminal history. From the digital archive, Daly learned that Gillespie had graduated from his hometown's Pittston Area High School in 2008. He could only assume that Gillespie had been in college during at least some of the intervening years. It looked like Gillespie had a Facebook page, but most of it was private. The profile picture showed a smiling well-groomed man wearing a shirt and tie with his sleeves rolled up. It appeared that Mr. Gillespie also had a dog and drove a Ford Five Hundred. Mr. Normal.

But.

To Daly, it seemed improbable that the same teacher would have been involved in the lives of three suicide victims. Three kids who went to different schools. There were thousands of high school students spread out over more than a dozen high schools in Luzerne County. And Mr. Gillespie was a young man. He wouldn't have had much time to substitute all over the county to get to know the kids.

And the fact remained that he didn't just know them. He appeared to have made a connection to each of them. For Justin and Emma, that connection was a felony. According to Jack Foster, Gillespie had just been talking poetry to Kimberly. But who knew how much Jack really knew about his daughter's personal life? Having a fling with a teacher wasn't something a teenage girl would likely bring up at the dinner table.

No, Daly felt certain it was no coincidence. Something nefarious was at work. It had claimed the lives of three young kids — kids who seemed normal and appeared to be on the right track in life. Until they met Mr. Gillespie. Daly felt determined to find out what was going on. He wanted to look Gillespie in the eye and find out what he knew. Most of all, Daly wanted to expose him for what he was: a wolf in sheep's clothing, a snake in the grass, a stalking lion.

A predator.

A predator lurking in the shadows, watching and waiting for his next victim.

But before he confronted Mr. Gillespie, Daly had one more bit of business to handle. Jack Foster had mentioned that other parents were upset with Mr. Gillespie because of the poems he was reading to students.

Daly intended to find out what other concerns they had. He was hoping the president of the Hanover Area Junior Senior High School parent-teacher association would be able to shed some light on Mr. Gillespie.

Judy Grant was a chubby woman with frizzy brown hair, thick, ominous eyebrows, and a square jaw. When Daly rang her bell, she'd come to the door with a suspicious scowl on her face that didn't disappear when he identified himself as a reporter. She listened to Daly with her left hand draped across her chin and her right arm wrapped across her lumpy sweatshirt. But when Daly mentioned Mr. Gillespie, Judy Grant stepped back and held the door open. As PTA president, Mrs. Grant had a solemn duty to spread gossip to anyone willing to listen. And this was a subject she apparently very much liked to discuss.

As Daly learned, Vincent Gillespie had come on as a substitute at the district the previous year. He was young and pretty recently out of college. Judy guessed he was in his late twenties.

Mr. Gillespie's appearance in the school landscape had gone mostly unnoticed until one day the previous May when Judy looked over the shoulder of her daughter Kyla and saw her reading a poem called "Howl" by Allen Ginsberg. Judy's hackles immediately went up. The poem was nothing short of obscene, she said.

"There's talk of sex and homosexuals and drugs," Judy said. "It's not literature. It's vulgar. And it's inappropriate for kids in high school."

Mr. Gillespie, it seemed, had a tendency to get close to his students. More than one parent had complained about him texting students with reading recommendations. Most of it was legitimate literature, but he wasn't recommending Mark Twain.

Mr. Gillespie's reading list was far more crude — and concerning — than that. Judy described him as a subversive. His book list suggested he was grooming children and trying to break down their inhibitions, rather than trying to educate them, she said.

Some of the parents had taken their concerns to the school board a few months earlier. They had no proof of wrongdoing, only disagreements about his reading recommendations. Several of the parents presented text messages Mr. Gillespie had sent to their children. While the messages contained nothing incriminating, some board members had expressed concern about teachers texting students. They assured the parents it wasn't against district policy, but it was frowned upon.

Daly also learned that another parent had spoken to the board about Mr. Gillespie: Sarah Foster. Kim's mother. Judging by Judy's account of the meeting, Sarah Foster was more concerned about Mr. Gillespie than her husband had been. Sarah had also found Kim reading "Howl" along with other risqué works that she found unsuitable for her teenage daughter. She'd discovered Mr. Gillespie had been texting Kimberly, chatting with her about poetry and school. For Sarah Foster, the exchanges had seemed a little too familiar. A little too close. Mr. Gillespie sounded like a friend, not a teacher.

But the most concerning part to Sarah was that Mr. Gillespie had been giving Kimberly things — presents. There was nothing big – a paperback or two and an app on her cellphone – but it was enough to make Sarah question the nature of the student-teacher relationship.

In the end, the school board president said he would talk to Mr. Gillespie about the concerns, but said he couldn't do much more. Nothing the parents had alleged was against school policy. Mr. Gillespie might be a bit unorthodox, but the board couldn't fault him for trying to get kids to read, the president had said.

"What was the app?" Daly asked. "That he put on her cellphone?"

"Oh, just some white-noise app to help her sleep," Judy said.

The blood in Daly's veins turned to ice. A chill shuttered up his back. It seemed David Kowalski wasn't the only one who had been using white noise to fall asleep.

"Was it called Soma?" Daly asked.

"Why, yes," Judy said. "How did you guess that?"

◆◆◆

Nestled along the banks of the muddy Susquehanna River, midway between Wilkes-Barre and Scranton, Pittston had been, in its heyday, a mining hub that brought scores of immigrants to the region, swelling the population of the city in the nineteenth century. In the early twentieth century, mines and coal fields in the Pittston area served as the backdrop for photographer Lewis Hine's work for the National Child Labor Committee — haunting black-and-white images of soot-covered boys that led to child labor reforms across the country.

When the Susquehanna River broke through the roof of the River Slope Mine in nearby Jenkins Township on January 22, 1959, the waters killed twelve miners along with coal mining in Northeastern Pennsylvania in what came to be known as the Knox Mine disaster.

The collapse of coal mining brought hard times to the region. The population dropped. The owners of Pittston's Main Street businesses boarded up their shops. Tight-knit rows of miner's houses began showing rust and wood rot.

But starting in the mid-1990s, city officials began a push to revitalize a downtown in disrepair. Local leaders began pushing public art and festivals. Riverfront condominiums rose up. Businesses opened their doors.

What once had been a bleak and despairing main drag had

been transformed into a bustling business district lined with bright murals and polished, inviting facades. As Daly made his way down it, he wondered what Mr. Gillespie would have to say to him. He guessed it wouldn't be much. But he was hoping Mr. Gillespie's eyes might give away something more.

Daly's global-positioning app directed him to a small house a few blocks off Main Street. The house had relatively new roof shingles and a fresh coat of paint. The lawn had been cleared of autumn leaves, and the grass seemed trimmed. It was a well-maintained yard. Over the front steps, a Philadelphia Eagles flag drifted gently in the breeze.

Daly turned off his car engine and got ready for the ambush. Most likely, Mr. Gillespie wouldn't want to comment. But sometimes people who don't want to comment blurt something out before slamming the door in a reporter's face. When that happens, the reporter has to be ready to catch it.

With his notebook and recorder in hand, Daly walked up the cracked sidewalk to the door and hit the buzzer. In all his years covering crime, Daly had seen doors slammed in his face and been threatened, but no one had ever actually gotten violent because of him knocking on a door. Then again, this would be the first time Daly had ever directly confronted a possible child molester who could be connected to three deaths.

Anything was possible.

When the door, opened, Daly saw the same face that had been smiling on Mr. Gillespie's Facebook page. The shirt and tie had been replaced by a Penn State sweatshirt. The smile had been usurped by a wary gaze.

"Yes?" he asked.

"Mr. Gillespie, I'm a reporter with the Wilkes-Barre Observer. I'm working on a story about a series of deaths we've had in local high schools recently. Your name has come up as being connected to the students from school. And some of the allegations I've heard are very serious."

As Daly spoke, the disinterested look Mr. Gillespie had on his face upon answering the door melted away. His gaze turned to a steely eyed expression of hate. Throughout his career, Daly had come across many killers. Some he'd even personally interviewed in their new accommodations at the Luzerne County Correctional Facility. Most of them displayed something that other people didn't have – some sort of an aura or demeanor or quality. Daly couldn't quite put his finger on it. The domestic killers – guys who shot their wives in a fit of rage or shook their crying babies to death in the middle of the night – usually didn't have it. They were mostly regular people who snapped and made bad choices in the heat of the moment. But something about the hardened killers set them apart from everybody else. It wasn't just the coldness in their gaze or the way they carried themselves as they shuffled along the courthouse corridors in chains. They exuded an aura that seemed to say they took what they wanted, whenever they wanted. And nobody would stand in their way.

That same vibe hit Daly now.

As Mr. Gillespie leaned out the front door, staring Daly down, Daly could tell from the look in his eye that he was not a kind man.

He was ruthless. He was a predator. Maybe even a killer.

"You came to my house to accuse me?" Mr. Gillespie said. "Get the hell off my property. Now."

No threat of calling the police, Daly noted. Mr. Gillespie didn't seem the type to waste taxpayer dollars on such a matter. He struck Daly as the kind of guy who handled trouble himself.

Daly went back to his car, switching off his recorder on the way. *For the story, a simple "he declined to comment" will be sufficient*, Daly thought.

As a journalist, Daly made every effort to stay impartial. He didn't comment on political posts on Facebook, nor did he "like" pages about sensitive topics. Crime reporters don't usually have to deal too much with the politics – everybody hates crime – but still he tried to be fair. When he wrote about an arrest, he always tried to reach out to the defendant, if possible, to give him or her a chance to comment. He prided himself on being fair and had built up a reputation for being honest and trustworthy as a result.

But as he sat in his car, getting ready to go back to the newsroom, Daly felt a growing rage inside of himself as he thought about the dead kids. In the months leading up to their deaths, Mr. Gillespie had been molesting at least one of them. In all likelihood, he had been doing something with Justin Gonzalez, too. And it was sounding more and more likely that Kim Foster was involved with Mr. Gillespie somehow as well.

Daly wasn't a man who usually saw things in black and white. There were at least two sides to every story. Usually, both of them had some merit. As Daly saw it, his job as a reporter was to grasp the nuance and present a balanced picture for his readers.

But right now, Daly was having trouble finding any nuance for Mr. Gillespie. What kind of a man could molest children? What kind of a man could play some sort of role – directly or indirectly, Daly still didn't know – in their deaths?

This wasn't a story with two sides. This was a story about a depraved monster who was using and discarding children for his own pleasure.

Forget the nuance. Forget impartiality. This piece of shit needed to go down.

# CHAPTER 16

*Thursday, April 5, 2018*
*4:12 a.m.*

In the darkness of the room at the Mountain Motor Lodge, Daly's eyes flashed open. For a moment, he looked around wildly, uncomprehending.

It was always the same after the dream. Beads of sweat collected on his head. His tee-shirt felt damp and had acquired the dull, musky odor of sweat. His eyes darted back and forth, trying to make out his surroundings in the dark. From the front window of the hotel room, the faint glow of the neon lights sliced like razors through small cracks in the curtains. To one side, Daly could hear Lauren breathing the steady rhythm of a girl at peace.

All was well at the Mountain Motor Lodge.

As Daly was lying down in the darkness, afraid any movement would wake Lauren, he tried to remember what had happened. It had been the dream again, of course, but it had somehow changed again. As he slowly regained consciousness, he tried to grasp the fleeting thoughts that had been his dream, knowing that if they escaped now he would never remember.

He could still picture the same desert motor lodge on the side of a dusty highway, and could still see Ed and Barbara Thompson sitting by the pool, sipping cocktails without a care in the world. Lauren was still the seventeen-year-old senior she had been the last time, but now she was down by the pool with her grandparents.

Rather than being in the bathroom this time around, Daly found himself down by the pool as well. And he had one terrifying thought.

Jessica was in the room by herself.

From down by the pool, Daly looked up to the room to see if anything appeared out of place. The faded off-white curtain was still closed in the window. The door was shut.

But Daly could feel something was wrong. He didn't know exactly what. He just knew something was wrong.

He climbed the stairs to the second-floor balcony, eyes fixed on the door to the room. When he got there, he found the door was not fully shut, as it initially appeared from downstairs. The faded and scuffed red door had not been latched, and had drifted slightly open in the gentle, hot breeze. A sliver of darkness peered out into the unforgiving desert sun.

Slowly, he put his hand to the door and pushed, bathing the room in the sun's golden glow. There was no gas can, and when he looked at his own hands there was no gun. But near the bed, where the shadow of the room still held fast against the encroaching sunlight, he could see Jessica's legs lying motionless.

He stepped through the doorway, allowing his eyes to relax as they entered the shadowy room. On the bed, he could see Jessica's playful smile projected upward. Her eyes gazed blankly toward the ceiling. That patch of drywall – not Daly or Lauren – had been the last thing she ever saw. As he moved closer to the bed, he could see the blood on the pillows and headboard. He began to weep. There was no murder to cover up this time. No crushing, overwhelming sense of guilt. Just sorrow for his beautiful, departed wife.

This had been uncharted territory for the dream. For years, Daly had awakened in a fit of terror or anger or shame at the thoughts that tormented him in the darkest hours of night. Now, seeing Jessica on the bed without feeling the guilt that came with holding the gun, Daly didn't know how to react. He stood there for a moment in a daze, confused about what to do next.

He decided to head back to the pool and tell the Thompsons what had become of their baby girl. He turned toward the door and his eye caught the flash of movement in the corner of the room. He stopped in his tracks. Looking to the darkened corner, Daly saw the outline of a figure standing there. He stood paralyzed with fear for a long moment, waiting for his eyes to adjust to the cave-like light at the periphery of the room. Then he was able to make out that the figure was a man.

Holding a gun.

"Hello, Mr. Gillespie," Daly said.

Then he woke up.

◆ ◆ ◆

Sleep was elusive after the dream. It always was. For a while, Daly lay in his bed, tossing, as though the problem were his physical comfort. Every time he rotated, he grew more frustrated. After more than an hour, he decided it was useless and abandoned hope of falling back asleep. He tossed the sheet back, put his feet on the ground and went over to a coffee machine he'd picked up at Walmart to start a pot.

He moved quietly in the dark, mindful about waking Lauren so early in the morning. But as soon as the coffeemaker began hissing and gurgling on the desk, Lauren's sheets began rustling. As she leaned up on her elbow, a tuft of hair fell over her glazed, half-closed eyes.

"What time is it?" she asked.

"Early," Daly said. "I'm sorry to wake you. Go back to sleep."

"I will when you do," Lauren said. "Was it the dream again?"

In the dull blue light, Daly nodded his head. "It was. But it's different. It's changing. For the first time in fourteen years, it's changing."

"What changed?" Lauren asked.

"There was someone else there. Someone new. Someone who ... who couldn't have been there," Daly said.

"Who was it?"

"A bad guy. At least, I think he's a bad guy. I don't really want to get into it," Daly said, reaching for the television remote control on the nightstand.

The local morning news was already on. Daly sat back against the headboard of his bed and sipped the bitter black coffee from a cheap mug. The weatherman was barely able to contain his excitement about the possibility of more snow over the weekend. It was already a couple of weeks into spring, but the cold and snow had not gotten the memo. Neither that nor the ungodly hour of day seemed to have put a damper on the weatherman's spirits.

Daly rose out of bed and walked to the window, peeling back the drab curtains to reveal the beginning of another gray, damp day. Light fog hung in the pine trees across the highway, giving them a mystical aura. Now and then, the headlights of a passing car flashed across the wet black pavement, but it was still early and traffic was light. Somewhere in the misty woods, a cardinal called out under the pre-dawn sky.

Such days made Daly feel somber and reflective. As he took another sip of coffee, he couldn't help but think about the kids whose deaths had consumed his life over the past few weeks. They all seemed like normal kids. Kids who flirted and fretted over tests. Kids who played and laughed. Kids who had just barely begun life when it was all taken away from them.

But while they each seemed normal, none of them was living a storybook life. Under the surface, they each had their own demons to fight. There was darkness behind the light, and each of them was working actively to stifle it. Kim Foster was a happy, well-liked cheerleader. She was also borderline anorexic. Justin Gonzalez was a church-going boy who loved his family. A family who couldn't bear the thought of him being himself. He chose a life of lies and secrecy rather than to demand they accept him for who he was. And Emma Nguyen had been smart and would probably have had no trouble getting into a top-notch medical school. Her family believed in her and would have footed the bill. But she couldn't even bring herself to tell them about her dying shame — her own baby.

They were just kids. Young, stupid kids who wanted nothing more in life than to be accepted. It was those around them who failed to give them the only thing they wanted. The only thing they'd ever wanted.

"Lauren? I've been thinking," Daly began. "I was wrong about you going to the prom with Kevin. It was wrong of me to judge him based on what his father did. You're free to go to the prom with whoever you want."

The shift in the conversation seemed to catch Lauren off-guard. She rose off her elbow and sat up in bed, turning to face her father.

"Thank you, Daddy. He's a really nice guy. I think you'll like him," Lauren said.

"I don't have to like him," Daly said. "But I do love you."

◆ ◆ ◆

The lights were still off when Daly got to the newsroom.

The only sound was the muted squawk of the scanner chatter in the corner. After setting down his coffee and logging into the computer, he set about trying to verify what the parents had told him, as best he could. Checking on Mr. Gillespie's presence at the schools had been fairly straightforward. The solicitors for all three districts were able to verify that Mr. Gillespie had subbed at the same schools as all three victims — although none of them had any exact dates available right away.

That showed Mr. Gillespie could have been involved. But it was still a far cry from showing he was involved. For that, Daly needed to call Wojcik to see if the police were also looking into him. A story about parents suspecting a substitute was molesting kids was a good basis for a defamation lawsuit. But a story about police investigating allegations of misconduct against said teacher was fair game.

Leaning back in his chair, Daly dialed the digits to Wojcik's cellphone and listened as Journey faded in, with Steve Perry beseeching him not to stop believing.

*Christ.*

Wojcik answered just after Perry finished advising Daly to "hold on to the feeling."

"Phil, I've been looking into these deaths some more and wanted to run a few things past you," Daly said.

"What do you got?" Wojcik asked.

"Well, some of the parents have told me they were concerned about a substitute. Vincent Gillespie. He was apparently giving kids some advanced reading assignments, and I've found indications that it might have gone further than that with some of them. Is he someone you're looking at?" Daly asked.

On the other end of the phone, Daly could hear Wojcik exhale deeply, followed by a long pause. The detective was thinking carefully about how to respond.

"Look, the only thing I can say on the record right now is that it's an ongoing investigation," Wojcik said.

"And off the record?"

"We're looking at him. We've got information that he was sexting Justin Gonzalez, and we think he may have been involved with the others somehow too. We've got warrants for Facebook and Verizon, and right now we're waiting for them to provide the records," Wojcik said.

"Where's that filed at?" Daly asked.

"It's sealed by court order," Wojcik said.

*Shit*, Daly thought. *Of course it is.*

"Fair to say he's a suspect?" Daly asked.

"I'd say we're very interested in what comes back on those warrants."

"When do you expect them back?" Daly asked.

"I'm hoping in a few more days. If it comes back the way I think it will, we'll have him in bracelets by the end of next week," Wojcik said.

By the time Daly ended the call, John Richardson was already at his desk in the editors' cube flipping through a copy of the Other Paper. As Daly walked over, he let the paper droop into his lap and peered over the top of his glasses.

"Making much progress?"

"We've got something big here," Daly said.

He proceeded to walk Richardson through his progress the last few days and what he'd learned about Vincent Gillespie. The explicit chats. The graphic poems. The parents' concerns. Gillespie's hardened stare.

"What about the cops? Where are they on this?" Richardson asked.

"Officially, it's still under investigation," Daly said. "Off the record, Wojcik told me they're looking at Gillespie hard. They've got warrants out for his social media and cellphone records. They could make an arrest next week."

"So what do you think we should do?" Richardson asked. It would be up to the editors to decide how to play the story, if at all, but Richardson liked to get input from his reporters first. It was a good way to gauge their news judgment.

"I don't think anybody else is on this," Daly said. "If we wait until they file charges next week, we're going to be in a pack of reporters at the arraignment. If we do something now, we can get ahead of the story and have a leg up when they file."

Richardson sat back for a moment, staring at the wall with his hands clapped together in front of his mouth. It was tempting to get the scoop on the Other Paper, for sure. But writing a story before charges were filed could be legally perilous. Especially if the basis for the story was simply the suspicions of prying parents.

What if there really was nothing there? What if the police never charged Gillespie? What if it was all a mirage conjured up by a few hysterical PTA moms with nothing better to do than gossip and conspire?

"I think we need to be careful with this one, Erik," Richardson finally said. "These are some serious allegations. I think we need more than just the fact that there is a search warrant – especially since we haven't even seen it."

"If we hold off on this, we could get beat," Daly said, fuming inside. He couldn't believe Richardson was willing to let a scoop so big slip through his fingers.

"We won't get beat," Richardson assured him. "I'm confident we're miles ahead of the Other Paper on this one. Worst case scenario is we both do the story the day of the arrest and it's a draw. But you'll already have the legwork done, so we'll be ready with the story on a silver platter while they're still reading through the complaint."

Daly shuffled back to his desk and slumped into his chair, reaching for his coffee. If they got beat, it wouldn't be on him. Richardson had made the call, and he would be responsible for the outcome. But that wasn't much solace to Daly. He tried to put it out of his mind as he began clicking through the online dockets, searching for new and interesting crimes.

In the movies, newspaper reporters are usually caricatures. They're either nuisances in brown fedoras with oversized press passes who lob softballs until the cops swat them to the side, or they spend months cultivating sources and meeting in dark garages to expose some grand wrong. The reality is that very few local newspapers have the resources anymore to do real long-term investigative journalism – but that doesn't stop them from trying. The reporters just have to do the investigation in between everything else that goes on. The daily beast is always hungry.

As Daly clicked through the docket sheets, his desk phone began to ring. He glanced at the caller ID but didn't recognize the number. He picked it up, hoping it wasn't some conspiracy theorist asking why the paper didn't investigate and expose the truth of some crackpot idea.

"Newsroom, this is Erik Daly," he said.

"Erik, this is Jack Foster," the voice said.

"Hey, Jack. What's going on?" Daly said.

"Not too much. I just wanted to let you know about Kim's journal," Jack said.

"Did you find anything?"

"Mostly it was just her writing about school gossip," Jack said. "You know, who likes who, who was flirting. Stuff like that. She also had some poems. Nothing too crazy. But toward the end of it, she had something that made my skin crawl."

"What was it?" Daly asked.

"It was written in the margin. Just scribbled like a note," Jack said. "It said, 'End it now. Before they find out.'"

Daly paused for a moment, startled by the bleak message.

"I'm sorry," he said. "Do you have any idea what it means?"

"I don't have a clue," Jack said. "As far as I know, Kim didn't have any secrets. There's nothing she could have done that would make us stop loving her."

Daly ended the call, not sure what to make of it. The words he thought might be there hadn't been there. Instead, there was a cryptic message that raised more questions. The last words that connected the three teens remained as big a mystery as ever.

As Daly leaned back in his chair contemplating what Jack had said, the scanner in the corner of the newsroom screeched to life with a report of a gunshot victim. The dispatcher called for Nanticoke police and firefighters to respond to a report of a male found with a gunshot wound to the head. Daly perked up and grabbed a pen to write down the address. When it came across, Daly paused for a second. He felt a sense of deja vu as he scribbled down the Noble Street address. Then it hit him.

It was David Kowalski's house.

# CHAPTER 17

*Thursday, April 5, 2018*
*11:24 a.m.*

When Daly pulled onto Noble Street, he could see from down the block that he wasn't going to find a spot in front of the house. The Ford Thunderbird was still in the driveway of a home with peeling paint and rusting furniture on the front porch. But the porch was now adorned with crime scene tape that police bent under as they came and went into the house.

Police dispatchers are trained to keep their cool, especially when the shit hits the fan. But when a serious emergency arises, the stress and excitement still show in their voices. The dispatcher on the scanner hadn't sounded very excited at all. From a single glance at the scene, Daly could tell the police weren't too excited either. There were only three patrol cars and a sport-utility vehicle from the coroner's office. The front of the house was blocked by crime scene tape, but the sidewalk and street were open. The cops and deputy coroner seemed to be going about business as usual.

Someone had clearly died, but the cops definitely didn't think it was a murder.

Already, a reporter from the Other Paper was standing a couple of doors down, trying to give the cops a respectful distance as he waited for someone to come tell him what happened. The TV stations hadn't yet shown up — if they were even coming. Daly walked over to stand by him.

"What's up, Derrick?" he asked. "They say anything yet?"

"No," he said. "One of the cops said the chief would be over in a few."

"You want to tag team it?"

"Sure," Derrick said. "It sounds like a suicide anyway."

If so, it almost certainly wouldn't be a story. *Unless it turns out to be David Kowalski*, Daly thought.

Some of the older newspapermen still held a grudge from the union strike that led to Wilkes-Barre becoming a two-newspaper town, but most of the younger ones were more concerned about their increasing workloads and job security. Daly fell into the latter camp. After years of covering the same perp walks and court hearings as reporters on the other side, he'd become friendly with many of them. He offered to do a joint interview because he figured there was no sense in trying to hide something from another reporter when the reporter would easily get the same information as soon as he talked to the cops.

That said, there was no way Daly was letting on he knew who lived at that house. Or how Kowalski was connected to the dying children.

Chief Jerry Fitzgerald was a portly man with a brown bushy mustache that had overrun his upper lip and sharp eyes that gazed out from behind rectangular rimmed glasses. As he sauntered over to Daly and Derrick, he raised a finger to his temple and brought it forward in salute.

"Nothing much for you here, boys," Fitzgerald said amiably.

"What happened?" Daly asked.

"We have a seventeen-year-old male with a gunshot wound to the head," Fitzgerald said. "His father found him in his room shortly after ten-thirty this morning. He was pronounced dead at the scene. No foul play is suspected."

"Suicide?" Derrick asked.

"We're still investigating, but right now we don't suspect foul play," Fitzgerald said, his mouth curling into a wry smile.

Daly could read between the lines. It was clearly a suicide, but Fitzgerald was reluctant to announce it to the world. He was worried about the family's privacy. What he didn't realize was that if he just confirmed it was a suicide, the reporters would walk away without a story. But by introducing some doubt to the case, Fitzgerald was actually increasing the chances of the death making the paper.

With some information in hand, the reporters backed away from the scene and got on their cellphones to report back to their newsrooms. After a brief conversation, Derrick got back in his car and drove off. Daly got back in his car but decided to wait it out.

David Kowalski was almost certainly the victim, and he needed to make a run at speaking to his father when police cleared the scene.

After about an hour, the deputy coroner and a few officers came outside, hoisting a shrouded corpse into the coroner's black SUV. Not long afterward, an officer began pulling down the yellow crime scene tape that had been wrapped around the front porch. After milling around for a few more minutes, the police began to disperse.

Daly waited about five minutes after the last cruiser had pulled away before popping his door open and heading toward the porch. The timing was hardly ideal. Within the past couple hours, Mr. Kowalski had discovered his son dead, most likely by his own hand. Now a reporter was knocking.

Mr. Kowalski opened the door almost as soon as Daly's knuckles left the door frame. He was a wiry man in a yellow-stained tee-shirt and blue jeans that were coated in a sickening layer of brown grime. The greasy hair that formed a perimeter around a bald patch up top extended in every which direction, giving him a crazed look. He appeared as though he'd been suddenly awakened from the deep sleep of a man who'd had a six pack or two the night before.

He probably had.

"Mr. Kowalski, I'm Erik Daly with the Observer," Daly said. "I was wondering..."

"No comment," Kowalski said, pushing the door closed. Daly put up his hand to stop it.

"Please, just hear me out for a minute," Daly said. "I have reason to believe your son didn't kill himself. At least, not on purpose."

Kowalski glanced up with a look of surprise in his glazed, bloodshot eyes.

"What do you know about my son?" he asked menacingly.

Daly told him about the deaths he was investigating. He explained how David's name had come up before and how he'd spoken to him a couple of times about his connection. How he had felt David was somehow connected but didn't know in what way. Now David had become the latest member of the suicide cluster, and Daly needed to find out what the connection was so he could try and stop it.

"Was there anything unusual going on with David recently?" Daly asked.

"Not that I can think of. He was having problems at school. Like usual," Mr. Kowalski said.

"There's a guy I've been looking at who has a connection to some of the other kids," Daly said. "Some of the parents think he might have been doing something ... bad. Do you know if David knew Vincent Gillespie? He's a substitute teacher."

"Can't say that I do," Mr. Kowalski said.

That didn't come as a surprise. Even if David had been seeing Vincent Gillespie every day, Daly guessed there was a pretty fair chance that Mr. Kowalski wouldn't have known. He didn't really strike Daly as the PTA type.

"I heard that David had an app that one of the other victims got from Mr. Gillespie," Daly said. "It's called Soma. It's a white-noise app to help you sleep."

"Oh yeah, I know about Soma. David's been using that for a while," Mr. Kowalski said. "Or had been, I guess."

"Are you sure he didn't hear about it from a teacher? Or someone at school?" Daly asked.

"No, he didn't get it at school," Mr. Kowalski said. "He got it from his psychiatrist. Dr. Radcliffe."

◆ ◆ ◆

Mr. Kowalski confirmed David had begun seeing Dr. Radcliffe over the previous summer. Their first meeting would have been in June, not too long before David used the app at camp. Therapy for David had been court-ordered when he got in trouble for his little fireworks experiment with the neighbors' cat. It was apparent that Mr. Kowalski didn't generally hold therapists in very high esteem – he seemed more the type to turn to Dr. Jack Daniels in his hour of need – but he seemed to think David was doing better since he started seeing Dr. Radcliffe. It seemed he measured progress primarily by how often the school contacted him about David's misbehavior. Fewer contacts meant less scrutiny on him as a father, which Mr. Kowalski recognized as a good thing. He was all about less government interference, especially when it came to his drinking.

On his way back to the newsroom, Daly kept trying to make sense of what he'd learned. His sights had been focused on Vincent Gillespie. He was a substitute teacher who worked at schools around Luzerne County. He had the ability to contact all of the victims. Daly had solid information that Mr. Gillespie had been sexually involved with Emma and Justin, and he had reason to believe something might have been going on with Kim as well. Mr. Gillespie looked like a predator who was preying on the students of the Wyoming Valley to fulfill his sexual desires. The cold stare he'd gotten at Mr. Gillespie's doorstep had only solidified Daly's suspicions.

But Dr. Radcliffe's resurfacing in the case could not be ignored. There were four victims spread across as many school districts and separated by miles. The likelihood that three of them would have been going to the same therapist seemed remote. And Daly couldn't stop wondering about the white-noise app Dr. Radcliffe had been handing out. It seemed a strange thing for a psychiatrist to be distributing. The App Store has dozens of white-noise apps. Most of them are free. Why would a doctor need to give his patient a special app?

By the time he got back to his desk, Daly decided it was time to take another look at Soma. The app wasn't easy to find in the App Store. He had to search for it by name and when it came up it had no reviews. Daly clicked onto the app's detail page and got little more information. The seller was listed as Sleep Song LLC. The app hadn't been updated in nearly a year and appeared to be very rudimentary. The logo was simply stock art of a pillow. When he clicked it open on his new iPhone, Daly was again struck by the fact that it appeared to have only one sound. *No wonder nobody is downloading this app*, he thought. *It's garbage.*

And yet.

At least two of Dr. Radcliffe's patients had used it. Daly popped a pair of earbuds in and clicked play on the app, trying to figure out its significance. All he heard was the low buzzing of static in his ears.

Daly pulled out the earbuds.

*Screw it,* he thought. *Maybe Dr. Radcliffe is just a psychiatrist. Maybe his connection is just a coincidence. There are only so many psychiatrists around here. Is it really so hard to believe that a few troubled kids seeing the same shrink decided to off themselves?*

As Daly sat thinking, Richardson called him over to the editors' cube. He wanted an update on the Nanticoke body. In his rush to get back and check into Soma, Daly had forgotten to let Richardson know what he found out at the scene.

"It sounds like a straight-up suicide," Daly said. "The father came home around ten-thirty and found the body. He'd apparently put dad's shotgun to his mouth. The cops said it was a seventeen-year-old male and didn't release a name. But I spoke to the father. It was David Kowalski."

"The same David Kowalski you've been talking to about the suicides?"

"That would be the one," Daly said. "I don't know at this point if there's a definite connection."

"Of course there's a connection," Richardson said. "Don't you have a picture of him with his arms around the other two?"

"Yeah, we do," Daly said. "But we still don't know what it means. Kowalski was connected to two of the other victims. I've also connected Vincent Gillespie to three of them and Dr. Marvin Radcliffe to three. If we go big on this now, all we're doing is showing our hand to the Other Paper."

"We're not doing a story saying anyone was murdered," Richardson said. "And those names aren't even going to appear in the same edition as this story – at least for now. But we need to get on record that another kid has died so that we can tie it all together when we figure out how it all connects."

Daly went back to his desk and dialed Wojcik's number from his desk phone. Before he wrote up the story, he wanted to figure out if this one had landed on the county detectives' radar.

It took Wojcik a while to pick up, and when he did he sounded distracted.

"Hello?" he said.

"Phil, it's Erik Daly. I'm getting ready to write up a suicide that happened in Nanticoke this morning. David Kowalski, age seventeen. I wanted to touch base and see if you were looking into whether this might be connected to the others."

"Right now, all I can say is it's an ongoing investigation," Wojcik said.

"Look, I've got a picture of him with his arms wrapped around Kim Foster and Justin Gonzalez," Daly said. "Are you telling me you think that's a coincidence?"

"I'm telling you it's an ongoing investigation," Wojcik said, pausing for a long moment. "Can we go off the record for a minute?"

"Sure," Daly said.

"Running that picture would be a mistake," Wojcik said. "We're getting close to making a move here. That picture is going to sound the alarm. I'm talking wholesale destruction of evidence. If that happens, we might not be able to get him."

"You know I'm not trying to screw you," Daly said. "But I've got the competition to think about. Can you give me anything?"

"Right now all I can say on the record is that we are looking into whether there could be a connection between the cases," Wojcik said. "Here's your quote: 'It's an ongoing investigation.'"

"What's that based on?" Daly asked. "Why do you think there could be a connection?"

"I said we're looking at whether there could be a connection. Off the record, I'll tell you there were similarities in the note that David Kowalski left to the others," Wojcik said.

"He left a note?" Daly asked. "Did he use the same phrase as the others?"

"This is absolutely not for publication. But yeah, he did," Wojcik said.

Daly hung up the phone, stunned. There was no doubt. Four deaths. Four matching sets of last words. There were too many similarities for it all to be a coincidence. Daly could hardly contain his excitement as he sped back over to the editors' pod with the information. The scoop. Five minutes later, he was back at his desk, typing furiously.

*NANTICOKE — A 17-year-old Nanticoke boy died of an apparent self-inflicted gunshot at home Thursday morning, according to police.*

*Authorities did not immediately identify the teen, but his father told the Wilkes-Barre Observer he was David Kowalski, a student at Greater Nanticoke Area Senior High School. The father, Jeff Kowalski, said he had returned home around 10:30 a.m. when he discovered his son dead in a bedroom.*

*"David had his issues, but he was a good kid," Jeff Kowalski said. "I can't believe he did this. He had so much to live for."*

*Detectives with the Luzerne County District*

*Attorney's Office confirmed they are looking into whether the death could be connected to a series of deaths in what appears to be a suicide cluster that has affected schools across the county.*

*Since February, at least three other area teens have died of apparent self-inflicted causes. The cases began Feb. 10 when 16-year-old Kingston resident Justin Gonzalez hanged himself in the family garage.*

*But it wasn't until March 22 that the cases gained widespread attention with the death of Kimberly Foster, a 15-year-old cheerleader at Hanover Area High School who fatally shot herself while recording a Facebook Live video. The footage subsequently went viral.*

*A week later, Emma Nguyen, a 16-year-old junior at Coughlin High School in Wilkes-Barre jumped from the Market Street Bridge and died after plunging into the Susquehanna River.*

*In each of the previous three cases, the victims used similar phrases in notes left prior to their deaths, prompting authorities to question whether there was a connection. Investigators on Thursday would not comment publicly on whether David Kowalski left a note or used similar words in a message prior to his death.*

*"We are looking into whether there could be a connection between the cases," Detective Sgt. Phil Wojcik said. "It's an ongoing investigation."*

Daly clicked save on the file and then released it for Richardson to read and post to the website. He wanted to try to anticipate the cops' next play and figure out when and where they might make their move. He already knew from his previous conversation with

Wojcik that they were looking at Vincent Gillespie. He hoped he could convince someone to tip him off about when the arrest would go down.

He grabbed his cellphone and pulled out the headphone jack as he prepared to get over to the courthouse and see if he could shake something loose from one of the cops or prosecutors wandering the corridors. As soon as the jack came out, his iPhone speakers blared a torrent of static. Daly realized he'd forgotten to shut down the Soma app.

*Shit*, Daly thought. The battery on his phone had already been dwindling. Now he'd left an app running for the better part of an hour while he worked. Hopefully, he'd have a few minutes to charge it in the car between stops.

He reached up to tap the stop button and end the static, but then hesitated. As he listened, the rushing, buzzing sound of the white noise seemed more than relaxing. It was almost hypnotic.

Daly listened on for a few more minutes and started to feel uneasy. He couldn't quite put his finger on it. But something didn't feel right. He was starting to visualize patterns in the static. It was almost like the static was coming in waves and was changing from the steady buzz he'd heard earlier. He couldn't tell if he was imaging it or not, it was so slight. But the thought sent a wave of goosebumps rising up his arms.

Somewhere, behind the crunching static, Daly could swear he heard a voice.

# CHAPTER 18

*Friday, April 6, 2018*
*9:51 a.m.*

Working for a small-town newspaper had its perks. In general, Daly had less oversight and more control over the process than he would at a major metro. He enjoyed being able to come in and, for the most part, decide what he was going to write about on a given day. But the limited staff also meant limited resources. The paper had a few photographers who were able to put together a decent web video, but nobody had any real expertise working with audio.

Fortunately, Daly knew a guy. His roommate at King's College, George Timmons, was a tried and true audiophile. When they met on move-in day, George had walked through the door just as Daly was putting an iHome docking station on his desk. After exchanging names, George hadn't wasted a breath impugning the quality of the off-the-shelf device.

"You don't listen to music on that, do you?" he'd asked.

Daly had a lifetime love of music and rarely drove for more than a block or two without something on the car stereo.

But he couldn't see the fuss about high-quality audio equipment. A set of mid-level headphones sounded just as good to him as any brand-name sets that cost two or three times as much.

When he told George as much, his new roommate had stood

there with a gap between his lips growing ever wider, until at last his eyebrows had come up and his face was frozen in a look of mock horror. He vowed to show Daly what was what. Over the next few years, they had spent nights sipping beers and listening to music together, talking women and arguing politics, sometimes until the sun came up. Daly had been forced to admit his iHome sounded pretty thin compared to George's sound system – although his Klipsch speakers had undoubtedly cost exponentially more.

After graduation, they hadn't stayed in close touch. They were still friends on Facebook and would talk whenever they bumped into each other, but the end of college had sent them on separate paths.

Daly had gone on to get married and to start a job in journalism. George had become an information-technology specialist with an insurance company.

They simply grew apart, as friends often do.

As he remembered his old friend George, Daly pulled out his cellphone and dialed the number. The call didn't go through. Daly was ashamed to realize that he no longer had even a working phone number for a guy he'd spent nearly every day with during college.

Daly logged onto Facebook and typed out a private message asking how things had been. He hit send and was about to close out the window when he saw a box pop up below his text. George was writing back.

"Doing good bro. Same old stuff going on here. What's up?"

"I need some editing done on an audio file. Do you think you could help?" Daly wrote.

"What, did you record yourself singing Mariah Carey?"

"LOL, something like that," Daly wrote back.

"No editing in the world is going to fix that. But I'm free after work tonight if you want to stop by," George wrote.

"Thx. Sounds good. I'll be by around 5," Daly wrote.

◆ ◆ ◆

George Timmons lived in a narrow white house in Wilkes-Barre's Heights section. The house was well-kept, but like much of the neighborhood it was old and showing its age. At a distance it appeared in good shape, but closer inspection revealed the white paint was beginning to crack. A pane or two of old glass that had cracked long ago had been left unchecked. Small pockets of rust reached out from under the eaves like fingers from the earth trying to reclaim its resources.

Daly threw his car into park and stepped out, holding a twelve-pack of Yuengling Lager to share with his host. He climbed the drooping staircase to the porch and rang the bell.

"Hey," George said as he opened the door, extending his hand. "How's it going?"

"What's up, man?" Daly said, clapping George's palm. "It's been a while."

"Too long," George said. "Come on in."

Almost immediately, Daly could tell George was still single. The living room was sparse but tastefully decorated with modern furnishings. But there were no plants, no soft colors, no family photos. Instead, the walls were adorned with framed posters for Pink Floyd and Metallica. One corner of the room was devoted almost exclusively to a bar lined with no fewer than four dozen bottles of booze. A large banner for the Philadelphia Eagles was on display on the wall above the TV.

It was a man cave, not a home.

They sat down at the kitchen table. George popped the tops off a couple of the beers and they spent the next hour catching up. It had been more than a decade since they had last seen each other at length, and they had a lot to talk about. Based on a few passing conversations and Facebook posts, they knew the broad strokes of each other's lives, but there was still much they had missed.

It turned out that George had almost gotten married, but things had fallen apart not long before. The woman, Jennifer, was a sales representative who seemed a perfect complement for him. She was smart, funny and loved music. He had met her on a Friday night when he was spinning records at a local nightclub. During his entire show, Jennifer had stood at the front of the room, watching him and swaying gently to the beat.

Things had been going great until George found out she was swaying to another beat as well. The wedding had only been a few months off when he found out. He dropped her on the spot.

"Hey, if she doesn't want to be with me, she can go," George said. "I'm not going to fight for someone who doesn't respect me."

"I don't blame you," Daly said. "I would have done the same thing. But hey, better to find out then rather than after you tied the knot, right?"

"Yeah, I guess," George said, taking another sip of beer. "So what was it that you needed? It must be pretty important for you to reach out after all this time and meet me the same day."

Daly hoped George was just riffing him. Otherwise, he'd feel guilty. He didn't want his friend to think he was using him.

"Have you heard about the suicide cluster?" Daly asked. "We've had four high school kids kill themselves in a pretty short time."

"Yeah, I read about it in the paper," George said.

"Well, I think I've got something that might be connected to it," Daly said.

"Connected?" George asked. "How?"

Daly filled George in on his reporting over the past few weeks and how he had come to believe that the deaths were not random. Someone was instigating them to do it, and he thought he had narrowed it down to one of two people: Vincent Gillespie or Dr. Marvin Radcliffe. He explained that he had almost settled on Gillespie when David Kowalski died and threw a wrench in that theory.

"Which is where you come in," Daly said. "Radcliffe has apparently been recommending this app – Soma – to help some of the kids sleep. It seems pretty low budget and doesn't look like it's gotten much use."

"So?" George asked.

"Well, when I first listened to it, it just sounded like static," Daly said. "But after a while ... I don't know. I could swear I heard something. Like a voice."

"What, like a subliminal message?" George scoffed.

"I'm not sure. But something was there," Daly said.

"All right. Let me see what I can do," George said.

He walked toward the back of the house to what was probably once a dining room. Now, it was George Timmons' personal sound studio, complete with tower speakers and dual turntables.

George woke up his computer and loaded up some sound editing software that would let him reduce the level of the static to see if any other tracks were playing in the background. Daly unlocked his iPhone and loaded the app. When he clicked play, the sound of static filled the room. They listened for a minute before George turned to Daly.

"Are you sure it wasn't just your imagination?" he laughed.

"I don't think so. Something was behind the static. I just couldn't hear what," Daly said.

"All right. Well, let me see it," George said.

He plugged a headphones jack into the iPhone and the hiss of the static disappeared. With a click of the mouse, an equalizer appeared on the screen, displaying the continuous, unflinching peaks of the static coming from the phone. George put the phone down and slumped down in an office chair, reaching for his beer on the way.

"What now?" Daly asked.

"Now, we wait," George said. "Right now it doesn't look like there are any other signatures. If something comes up, I'll hit record and then we can use noise reduction to manipulate the recording so we can hear what it is."

Daly dropped to another seat and took a long sip of beer. The last time, it had been more than an hour before he noticed something in the sound. It sounded like it could be a while.

He asked to borrow George's phone and called Lauren to let her know he wouldn't be home for dinner. She was still at her friend Jessica's house, where she spent most of her recent afternoons, and sounded happy to be able to stay there for dinner. The near-nightly outings to Leopold's Pizzeria at first seemed to be a blessing, but after a few weeks, Daly and Lauren both found themselves craving a home-cooked meal.

With Lauren taken care of, Daly snapped open his work laptop and logged in. He had a bit of business to check into while he waited. The App Store had identified the maker of the Soma app as Sleep Song, LLC. But when Daly did a Google search for the company before, he came up empty. There was no website, no mailing address, no phone number. But he knew there had to be some record of it. He decided to run the name through an online searchable database of all corporations registered with the Pennsylvania Department of State. If Sleep Song was registered in Pennsylvania, it would be there.

Daly keyed in the name. A moment later, a single result popped up. The business was indeed registered in Pennsylvania and was based at an address in Kingston. Daly moved the cursor over the hyperlink on the corporation name and was about to click it when George interrupted him.

"I think we've got something," George said.

Daly looked up from his laptop and squinted as his eyes adjusted to see the equalizer on the screen in front of George. He could still see the line of steady waves moving across the screen. But now there was activity on a second channel. George leaned in closer to the screen and reached for the mouse. With a soft click, he began recording the sound Soma was producing. They sat and waited in silence, watching the sound waves rise and fall. After about ten minutes, Daly couldn't take it anymore.

"Okay, that's enough," he said. "Let's stop recording and see what we got."

George clicked the stop button and saved the recording to his desktop. Then he closed the equalizer window that had been displaying Soma and started a new project. When he clicked play, the familiar sound of static began flowing through the speakers. But again, below the surface, Daly thought he could hear something.

"Do you hear that?" he asked. "It sounds like there's a voice or something."

George leaned in and began clicking through the effects in the program, trying to reduce the level of the static on the first channel. Soon the hissing static began to fade, exposing a man's voice. The speaking was calm, almost monotone, like Ben Stein delivering an economics lesson. But the message was much darker. In the absence of the static, the voice sounded certain and unrelenting. The message kept repeating at even intervals, like the slow drop of water coming from a leaky faucet.

As he listened, a chill went up Daly's back.

"They're watching me always. Nothing can make it stop," the cold, unflinching voice said. "End it now. Before they find out."

They sat there in stunned silence, listening in disbelief until the recording came to an end. The voice hadn't wavered once through the monologue. The message hadn't changed. There it was, verbatim: the kids' last words and the cryptic note Kim Foster had left in the margin of her journal.

"Damn," George finally said, scratching his head. "That's some fucked up shit. Where did you say you got this?"

"The App Store," Daly said. "I think someone was using it to brainwash the kids or something. Maybe it was, like, subliminal messages."

"Does that stuff really work?" George asked, his eyes narrowing in disbelief.

"I don't know. But at least a couple of the victims were using it," Daly said. "Apparently their doctor was recommending it to them."

"Who's that?" George asked.

"Dr. Marvin Radcliffe. He's a psychiatrist in Kingston," Daly said.

"Do you think that's him on the recording?" George asked. "That's really screwed up, especially for a shrink."

Daly sat for a moment, thinking. He needed to get this information to the police. Phil Wojcik might already know about it, but if he didn't he needed to, and fast. Daly went to grab his laptop and realized he still had the search page open on the Department of State's website. He set the computer back down and used its touchpad to click on the hyperlink he'd all but forgotten about. The corporation details appeared on the screening, showing the business had been created in May 2017 and had an active license. The only filing was the articles of incorporation. With George leaning over Daly's shoulder, the friends' eyes moved across to the list of company officers.

"Son of a bitch," George said. "There he is. Marvin Radcliffe. President of Sleep Song, LLC."

Daly stared at the screen in disbelief. He'd expected to see Dr. Radcliffe as a company officer. What he hadn't expected was the name below Radcliffe's. There, appearing for the first time next to Dr. Radcliffe, was Mr. Vincent Gillespie.

Vice president of Sing Song, LLC.

# CHAPTER 19

*Monday, April 9, 2018*
*10:22 a.m.*

After discovering the recording Friday night, Daly loaded a copy of the edited recording onto his computer and gave George a rushed goodbye before running from the house.

His first thought was to call Phil Wojcik and tell him what he'd found. But he hesitated as he grabbed his cellphone and pulled up his contacts. On one hand, he'd uncovered some pretty damning evidence that Dr. Radcliffe was directly involved in the suicide cluster. On the other, he was a journalist who was expected to be separate from the police. For him to be credible, he couldn't be seen as a mouthpiece for the cops. Not only that, but at any time he could be called upon to write about an officer or lawyer accused of misconduct. So while they often talked and joked with each other, Daly made it a practice not to share notes.

Still, this was a far cry from identifying a source or giving the police some correspondence. Daly had uncovered actual evidence of a crime. Not only that, but a crime that was in all likelihood still in progress. Waiting to talk to an editor could mean more kids were downloading the app. More kids could die.

Daly decided his civic responsibility outweighed the journalism ethics debate. He made the call, knowing he might become a witness and be conflicted out of covering the story.

Even though it was Friday night, Wojcik agreed to meet up

with him. Wojcik could hear in his voice that Daly had something to show him. Something urgent.

When Daly pulled into the coffee shop parking lot, Wojcik was already waiting in his car. They shook hands and Daly plunked his laptop down on the trunk of Wojcik's car. The detective looked perplexed as Daly logged on to his computer and pulled up the VLC media player. After a moment's hesitation, Wojcik took the headphones.

Daly watched as Wojcik's mystified expression melted into disbelief.

"Where did you get this?" Wojcik said, pulling the headphones off his ears.

"The App Store. It's hidden in a white noise app called Soma," Daly said. "And you're not going to believe who the company officers are."

"Vincent Gillespie?" Wojcik asked.

"He's the vice president," Daly said. "The president is Dr. Marvin Radcliffe."

"Oh my God," Wojcik said.

Wojcik immediately downloaded the app himself and asked Daly to send him the edited audio clip. Then he started talking, apparently feeling generous in the face of such an unexpected break in the case.

The police, it seemed, had already been closing in on Mr. Gillespie. Wojcik told Daly that he and a few other detectives had raided Gillespie's house two weeks before and seized his computer. There had also been some external drives and camera equipment. Vincent Gillespie, it seemed, hadn't been simply involved with his students. He was documenting his exploits and selling videos online.

Gillespie knew he was caught, so he had cooperated. He'd told the police he had been finding customers in online chat rooms, places with names that would make most people's skin crawl. The customer would transfer the money to Gillespie and he would allow the file to be downloaded to the customer's computer via a peer-to-peer network.

For the past couple of weeks, the police had their hands full sorting through thousands of pictures and videos.

They had already found Kim Foster and David Kowalski. Wojcik thought it was only a matter of time until Justin Gonzalez and Emma Nguyen turned up in Gillespie's video library as well.

Wojcik figured they would probably be ready to move on Gillespie and do the perp walk in a few more days. But Soma changed that. Now they needed to revisit their conversation with Gillespie.

The last time there had been no mention of a business partner. Now they had the dirt on Gillespie and proof he wasn't working alone.

◆◆◆

The newsroom was still quiet as Daly leaned forward at his desk to get a better look at the image on the screen. It was just a thumbnail image, but it was all he'd been able to find. Dr. Marvin Radcliffe was a portly man with glasses and shaggy brown hair. The gray suit he wore in the photo looked a few sizes too big for him and clashed with the curled mop of hair up top. Dr. Radcliffe had a graying beard and a red nose, with beady brown eyes. His mouth was curled into a slight smile, but his eyes weren't smiling. Daly found the expression cold and flat.

He right-clicked his mouse and saved the picture to his computer – one never could tell when a picture might disappear from the Internet – and scrolled back up to the top of Dr. Radcliffe's website to find his office phone number.

Wojcik had promised to give Daly a heads-up with enough warning that he would be first when the police made their move, but he still had work to do on his end. It wasn't just enough to have the story first. He wanted to be so far ahead of the Other Paper that the unsuspecting reporter whose lap it fell into would be taking notes on his coverage.

He reached for his phone and dialed the number listed on Dr. Radcliffe's website.

"Good morning, Dr. Radcliffe's office," a woman said.

"Hi, I'm Erik Daly with the Observer. I'm trying to reach Dr. Radcliffe."

"What's it in regard to?" Her voice had lost the false chipper tone it had when she answered.

"I wanted to ask him about some of his former patients ..."

"He can't talk about any patients," the woman cut in. "It's against our policy."

"I'm not trying to discuss the patients' treatment. I just want to ask about some allegations that came up about Dr. Radcliffe," Daly said.

"Well, he doesn't talk to reporters," the woman said. All pretense of being polite was now gone.

"Can we at least ask him and let him decide?" Daly asked.

A long pause was followed by a disinterested voice asking for Daly's name and to repeat which paper he was with.

"I'll have him call you," she said.

"What about my phone number?" Daly asked.

"Oh, right," the woman said. "What's your number?"

Daly dropped the phone into its cradle, knowing there would be no return call. He needed to get to Dr. Radcliffe, and he wanted to do it before the media circus descended at the perp walk. Once the handcuffs went on and the TV camera lights were shining, most of them shut down. If he could catch Dr. Radcliffe off-guard, he might talk. Even better, he could make an admission.

Rather than sit and wait for a call he knew wasn't coming, Daly decided to stake out Dr. Radcliffe's office. Lunchtime was approaching. With any luck, he would catch the doctor on his way out for a sandwich.

He arrived at the office in Kingston fifteen minutes later and pulled into a parking space along the street. From his vantage point, he could see the front door to the office as well as a side entrance that probably led to employee parking in the back. He cut the engine and waited.

The narrow boulevard was lined with maple trees with branches that met above the pavement, creating a jungle-like canopy that permanently shaded the neighborhood. Lining the strip were small law and medical offices, broken up by the occasional convenience store or deli. All the properties had fresh paint and trimmed lawns. It was a good neighborhood in a worn-down and struggling region, an island in a stormy sea.

Occasionally, small groups of people emerged from the offices and walked down the sidewalk past Daly, heading to a nearby lunch spot. But the door to Dr. Radcliffe's office hadn't twitched. For more than an hour, Daly sat in his car listening to Fats Waller hammer away on his piano. After witnessing most of the lunchtime crowd make their returns to work, Daly decided he'd had enough. He pulled out his key and slammed the door, making a bee-line to the front door of Dr. Radcliffe's office. His receptionist probably wouldn't be any more endearing in person, but Daly was prepared to wait Dr. Radcliffe out if he refused to see him.

But before Daly reached the front door, he heard a faint bang from the side of the building. He stopped in his tracks, then turned and headed toward the noise.

The noise of a slamming door.

Daly rounded the corner in time to see a suited figure disappear behind the back corner of the building, walking quickly down the sidewalk to an employee parking area. Upon seeing the figure, Daly burst into a sprint to catch up. He'd only seen a glimpse from the back, but it could have been the man he'd seen on the website.

The office appeared to be a reconfigured old house, as many in the area were. It was a quick sprint for Daly to get to the back. When he did, he saw the man pulling at the door handle of a shining black Lexus LS. The man looked up, startled, as Daly emerged from around the corner about ten feet away.

*That's him*, Daly thought. *That's Dr. Marvin Radcliffe.*

"Dr. Radcliffe?" Daly asked.

"Yes?" he said, a slightly nervous smile appearing on his lips and a look of confusion flashing in his eyes.

"I'm with the Observer. I wanted to ask you a few questions about some patients," Daly said.

"I can't talk about patients," Dr. Radcliffe said.

"Your receptionist told me," Daly said.

"Well, then you know."

"Did she tell you I called?" Daly asked.

"No. But I just left through the back, so she didn't see me," Dr. Radcliffe said. "What did you say your name was?"

"Erik Daly. With the Observer."

With that, the smile, the perplexed expression, and the cordiality were gone. In their place was a flat, hard stare on Dr.

Radcliffe's pale white face. In his eyes, Daly thought he could see a flash of something. Hatred, perhaps. Or anger.

Whatever it was, it was clear that there was not going to be any interview this afternoon. But just when Daly thought Dr. Radcliffe would throw him off the property, the doctor began speaking in a low voice.

"You're not secretly recording this, are you?" he asked.

"No. I wouldn't record without you knowing," Daly said.

"Erik Daly, huh?" Radcliffe said, his expression relaxing. He took a couple of steps toward Daly and looked upward to some squirrels scampering across a power line.

"I remember hearing your name," Dr. Radcliffe said. "What was it? Oh, that's right. Wasn't there a fire at your house?"

"That's right," Daly said, not sure how to respond.

"You lost everything, right? Even your precious daughter almost went up in flames, from what I heard," Radcliffe said. "I'm surprised you got out."

The expression on Dr. Radcliffe's face had turned to something else. He squinted slightly as he looked to Daly, his unblinking eyes never wavering from Daly's gaze. When Daly looked down, he could see Dr. Radcliffe's hands clenched into fists, his knuckles turned white with anger. He was no longer a doctor. He was a caged animal.

For the first time, Daly felt in danger. He cursed himself for running into the secluded lot behind the office, and for not telling John Richardson where he was going. He found himself feeling some relief that he'd left Radcliffe's website open in the browser of his work computer when he left. *At least they'll know where to start looking*, he thought.

Instinctively, Daly took a few steps back as Radcliffe advanced toward him.

"How did that fire start? The papers didn't say," Radcliffe said. This time, Daly waited in silence.

"You really should be more careful, having a beautiful daughter like Lauren around," Radcliffe said. "I can't imagine what a loss that would be. But I guess you can, can't you?"

Radcliffe turned and took a step back, pushing a button on his key fob to unlock the car.

"You take care now, Mr. Daly," he said as he walked to the door. "And do be careful. Remember, curiosity killed the cat. You never know when someone might decide to throw a firebomb through a window at the Mountain Motor Lodge."

# CHAPTER 20

*Monday, April 9, 2018*
*3:43 p.m.*

Daly hadn't even finished telling John Richardson what happened when his editor jumped in and cut him off.

"You're off the story," Richardson said.

The move was expected, but it still stung to hear the words. Daly thought about putting up a fight; after all, there was nothing concrete to conflict him out of the story. But he decided it would be futile. He had become a possible witness in the case, which meant he could be called to testify. Which obviously meant he couldn't cover the story. And while Radcliffe had not come out and admitted involvement in firebombing Daly's home, his thinly veiled threats made clear how he felt about it. It was enough to warrant taking him off the story to avoid the perception of bias.

It was the biggest story of his career and he lost it because someone burned down his house and nearly killed him.

*Goddamn it.*

Richardson called across the newsroom and summoned the city reporter, Joe Reed. Reed was a lanky guy with a mop of shaggy brown hair that always hung down into his eyebrows. With his perennially rolled shirtsleeves and unfastened top shirt button, Daly couldn't help but think Reed looked more like the member of a boy band than a serious journalist. But although Reed was relatively new out of J-school and still in his late twenties, he was

171

a solid reporter with a flair for words and a knack for sniffing out good stories.

Between reading the coverage and the newsroom chit chat, Reed was pretty well familiar with the story. Richardson took a few minutes to bring him up to speed on why he was inheriting the crime story of the year and then wished him luck.

"So you're a witness?" Reed asked as they headed back to their cubicles. "I might need to get a quote for the story."

"Are you ready?" Daly smirked. "Write this down: Go fuck yourself."

◆ ◆ ◆

The text came in a few minutes before six o'clock. Daly had been about to log out of his computer and head home when the phone dinged in his pocket.

"Picking them up. Holland's at 7."

It was Phil Wojcik. The cops were making their move. Radcliffe and Gillespie would be paraded in handcuffs into Magistrate Brian Holland's office for arraignment at seven o'clock.

Daly jumped out of his chair and ran over to Reed.

"They're picking them up now. We need to get over to Holland's," Daly said. "Can you let photo know?"

"Ten-four," Reed said, picking up a notepad as he rose.

Reed walked over to the photo department to get a photographer and Daly went to Richardson to tell him the news.

"They're picking up Radcliffe and Gillespie now," Daly said. "Joe's getting photo on it, then we're going to head over there."

"We?" Richardson asked, raising his eyebrows.

"I just want to be there. I want to see them," Daly said. "After everything I've been through, I deserve at least that much."

"It's a public courtroom," Richardson said. "But this is Joe's story. We can't have you even helping on it anymore."

"What about posting it?" Daly said. "Should we go live now or wait until they're arraigned?"

"Is anyone else on it?" They both knew the Other Paper would get the story sooner or later. They just needed to be first.

"I'm not sure. I don't think so, but if the cases are already docketed someone could find it," Daly said.

"Check the docket. If it's in the system, let's break the story first," Richardson said.

Daly went back over to his computer and ran a search through the online court dockets. There they were: Vincent P. Gillespie, age twenty-eight, and Marvin G. Radcliffe, age fifty-six, were charged with causing suicide as criminal homicide, involuntary manslaughter, criminal conspiracy, and producing child pornography. Daly couldn't help but notice that a charge of arson was absent from each of the docket sheets.

*Maybe it's still pending*, he thought. Then he pushed the question out of his mind. At the moment, there wasn't time to consider the legal nuances. Daly printed out the docket sheets and went to the door to meet up with Reed.

As they ran down the stairs and headed to the parking lot, Daly paused. This could be an opportunity to get exclusive video of an arrest in a major case. He wasn't supposed to be on the story, but he figured it couldn't hurt for him to shoot some video with his cellphone. There wasn't time to run Radcliffe through the system and find his address. But Daly had already been to Gillespie's house.

"You know what? I'm going to take my own car," he said. "I want to see if I can get video of them arresting Gillespie."

"You sure?" Reed asked. "By the time you get to Pittston, they could already be gone."

That was true. But Daly also knew that the wheels of justice turned quite slowly. He figured there was a fair chance that the cops hadn't even left yet to pick them up.

"Yeah. I'll just take a look and then meet you at Holland's office," Daly said.

Daly jumped in his car and headed north toward Pittston, hoping he wasn't too late.

◆ ◆ ◆

Gillespie's street was still. As Daly turned onto the narrow lane, he crept forward at barely an idle as he squinted his eyes, trying to see if there was any activity ahead. When he was convinced there wasn't, he let off the brake and let the car roll down the street slowly, looking for anything out of place. There were no signs of a disturbance, no police lurking in SUVs with tinted windows. The street was quiet except for the faint rush of traffic that could be heard coming from Main Street. Daly watched as a cat lazily crossed the street and a slight breeze ruffled the Eagles flag dangling over Gillespie's well-kept lawn.

After passing the house, Daly continued on down the street and then went around the block. Gillespie had no reason to expect anything was about to happen, but Daly was conscious that a car turning around in front of his house could draw suspicion. He completed a full circuit around and then pulled over between two parked cars a few doors down from Gillespie's house. From there, he could see the door as well as anyone pulling on to the street.

He waited for five minutes, then ten, then twenty. There was nothing but a mail carrier working the street, shuffling door-to-door dropping junk into mailboxes.

Daly started wondering if he'd missed it. He reached for his phone to text Reed if there had been any progress on his end. But as he unlocked the phone, he caught a glimpse of movement in his rear-view mirror. He looked up and saw a dark SUV with tinted windows finishing the turn onto the street. Instinctively, Daly reached for his voice recorder and turned it on so it would be ready to go. He also closed out of the text app and got his cellphone camera ready.

Getting out of the car now would be a sure way to piss the cops off, but Daly needed to be ready to go as soon as they got into the house.

Through the rear-view mirror, Daly watched as the SUV slowly rolled down the street, growing larger in his view as it went. Whoever was behind the wheel didn't seem in too big a rush. Then, as the SUV glided past, Daly could see why: The driver was a woman who looked like she probably remembered hearing radio reports about the Japanese attack on Pearl Harbor.

Tossing his recorder on the dashboard, Daly closed out of the camera and began typing the text to Reed.

The tap at the window startled Daly. When he turned and looked up, he was face to face with the barrel of a forty-caliber Sig Sauer pistol.

"Hello, Erik," Gillespie said. "Put the phone down. Now."

Daly was petrified. Slowly, he reached up and put his iPhone on the dash next to the recorder. He thought about hitting send on the unfinished text to tip off Reed, but Gillespie was watching intently. There was no chance of getting it off unnoticed. Even if he did, Reed would probably just think he had fat fingers.

"Get out," Gillespie said, pulling on the door handle. "Let's take a walk."

Daly leaned out and stood up, trying to calculate the chances of him getting away unscathed if he took off running. The gun was about eight inches from his chest. Gillespie's finger was on the trigger. Even if he were a terrible shot, Gillespie would be hard-pressed to miss at that range.

"My editor knows I'm here," Daly said. *Then again*, he thought, *this guy is already charged with killing four people. He probably doesn't give a shit.*

"Well, then they'll know where to look, won't they?" Gillespie said.

As he finished speaking, he turned his gaze up the street. Rounding the corner were two black sedans with tinted windows. The antennas and light bars were dead giveaways. The cops had arrived.

"Move," Gillespie said, pushing the gun into Daly's side. "To my house. Now!"

With the gun dug into his ribs, Daly began moving across the street in the direction of Gillespie's house. As they walked, Daly looked to the approaching police cars, hoping someone would recognize him before it was too late. Gillespie noticed.

"Eyes front!" he snarled. "You've got five seconds to get to the door."

Daly quickened his pace. But he could hear the police cars gaining speed. From the corner of his eye, he could make out that Gillespie was looking in their direction. Without shifting his gaze, he reached into his pocket, grabbed his wallet and tossed it in the street. At least the cops would know he was inside if they raided the place.

"Hey!" Gillespie said. "Last warning!"

They reached the front door just as the first police car screeched to a stop at the curb. Gillespie reached around Daly and turned the knob, pushing Daly into the dark room just as the first officer's boot hit the blacktop.

Gillespie gave Daly a push, relieving the pressure of the gun muzzle from his lower ribs. As Daly's eyes adjusted to the dim light of the living room, he heard the door slam home and the metallic click of a deadbolt engaging. The room was surprisingly neat, considering the sole occupant of the home was a twenty-eight-year-old man. There were two white plush couches forming a corner around a coffee table. A flat-screen TV was mounted on the wall, looming over the room as the empty chairs faced it obediently. A bowl full of potpourri on the glass coffee table gave the room a slightly lavender smell, masking the faint hint of light cigarette smoke that clung to the drawn drapes.

In a corner, a small desk displayed loose wires projecting from the dark space beneath like tentacles. A blank monitor remained, but the computer tower had been seized. A tripod stood next to the desk, but no camera was left to record scenes from the couch directly across from it.

"Sit down," Gillespie directed, pointing the black tip of the pistol toward the couch.

For an instant, Daly hesitated. Then he did as he was told. As he sat down, he felt angry and impotent. He'd always imagined himself capable of stunning acts of bravery if it ever came down to it. When he saw Bruce Willis running across broken glass with bare feet in "Die Hard," he figured he could do the same. And there had been no doubt Daly would have lathered up the mud and gone on a killing spree just like Sylvester Stallone in "Rambo: First Blood Part II," had the right circumstances arisen. But now, confronted with an actual life-or-death situation, Daly found himself cowed, agreeing to sit on a couch peacefully because he was afraid of a man with a gun.

The sound of a fist hammering on the door broke the silence, sending vibrations echoing through the house.

"Police!" a cop shouted from outside. Daly recognized the voice. It was Phil Wojcik. "Open up!"

"I've got a gun," Gillespie called back. "If anyone comes through that door, this guy gets it."

There was a brief pause before Wojcik spoke again from the other side of the door. This time his voice was more subdued.

"We just need to talk to you," he lied. "Put the gun down and come out with your hands up. Nobody needs to get hurt."

"I can't do that," Gillespie said. "It's too late now. You've seen my computer. You heard what's on that app. They're never going to let me go."

"I don't know that," Wojcik said. "You've been cooperative. You gave us a statement. And now you're in a position to help us get Dr. Radcliffe. If you keep on cooperating, the judge will take that into account. This isn't a death sentence."

"It might as well be. I'm done," Gillespie said.

"Now hold on," Wojcik blurted out quickly, sensing the desperation in Gillespie's voice. "Don't do anything rash. Is there a way we can talk without shouting through the door? Can we give you a call?"

Outside on the porch, Wojcik raised his eyebrow and exchanged a look with the handful of other cops standing with guns drawn by his side. They strained to hear any type of response or movement from inside the house. All they got was silence.

"Okay, we're going to need some backup here," Wojcik whispered. He pointed at two uniformed Pittston city cops. "You two go around back and post around the corners. The rest of you form a perimeter up front. Nobody gets in or out."

The officers jogged to their assigned positions, forming a box around the home. Wojcik ran back to his unmarked car and grabbed the handset to his radio.

"County, this is X-Ray 314. We're going to need SERT at this location," Wojcik said.

The Pennsylvania State Police Special Emergency Response Team would arrive within minutes to try and talk Gillespie out. But there was no doubt he would be coming out, one way or another.

# CHAPTER 21

*Monday, April 9, 2018*
*5:35 p.m.*

B ack at the newsroom, John Richardson was at the city desk reading early copy and waiting for an update from Joe Reed when the scanner crackled to life with an urgent voice.

"County, this is X-Ray 314. We're going to need SERT at this location," the grainy voice broke through the static.

Richardson immediately perked up. The SERT team meant something big was happening. And Richardson had a good hunch it had something to do with the cops picking up Gillespie and Radcliffe.

"Where was that?" he asked no one in particular.

Jennifer Talmadge, the night police reporter, popped her head up from her cubicle.

"Pittston," she said. "Off Main Street. You want me to check it out?"

With a phone cradled against his shoulder, Richardson raised a finger gesturing for Talmadge to stand by. Then he hammered out the digits to Daly's cellphone. Four rings, and it went to voicemail.

"Christ," Richardson said, disconnecting and immediately dialing the number again. "Where the hell is he?"

For the second time, Daly's phone went to voicemail. It was an uncharacteristic lapse in communication, and Richardson was growing frustrated. He disconnected again and then dialed up Reed, who picked up on the second ring.

"Joe, is Erik with you?" Richardson asked.

"No, I'm just waiting outside Holland's office. Nothing's happening yet," Reed said. "Erik went up to Pittston to try and get video of Gillespie's arrest."

For a moment, the hairs on Richardson's neck rose up and he got a chill. There were coincidences in the news business, to be sure, but he had learned that where there's smoke, there's usually fire.

"What's going on?" Reed interrupted Richardson's thoughts.

"They just called for SERT up at Gillespie's house. And I can't reach Erik," Richardson said.

"Do you want me to get up there?"

"No. You stay put. They'll still be bringing Radcliffe in. I'll get someone else to see what's going on up there," Richardson said.

"I'm on my way," Talmadge said before the phone hit the cradle. She grabbed her keys and a notebook as she marched out the newsroom door.

◆ ◆ ◆

The fear had mostly left Daly. For hours he had been sitting on Gillespie's couch, wondering how to escape. For a while, Gillespie had paced between the kitchen and living room with his pistol at his side, clearly agitated by the rapidly growing police presence outside his home. Occasionally, he peaked out through the blinds to see what the cops were doing. The cops just watched him back, revealing nothing. After a while, Gillespie had grown tired of pacing and had taken a seat at the computer desk across from Daly. His mutterings about what the cops were up to had ceased. Now, Gillespie just hung his head with his elbows on his knees, dangling the pistol in his fingertips.

"Why did you do it?" Daly asked after a long silence. "Was it just about the money?"

"Shut up," Gillespie said, looking up at Daly with a glint of danger in his eyes. "This isn't a fucking interview."

The words stuck in Daly's throat. He wanted to ask more. But then he thought about Lauren and their comfortable life and he grew afraid again. He was all she had left. If he pushed it too far, she would be alone in the world. She would have nobody left to hold on the couch when she watched scary movies. Nobody to take her to Leopold's Pizzeria. Nobody to walk her down the aisle when her special day came.

It was easier to just say nothing. But Daly knew it wasn't the right thing to do. The police outside weren't risking any less than he was, and many of them surely had families waiting at home. The families of the dead children had already lost everything, and they deserved answers. This might be the only chance Daly ever had to confront Gillespie and get meaningful answers from him.

He had to man up and try.

"You know that this is going to be a story, no matter what happens from here on out," Daly said. "I'm sure the TV news trucks are already out there. This is your chance to tell people your side of the story."

"Be quiet!" Gillespie said.

"You don't want people to think you're a monster, do you?" Daly said. "The cops said you were helping them. You must feel bad about what you did."

Gillespie took a step back from the window and pinched the tip of his nose, then ran his hand back over his hair. He was defeated and he knew it. There was no escaping. He would go down in history as a sexual predator who raped children for money.

"Of course I feel bad," he said. "I never wanted to do it."

"Then why did you?" Daly asked.

"Why? Because Dr. Radcliffe made me, that's why."

"How did he make you?" Daly asked, skeptical.

"It's not like he put a gun to my head," Gillespie said, picking up on Daly's disbelief. "He had stuff on me. I'd been seeing him for years."

"What kind of stuff?"

It seemed Gillespie had started going to counseling with Dr. Radcliffe when he was still a kid, barely fourteen years old. He had gotten caught shoplifting at Walmart, and his outraged mother wouldn't stand for her son tarnishing the family legacy. Her husband had been a county councilman before his death, and the Gillespies were known as respected members of the community. Shoplifting was simply not something they did. The only explanation that made sense to Gillespie's mother was that there was something wrong with her son.

The irony was that Gillespie had gone into therapy a mostly normal kid and emerged a damaged and scarred young man.

For more than a year, the treatment had been routine. Gillespie went to see Radcliffe and talk about the mundane happenings of his life. It was boring, and he felt his mother got far more out of it than he did. Eventually, Radcliffe had approached Gillespie's mother and confided in her that he thought her son was a terrific young man who was capable of great things. He wanted to take young Vincent Gillespie under his wing and hire him as an assistant. Of course, Mrs. Gillespie had been floored by the acknowledgment of her son's talents. She hadn't even considered the strange nature of the request. By the week's end, Vincent Gillespie had the job.

At first, the job seemed routine: filing papers, answering phones, adjusting the calendar. But over time, Gillespie noticed Radcliffe was getting increasingly familiar in their interactions. He was standing closer, touching him more. The jokes grew dirtier and the hours grew later.

Then came the evening Radcliffe had asked for a handjob. Gillespie had been mortified at the idea. He wasn't gay, so why was this man trying to get him to do such a thing? But he was young and alone and under pressure. He caved and did as he was told, hoping that would be the end of it.

But it was just the beginning.

The abuse lasted several years, until he was about eighteen and started sprouting the first wisps of a beard. He had grown too old for Radcliffe's tastes.

Radcliffe, however, had not been ready to give up his hobby. Instead, he asked Gillespie for help finding new helpers. At first, Gillespie resisted. He wanted no part in making other kids go through what he had. But Radcliffe had videos. He reminded his young assistant what those videos showed, and how embarrassing it would be for his friends and family to see them.

In his naivety, Gillespie hadn't even considered that publicizing those videos would be a sure ticket to prison for Dr. Radcliffe. All he could picture was the everlasting humiliation he would endure if they ever got out.

So he made a deal with the devil.

Vincent Gillespie continued working as an assistant for Radcliffe all through college, although his responsibilities had shifted from alphabetizing paperwork to shooting pornographic videos of himself with younger kids. A few of the kids he passed up to Radcliffe for some personal attention, but most of them the doctor saw only on film. Gillespie's job responsibilities also included selling the footage online to help finance the operation. He learned that there was no shortage of perverts out there willing to pay top dollar for scenes they could never find in Hustler.

"How many were there?" Daly asked.

"I'm not exactly sure," Gillespie said. "About a dozen, I'd say."

"What about Soma? Why did you start using that?"

"Dr. Radcliffe was getting paranoid," Gillespie said. "He kept worrying that someone was going to tell. I told him that they were scared and didn't want anyone to find out, but he wouldn't listen. So he started doing some research and designed the app. He made me record the message and then he spliced it into the audio feed. When he saw the kids during counseling, he recommended the app and talked them into using it. He also worked on them during the sessions, trying to convince them they were worthless. He filled their heads with talk about how everyone was going to find out what they had done and how embarrassing it would be."

Gillespie paused, wiping a few beads of sweat from his forehead with the back of his hand, waving the gun up over his temple. He sniffled before continuing.

"He took a bunch of scared kids and used them, then turned their hopelessness against them," Gillespie said, staring blankly toward the front of the house and contemplating the police blockade surrounding them. "And I helped him do it."

He could have been lying. It was clear he was caught. He was caught on video, caught in online chat rooms, caught by his proximity to the kids. His choices were to go tilting at windmills and fight a losing battle against a mountain of evidence, or turn state's evidence and hope for leniency. It didn't surprise Daly that Gillespie portrayed himself as a victim, another pawn being manipulated by a malevolent force. Such was often the case when co-conspirators part ways. But for some reason, Daly believed him. It didn't excuse what Gillespie had done. But it did help explain it.

Suddenly, the phone rang, giving both men a start. They looked to the handset sitting on a charger on the kitchen counter, illuminated in the darkened house only by the reflections of police spotlights that penetrated the curtains.

"Are you going to answer that?" Daly asked after the fourth ring.

Gillespie was silent. He turned his head back to the floor, ignoring the call. When the phone went to voicemail, the caller hung up. A couple of minutes later, the silence was again shattered, this time by the sound of a bullhorn out on the street.

"Mr. Gillespie, this is Corporal Mike Durden with the Pennsylvania State Police," the voice boomed through a grainy loudspeaker. "I would like to talk to you. Can you please pick up the phone?"

Another moment of silence, then the phone buzzed back to life. This time Gillespie didn't even look at it. Instead, he jumped up and marched to the front window to peer out from behind the blinds.

"I have nothing to say to you," Gillespie shouted.

"Why don't you talk to them?" Daly asked quietly from the couch. "Tell them what you told me. They would ..."

"Enough!" Gillespie shot back. "No more talking."

He turned on his heels and made a beeline back to the computer desk to reclaim his seat. No sooner had his backside hit the cushion than the silence in the room was shattered by the splintering tinkle of breaking glass. Daly barely had time to register a small canister coming through the front window when everything went blank.

A blinding burst of white light seared the men's eyes as the flash-bang grenade burst in front of the coffee table. The flash was accompanied by a deafening crack that sounded like Zeus himself had descended from the heavens. A paralyzing shock wave hit the men, rendering them both momentarily senseless. From his perch on the couch, Daly fell forward, simultaneously trying to massage his blinded eyes and pounding headache. He could see nothing. Through his stupor, he heard the sound of a door being kicked open and police barking commands. Then came a volley of gunfire. Rapid bursts of lead transformed the living room into a five-yard-wide battlefield, with Daly curled in a ball in no man's land. He prayed the cops would see him as a victim. He prayed that the gunshots Gillespie was blindly hurling at anyone at the front of the house would somehow miss him.

The last thing he remembered was a sharp pain burning through his stomach. Then all went dark.

# CHAPTER 22

*Monday, April 9, 2018*
*9:12 p.m.*

For the past several hours, Jennifer Talmadge and other members of the media had been camped out at the edge of a police perimeter waiting for information about what they could neither hear nor see. At one point, Pittston Police Chief Joseph Rossi had come to the edge of the perimeter to dole out a few tidbits to the hungry reporters. Speaking in a gruff, terse voice, the chief had confirmed what the reporters already knew – that the police were involved in a standoff with a subject they had been trying to serve with a warrant.

"That's all I can say right now," Rossi told the reporters, expressing regret he did not feel. "It's an ongoing investigation."

Aside from that impromptu news conference, the reporters on scene had mostly occupied themselves with getting reaction from shocked residents and then, when that grew monotonous, making small talk as they waited for another update.

Talmadge had sent in a short story for the website saying police were involved in a standoff with an unknown suspect. Richardson had decided, for the moment, at least, to hold off on revealing that Daly had been in the area to cover a major arrest and was now missing.

When the gunshots rang out on the street, Talmadge and the other reporters perked up and craned their necks toward the sound as it echoed like distant fireworks. There was no mistaking the volley of explosive violence that penetrated the night sky.

Cameramen grabbed their gear and aimed their lenses into the darkness, focusing on action they could not see. The newspaper reporters flipped open their notebooks and began scribbling descriptions of the sound and of the reactions of the people on the street.

Not a single person – not the media, the gawkers, or the firefighters and medics standing by – tried to seek cover. Everyone watched in earnest, trying to catch a glimpse of the gunfight.

Talmadge counted about a dozen shots that blasted off in quick succession before it was over. A dozen shots shattering the nighttime quiet, leaving only silence and mystery in their absence.

For a moment, the throng of reporters stared toward the void. Then, as the perimeter collapsed and officers rushed toward the action, they pushed forward as far as they could before the road guard halted their advance, leaving them to shout questions for the commanders to ignore.

Talmadge, though, sensed her opportunity. She was only a few years out of journalism school but had learned the ropes quickly. She was sharp and had a friendly, outgoing personality that helped her build sources quickly. People liked to be around her. And, truth be told, her golden, curly hair and her deep, blue eyes never hurt when it came to endearing herself to new sources. She was a solid journalist who didn't need to get by on her looks, but she was also an opportunist who didn't think it below her to bat her lashes a bit if it might entice a source to part with some key information.

Trying to be discrete, Talmadge lowered her notepad and walked to the side of the closed street, away from the craning necks of her fellow reporters. The last thing she wanted was the cameramen to see her and come running over. She made her way quietly to a uniformed cop standing along the perimeter.

"Excuse me," Talmadge said. "I'm with the Observer. I was wondering ..."

"You've got to talk to the chief. He's in there," the cop said, raising a thumb toward Gillespie's house.

"I'm not trying to get a comment," Talmadge said. "We had a reporter in the area before the standoff. Erik Daly. He was going to Vincent Gillespie's house, and we haven't heard from him since this started."

The uniform looked at Talmadge blankly for a moment, as if trying to decide whether she was pulling one over on him. Talmadge stared back evenly, batting a lash or two.

"Wait one," he grumbled back.

The uniform turned away and reached up to key the radio microphone mounted on his shoulder. He exchanged inaudible chatter with someone on the other end, then turned back to Talmadge.

"Chief's coming," the cop grunted, turning back to watch the action.

A few minutes later, a shadowy figure appeared in the darkness down the street, lumbering toward the perimeter and the uniform who clearly wanted to be closer to the action. Chief Rossi sauntered up to the line, pointed at Talmadge and gestured for her to cross the yellow crime scene tape. Talmadge hooked a thumb under the plastic tape and ducked underneath as a couple of television reporters exchanged incredulous looks.

Rossi turned his back to them and escorted Talmadge to a pair of police cruisers parked at angles in the street, blocking traffic.

"Jen, what I'm about to tell you is not for publication. Are we clear?" Rossi asked.

"Understood. We just need to know if Erik is all right," Talmadge said.

"He got here before us. And Gillespie got to him first. Brought him into the house just as our guys were arriving on scene," Rossi said.

"Is he okay?" Talmadge asked, growing impatient.

"He sustained a gunshot wound to the torso. It didn't look good, but we're hopeful he'll live," Rossi said. "Medics rushed him to the hospital. What I need from you is how to get in touch with his people."

For a moment, Talmadge looked at — or more precisely, through — Rossi with a blank stare. The words couldn't make their way past her lips as she tried comprehending what the chief had just said.

Erik could die.

What about Lauren?

"Jen," Rossi interrupted her thoughts. "Do you have a number for his family?"

"He's not married," Talmadge muttered. "He has a daughter. Lauren. We probably have her number back at the newsroom."

"How old is she? A kid?" Rossi asked.

"No. I mean yes. I mean, she's in high school. I think she's a senior," Talmadge said.

"Okay. Can you call work and see if you can get me her number? I want to get to her before you guys blast this all over the place," Rossi said. "No offense."

"None taken," Talmadge said.

She pulled out her phone, swiped the screen and keyed in her passcode. Rossi could hear her repeating the story to someone on the other end of the phone who, by Talmadge's reaction, was as shocked as she had been just moments ago.

"I know," Talmadge said into the phone. "I can't believe it."

She flipped open a notepad and scribbled down a number, then ended the call. Talmadge turned back to Rossi and then read him back the number.

"Her name's Lauren," she said. "Listen, what hospital did they take him to? My editor wants to get a few people over there. For support."

"They brought him to Geisinger Wyoming Valley Medical Center," Rossi said. "Remember, I don't want any of this getting out, at least until we can contact Lauren."

"You've got my word," Talmadge said, turning to return to her position along the perimeter.

◆ ◆ ◆

Wojcik's black unmarked cruiser rolled up to the entrance of the hospital's emergency department and the passenger door popped open before he put the car in park. Lauren jumped out in a panic, leaving the door open behind her as she rushed inside.

"Where's my father?" she blurted breathlessly to the receptionist, her eyes on the verge of tears.

"Who's your father?" the woman asked flatly.

"Erik Daly. He was shot."

The woman hammered on her keyboard briefly then turned her eyes back up to Lauren.

"He's still in surgery. You can have a seat in the waiting area and someone will come get you as soon as he's out."

Calming earth tones and padded chairs greeted Lauren in the waiting room. Health magazines laid out on the tables discussed issues that no one waiting for a loved one in surgery would ever care to read about. From a television hanging on the wall, a cable news anchor droned on, joined by the omnipresent "breaking news" graphic.

Lauren tuned it out and spent the time waiting on her phone, texting friends. Wojcik sat next to her in uncomfortable silence.

Eventually, Lauren put her phone down and joined the detective in staring blankly across the waiting room.

"Why'd he do it?" she asked finally. "Why did this guy try to kill my dad?"

Wojcik paused a moment before answering.

"I don't know if he was trying to kill him, necessarily. I think he just panicked because he knew he was caught," Wojcik said.

"Caught doing what?" Lauren asked.

"You should probably ask your father when he's done. I don't think it's my place to tell you," Wojcik said.

Lauren's cheeks flushed and her eyes narrowed. Her chair slid slightly away from Wojcik as she turned to face him.

"My father almost died!" she snapped. "He was shot in the stomach while you guys were trying to arrest someone. I think I deserve to know why it happened."

"You do," Wojcik agreed. "I'm not trying to hide anything. I just don't know if your father would want you to hear it from me."

"My father could be dying right now," Lauren sobbed, putting her face in her hands. "He's on a slab and you're worried about who gets to tell the story."

Put that way, it did sound foolish, Wojcik had to admit.

"It's just that it's graphic," Wojcik said. "We had two guys who were abusing kids. The teacher, Vincent Gillespie, was selecting them and grooming them so that he and a psychiatrist could make videos of them. When we first went to Gillespie's house a couple weeks ago, we found a bunch of videos on his computer.

Videos of him with teenagers. We believe he was working with Dr. Marvin Radcliffe to make them."

"Oh my God," Lauren said. "That's disgusting. But why did he go after my father?"

"Your father found out they had created a white-noise app that had subliminal messages in it," Wojcik said. "When we reinterviewed Gillespie, he admitted that they created it to mess with the kids' heads. Radcliffe was also seeing them for therapy. Gillespie told us that Radcliffe was trying to instill them with a sense of hopelessness so they would kill themselves. These men were just trying to protect themselves. They didn't give a crap about the kids."

Lauren sat in stunned silence for a minute. The thought of two men in positions of trust using unsuspecting kids for their pleasure and then discarding them was beyond depraved.

It was outright evil.

"What's going to happen now?" Lauren asked.

"Well, Gillespie's gone. He didn't survive the raid," Wojcik said.

Lauren felt a little embarrassed to admit it, but she was glad.

"What about Dr. Radcliffe?"

"We took him into custody without incident around the same time as the standoff with Gillespie began," Wojcik said. "We got him."

# CHAPTER 23

*Tuesday, April 10, 2018*
*12:27 a.m.*

John Richardson hurried through the hospital doors and into the waiting room. He scanned the bored occupants, seeking recognition and getting only mild interest from people with nothing else to do but watch a disoriented newcomer.

When at last his eyes settled on Lauren and Wojcik in the waiting room corner, Richardson made a beeline in their direction.

"How is he?" he said too loudly, drawing a reproachful eye from the receptionist.

"He's out of surgery," Wojcik said. "The doctor says he's going to be all right."

"Thank God," Richardson said. "I got here as soon as I could. What did they say?"

"He was shot in the stomach," Lauren said. "It's going to take a while, but the doctor said he should make a full recovery."

Richardson gave Lauren a squeeze around the shoulders, the awkward gesture of a man who feels he needs to console a near-stranger. After a moment, he released his hold and Lauren fell back into her seat. After all the emotions she'd faced over the past few hours, she wasn't much in the mood for keeping up appearances. She slid her phone out of her pocket and got back to texting.

Wojcik looked to Richardson.

"Listen, could I talk to you for a minute?" he asked. Alone, he didn't need to say.

"Sure," Richardson said. "Lauren, we're going to go grab a cup of coffee. Do you want anything?"

"No thanks," she said, not looking up.

The men walked down the white tiled floor to the vending machines. Wojcik pushed a dollar bill in the slot of the coffee dispenser to the sound of gears humming and pushed the button for French roast. No cream, no sugar.

"What are you having?" he asked.

"The same. Thanks," Richardson said.

The steaming coffee trickled into the cheap paper cups with a spattering sound. Wojcik waited until both cups were full before speaking.

"I know this really isn't the best time to bring this up, but you guys really screwed us on this case," he said.

"Jesus," Richardson said. "You've got that right. About the timing, anyway."

"I know. I'm sorry," Wojcik paused to collect his thoughts. "It's just that we were closing in on them. We were about to get them. And trust me, I know Erik helped us connect it to Radcliffe ..."

"Helped you?" Richardson cut in. "Cracked the case for you, the way I see it."

"You're right. I'm not trying to minimize what he found. But when he went to Radcliffe's office and confronted him ... I know he was just trying to do his job, but he showed Radcliffe our hand," Wojcik said.

"Well, Phil, you know we're willing to work with you guys, to an extent. But we've got a different mission than you," Richardson said.

"To sell papers?"

"To report the news. We're trying to tell stories that matter to our readers, and we can't always wait for the opportune time according to your timeline to break the story."

"Spare me that bullshit," Wojcik said. "I told Erik I would tip him off before the others. He had the story in the bag. Then he pulls this crap and flushes the case down the toilet."

"I think that's being a bit dramatic. You've already arrested Radcliffe," Richardson said. "He's done."

"If he is, it won't be because of what you guys pulled," Wojcik said. "This is off the record, agreed?"

"Agreed."

"When we searched Gillespie's home we found equipment and videos. A lot of videos," Wojcik said. "But so far he's the only one we can recognize in them, aside from the victims. Radcliffe isn't in them — or at least you can't make him out. And when we took Radcliffe his house was clean. Not a single computer or a hard drive. Not even a goddamned Xbox. His office had a mahogany desk with a ring of dust around where the computer used to be. He knew we were coming and he got rid of it all."

"Well, get out there and find it," Richardson said, getting short. "Isn't that what you're paid to do, detective?"

"We're trying," Wojcik nodded. "But if we don't we could be in trouble. Gillespie was our link to Radcliffe. And he isn't talking anymore."

◆ ◆ ◆

The sun was just breaking over the mountains to the east, cutting through thick fog blanketing the forests and valley below, when Daly began stirring in his bed. The dim room flickered with the light from a muted television no one was watching. A cardiograph next to the bed beeped at regular intervals, assurance that life still pumped through Daly's veins. By the window, Lauren sat slumped in a lightly padded chair that was clearly never intended to double as a bed. Her body twisted at odd angles through the night as she tried finding comfort where none was to be had.

Under the snow-white sheets, Daly's arm raised slightly and his eyelids began to flutter. Slowly, he reached for the intravenous needle protruding from his arm, which registered in his mind only as a sharp pain in the crook of his elbow. Feeling the plastic catheter extending from his body, Daly slightly perked up, growing more aware of his surroundings. At once, he noticed an oppressive antiseptic hospital smell.

He glanced to the window and was relieved to see Lauren curled in the chair. She was safe and by his side. That was the most important thing.

But why was he here? He had no idea. He tried remembering the last thing he had done. All that came were fleeting images floating by like snippets of an old forgotten dream. Unsure of the reason for his current situation, Daly began giving himself a once-over. He leaned forward a bit to sit up in bed and unwittingly discovered the likely culprit: searing pain in his stomach. Tenderly, Daly lifted the sheet like a kid opening a squeaky door in a horror film. Underneath the hospital gown, he found a large gauze bandage covering the lower left side of his abdomen. After a moment's hesitation, he decided to peel the tape away to get a look.

"Dad?" Lauren said, perking up in the chair. "Dad!"

She jumped up abruptly and wrapped her arms around Daly's neck, squeezing tightly and pulling him toward her. He said nothing of the pain.

"You're going to be all right," she assured him. "The doctor said ..."

"What happened?" Daly cut in. "I can't remember anything."

Lauren froze for a moment, at first unsure if her father was making a joke and then mortified at the possibility that he might not be.

"You don't remember?" Lauren asked. "They said you were on a story. You went up to Vincent Gillespie's house and ..."

"Gillespie," Daly said, as if in a trance. Lauren could see there was no comprehension in his eyes.

The door swung open and a doctor strode in, glasses perched high on a narrow nose protruding from an olive face. The ends of her jet-black hair had brown highlights that stood in stark contrast to the shimmering green eyes that flashed behind the spectacles. She wore the requisite white overcoat with a stethoscope around her neck, but her youthful age and beaming smile gave her a more casual air than most emergency room doctors. She was short but confident, smart but not condescending.

She immediately extended a hand to Lauren.

"Hi. I'm Dr. Maria Torres," she said.

Lauren turned to her with a pleading look in her eyes.

"Something's wrong," she blurted, on the verge of tears. "He doesn't remember. He doesn't know why he's here."

"Memory loss?" Dr. Torres looked at Daly.

"I can't remember what happened," Daly said. His voice was confused, but there was no panic in it.

"Do you know your name?" the doctor asked.

"Erik Daly."

"What do you do for a living?"

"I'm a reporter with the Wilkes-Barre Observer."

"Who's she?" Torres said, gesturing to Lauren.

"Lauren. My daughter."

"What year is it?"

"What year is it?" Daly parroted, looking dazed.

Dr. Torres nodded and went over to the cardiograph, reading the results before opening Daly's chart. She scribbled a few notes, checked her watch and entered the time, and then returned the chart.

"How did I get here?" Daly asked. "Can you tell me how I got here?"

"You suffered a gunshot wound, but you're going to be okay. The bullet missed your vital organs and we've stopped the internal bleeding. As long as we can fight off infection, you should be fine," Dr. Torres said, turning to Lauren. "As far as the memory loss goes — I'd like to do some tests, but I don't think it's anything to be too concerned about."

"He just keeps repeating the same thing," Lauren said.

"It's called perseveration," Dr. Torres said. "It's common in cases of transient global amnesia. We'll run some tests to exclude anything else as being the cause of the memory loss, but he doesn't have any trouble understanding words or any paralysis, which would indicate something more serious. If it's transient global amnesia, it should clear up within a day."

Seeing Lauren relax, Dr. Torres excused herself and left them alone once more in the recovery room. Lauren immediately moved to the edge of the bed and sat next to her father, putting her arm around him and holding tight.

"I'm going to be fine," Daly reassured her, despite not feeling reassured himself.

The last thing Daly wanted to do was spend the day in the hospital being poked and prodded. He felt fine and was anxious to get back to work and learn more about what had happened — and what was going to happen next. But he recognized that Lauren was terrified and wouldn't rest easy until she had some definitive answers.

He lay back in bed and tried to get comfortable, turning up the volume on one of the network morning shows that was light on news and heavy on health tips and entertainment promotions. He held Lauren tight against his side, watching the television without interest as he tried to remember what had happened. Over the next few hours, the details of the past few weeks flitted back into his head like snapshots, revealing individual scenes from his own life without context. When he eventually regained control of his mind and memories, Daly comprehended for the first time how close he'd come to losing Lauren. He'd been so caught up in chasing the story that he hadn't bothered to think about what she'd been through. She was just a girl trying to decide who to take to the prom and where to go to college. A typical teenage life. But because of his actions, her mother was dead. Her house was reduced to ashes. Her father was in a hospital bed.

The thoughts turned to anger in Daly's mind. Anger at himself for his stubbornness. For his thoughtlessness. For his selfishness.

The anger melded to guilt, and Daly found himself wondering how long it had been since his last drink. *Too long*, he thought.

*Hopefully, I'll be out of here by tonight,* he thought.

"Dad?" Lauren pulled him from his thoughts. "Is everything going to be okay? I mean with your work?"

"Of course. Why wouldn't it be?" he asked.

"Well, when you were ... out ... your boss was here with that cop. When they went to get coffee I could hear a little of what they were saying. The cop sounded mad. At you," Lauren said.

"Well, I suppose he might be a little mad at me right now. He probably thinks I was getting in the way," Daly said.

"But won't you get in trouble?"

"Nah," Daly said, as casually as he could manage. "John's a good editor. He knows I was just doing my job. Sometimes that means not doing what the police would like. They've got their job and we've got ours."

Daly gave Lauren a squeeze and a peck on the forehead.

"I've been thinking," he said, changing the subject. "I don't want to stand in the way of your dreams. It will be tough, but we can take out some loans and make it work, I think. So if you really want to go to Stanford, it's your call."

Lauren turned her eyes from the television screen and pulled her head away from her father's shoulder to take his face in. Her eyes were saucers, beaming like a kid on Christmas morning — but just for a moment. Then it was Daly's turn to get a peck on the forehead, and Lauren returned her head to its spot against his chest.

"Thanks, Dad," she said.

"What?" Daly asked, perplexed. "You don't still want to go to Stanford?"

"I do," Lauren said. "It's just ... well, it's just like you to say I can go to California while you're laid up in a hospital bed."

# CHAPTER 24

*Monday, June 3, 2019*
*9:05 a.m.*

The Luzerne County Courthouse towers over the banks of the Susquehanna River, serving as a domed cathedral to the law for well over a century. Its high sandstone walls are adorned with cherubic images espousing justice and paintings of forefathers now long dead. Through its halls, the most petty of thieves and the most heinous mass murderers have made the long march to the third-floor courtrooms where judges in black robes sealed their fates from their dark wooden benches.

In the basement, Daly made his way through the security checkpoint, waiting his turn through the metal detector along with the mass of defendants and their family members arriving at court for the day. Most of them were well acquainted with the procedure.

It was the day Daly had been anticipating for over a year: the opening of Dr. Radcliffe's trial. But rather than feeling the usual adrenaline rush that came with covering a high-profile case, Daly wore a glum expression as he sullenly picked up his wallet and cellphone from the X-ray machine's conveyor belt.

He'd fought to stay on the case after Gillespie's death, but Richardson had been adamant that there could still be a conflict of interest. Then Wojcik had shown up at the newsroom one morning and slapped a subpoena on the desk, ending all debate on the matter.

So rather than coming to cover one of the most sensational cases to ever wind up in the storied courthouse, he was scheduled to appear as a witness.

Although he was off the story, he had been closely following the case, reading about developments and picking Talmadge's brain for details she didn't include in her articles. He had a pretty good idea of what to expect in court, and that knowledge did not help his dour mood.

In the morning paper, Talmadge had a front-page preview story about the case. It didn't mention Daly by name, but anyone who knew anything about the case knew what was what.

*WILKES-BARRE — The criminal homicide trial against a Kingston psychiatrist accused of manipulating four teens into committing suicide is set to begin today.*

*Marvin G. Radcliffe, 57, is charged with causing suicide as criminal homicide, involuntary manslaughter and criminal conspiracy in the deaths of four youths who died last year.*

*Radcliffe's alleged accomplice in the crimes, substitute teacher Vincent P. Gillespie, 28, was killed in a shootout with police in April 2018.*

*Prosecutors allege the two men were producing child pornography involving the four victims. In an effort to avoid detection, the men created a white-noise app called Soma that contained subliminal messages urging the youths to commit suicide, according to prosecutors.*

*In addition, Radcliffe, who was also counseling the teens, coaxed them into suicide during sessions, according to prosecutors.*

*Both men were initially charged with producing child pornography, but prosecutors dropped that charge against Radcliffe after Gillespie's death. Prosecutors say they believe Radcliffe destroyed his computers and other evidence, and that Gillespie had been their link to connecting him with that offense.*

*"Unfortunately, these suspects were tipped off about their impending arrests ahead of time," District Attorney Robert Phillips said. "Despite that setback, my office is committed to ensuring that these victims get justice, and that Dr. Marvin Radcliffe will be held accountable to the fullest extent of the law."*

*The deaths began with the Feb. 10, 2018, hanging death of 16-year-old Kingston resident Justin Gonzalez, but the case did not make news until Kimberly Foster killed herself on March 22, 2018.*

*Foster, a 15-year-old cheerleader at Hanover Area High School, fatally shot herself in a live web video that went viral.*

*A week later, Emma Nguyen, a 16-year-old junior at Coughlin High School in Wilkes-Barre, committed suicide by jumping off the Market Street Bridge.*

*The final death connected to the case was that of David Kowalski, a 17-year-old Nanticoke boy who shot himself at home on April 5, 2018.*

*The trial is expected to last the week.*

The article incensed Daly — and he hadn't even bothered to look at the Other Paper's version, which no doubt identified him as an Observer reporter, if not by name. There was no mention of the fact that Radcliffe could still spend decades in prison. In fact, a conviction on the remaining charges would still be tantamount to a life sentence for a man of Radcliffe's age. To Daly, it was a transparent attempt by the DA to set up a scapegoat in case he couldn't bring home a tough, high-profile trial. But the media, ever-quick to spotlight drama, had eaten it up without even pausing to question the DA's motivation for making such a statement.

Daly thought about taking the elevator, then thought better of it. The long climb to the third floor would give him a bit of exercise before a long day in court and cut back on the chances of him running into someone he didn't want to see — such as Jennifer Talmadge or Robert Phillips.

Daly reached the top of the worn stone staircase and encountered dozens of defendants conversing with attorneys outside the courtrooms. Every chair and stretch of railing on the interior balconies surrounding a vast rotunda seemed to be occupied. From the balconies, the defendants could look down to see people scurrying up the stairs from the first floor or look up to see stained glass windows and intricate murals painted onto the dome above. Most of them occupied themselves by pecking at their cellphones and hushing crying babies.

As Daly rounded the bend to Courtroom Four, he could see Phil Wojcik was among the people gathered around waiting for opening statements to begin.

"Shit," he muttered under his breath.

Although it had been more than a year, things had not quite returned to normal between Daly and Wojcik. After a brief and awkward meeting at the hospital, Daly hadn't even seen Wojcik for a few months while he was out of work recovering from the gunshot wound. When he came back, he'd tried to rekindle the relationship, but he could tell Wojcik was cooler than he had been before. He still returned Daly's calls and fed him the occasional tip, but Daly could tell Wojcik was keeping him at a greater distance than in the past. They had never been drinking buddies, but they had been closer to friends than business associates before. That had changed since the shooting.

"Hey Phil," Daly said, extending a hand.

Wojcik reached out and clapped it with an athlete's exaggerated bravado.

"What's happening, my man?" he said. "You ready for your big day?"

"As ready as I'm going to be," Daly said.

"You'll be fine. Just tell the jury what happened and stick to the facts. Piece of cake," Wojcik said, clapping Daly on the shoulder with a meaty hand. He nodded over Daly's shoulder as the county's top prosecutor got off the elevator. "Bob wasn't too happy with you after what happened with Radcliffe, but he isn't going to throttle you on the stand. You're his witness, after all."

The district attorney, Robert Phillips, had a stout frame perpetually shrouded in immaculate pinstripe suits. He wore Italian leather shoes, gold watches, and red power ties that complimented his slicked salt-and-pepper hair. Over the years, he had built a reputation for being a hard-charging and aggressive prosecutor. He'd been with the office as an assistant district attorney for nearly two decades, during which he'd led the prosecution to victory on some of the most high-profile and heinous cases in county history. When his predecessor retired, Robert Phillips decided to make a run for the office and won a landslide victory with overwhelming support from the legal community.

Phillips was a deeply personable man, despite his excesses and drive for victory. He was the sort who would cross the room to shake hands with anyone and everyone to say hello and ask about the wife and kids. Making his rounds through the courthouse, he would talk sports with the law clerks and weekend plans with the secretaries. His natural charm ensured he had few enemies. Juries found him charming. Journalists found him quotable. Cops found him tough on criminals. Defense attorneys found him unflappable and fair.

Phillips strode briskly toward the heavy wooden courtroom doors without meeting Daly's gaze, even though he'd given Wojcik a nod. Without breaking stride, Phillips led his entourage of assistant district attorneys, detectives, and trial assistants through the portals into Courtroom Four. Inside, the grand mosaics and white Italian marble that brightened the rotunda gave way to perpetually drawn burgundy silk velour draperies that cast shadows over the dark mahogany furnishings. Two large tables at the front were set up in front of the jury box for the prosecution. Opposite them, on the far wall from the jury, was a single large desk set aside for the defense. Without bothering to acknowledge Radcliffe or his attorney, the prosecution team made a beeline to the front of the room and settled in at their desks. Wojcik excused himself from Daly's company and followed suit.

Daly entered the courtroom and sat down at the back of the hard wooden pews lining the gallery. He looked toward Radcliffe with interest to get the first glimpse of the man that he'd had in months. Radcliffe looked somewhat slimmer than the last time. The menu at the Luzerne County Correctional Facility sometimes had that effect. Radcliffe's salty hair looked to have been freshly trimmed, and he was clean-shaven. The time behind bars had not helped with the furrow lines on his forehead, but Radcliffe's cheeks and nose still had their rosy sheen. He was also wearing a Navy blue jacket with a light blue tie — a marked improvement from the yellow prison jumpsuit and slippers he'd sported the last time Daly laid eyes on him.

Radcliffe was leaning close to the ear of his attorney, Melissa Cooper, and speaking in earnest about something that clearly had him worked up. Cooper was nodding and holding a hand up to placate Radcliffe, signaling that whatever problem he was having would be resolved.

Cooper wore a black dress suit and an ivory-hued blouse that stood in stark contrast to her jet black hair, which was pulled back into a ponytail. A former prosecutor who had switched teams, Cooper had a piercing gaze and firm handshake. She was a short woman, but any defendant who took the stand thinking he could intimidate her had another think coming. Over the years, Cooper had developed a reputation for being a bulldog in the courtroom. She was known for her aggressive cross-examination style and her ability to quickly process new information and adapt.

While Phillips had a reputation for his warmth, Cooper was known for what some saw to be a chilly disposition. She wasn't the sort to engage in small talk; when she was in court she was all business. To some, she came across as distant. But over the years, Daly had gotten to know her and he knew she was really just intensely focused on her work. And that intensity paid off: she had a talent for making juries find doubt when none should have existed. More than once, talk of the courthouse had been dominated by the stunned whispering of attorneys who couldn't believe the jury had sat through the same case they did.

That ability came at a steep price. Cooper was one of the most expensive attorneys in the county, but those who could afford her gladly paid what she asked. It wasn't possible to buy one's freedom in Luzerne County, but hiring Melissa Cooper was the next best thing.

From the back of the courtroom, Daly craned his neck to try and learn why Radcliffe was upset. In his hands, Radcliffe held a report that he was reading with what seemed to be a growing sense of alarm. One of the thin, flexible pens that the county jail issued to prevent weaponization tapped rhythmically against the desk. Underneath, his right knee was pumping like a piston.

Before Daly was able to get a look at the cover of the report, the tipstaff called out from the front of the room.

"All rise," the voice echoed through the cavernous courtroom.

Judge Thomas Perry glided across the white-tiled floor and ascended the bench with the black robes of justice flowing in his wake. He set a steaming cup of coffee on the bench next to the gavel and sat back in his plush leather chair, shifting his gaze between the lawyers.

"Good morning, counsel," Perry said. "Are we ready to proceed?"

Phillips was out of his seat before the words left the judge's mouth, ready to address the court.

"Good morning, your honor," he said. "Before we do, there is one matter that has come to our attention."

"Very well. Will counsel approach?"

Cooper joined the prosecution team and approached the bench so that the parties stood directly in front of the judge to address the court.

"Your honor," Phillips began, "Over the weekend, a situation was brought to my attention that has great bearing on this case. I learned that late last week the police received a tip about the location of the defendant's missing electronics. Our investigators conducted a search at the location in a wooded area and recovered a number of items, including a computer, a hard drive and several thumb drives. The items appeared to have been smashed and burned. Obviously, we have not had enough time to conduct a thorough investigation into this information, but our detectives have reason to believe these items could contain evidence of Dr. Radcliffe engaging in illicit sexual activity with minor children."

Judge Perry's eyebrows rose up as Phillips paused for dramatic effect, ensuring the reporters in the courtroom had a chance to finish scribbling the quote.

Cooper saw her chance to interject and quickly stepped in, drawing a sideways scowl from Phillips.

"Judge, we picked a jury in this matter last Friday," Cooper said. "We all showed up here this morning ready to begin the trial. Now, at the moment that the Commonwealth is supposed to be delivering its opening statement, Mr. Phillips comes in saying he's potentially found photographic evidence of my client committing a crime. This evidence was not included in discovery, and from the sound of things Mr. Phillips hasn't even seen it yet. As your honor well knows, the defense has the right to inspect any and all evidence presented by the Commonwealth. For them to come in with this now — this isn't the eve of trial. This isn't even an eleventh-hour surprise. This is an outright ambush."

"Your honor, the defense did not receive these materials in discovery because the Commonwealth did not have them," Phillips retorted. "As soon as this was brought to my attention, I contacted Ms. Cooper to bring her up to speed."

Judge Perry squinted at Phillips a long moment, seemingly trying to assess whether the prosecutor was in earnest or blowing smoke. The judge had been a defense attorney prior to taking the bench. That had been more than twenty years earlier, but he never seemed to have lost the defense attorney's underdog spirit. Most courthouse watchers would say he was a fair judge. But he also wasn't afraid to buck popular opinion and rebuff the prosecution, even in a high-profile case.

Sitting on the bench, Judge Perry pulled at his chin and peered out at the courtroom through thick-rimmed black glasses before speaking.

"The defense has the right to discovery — all of it. There's no question," he said.

"Of course, your honor," Phillips said, trying to sound agreeable.

"If I let this come in now, the defense will be highly prejudiced. How can Ms. Cooper effectively defend against something she knew nothing about before the morning of trial?" the judge asked.

"Again, your honor, I do apologize for the timing, but it was simply out of our control," Phillips said. "Perhaps the appropriate remedy here is for this matter to be continued to allow the defense to examine the data?"

"That could solve the issue. Ms. Cooper?" the judge turned to the defense.

"Your honor, I do not believe that would be appropriate," Cooper said. "As the court, I'm sure, is aware, Dr. Radcliffe has the right under rule six-hundred of the Pennsylvania Rules of Criminal Procedure for his trial to commence within one year of being charged. The defense has not requested a single continuance in this matter. This case has only been subject to a couple of brief continuances because of court-scheduling conflicts. Put simply, the Commonwealth is running out of time. If the prosecution requests a continuance, I will have no choice but to file a motion seeking dismissal of all charges, with prejudice."

"Mr. Phillips?" Judge Perry turned his gaze back to the prosecution.

"I believe that a continuance at this juncture is the appropriate remedy and that the time should run against the defense," Phillips said. "The Commonwealth cannot be expected to scour the ends of the Earth for evidence that a defendant purposefully hid. The delay in finding this evidence is solely the result of Dr. Radcliffe's actions. Barring evidence under such circumstances would be tantamount to encouraging wholesale evidence dumping."

"I'm sure the Commonwealth has been eagerly seeking this evidence for over a year," Cooper shot back. "The anonymous tip makes it clear that someone knew where it was. It also makes clear that the Commonwealth failed to identify that person in a timely manner, even though it must have been someone close to Dr. Radcliffe. The Commonwealth failed to exercise due diligence, and now they're asking Dr. Radcliffe to pay the price by sitting in jail while they get to work."

Judge Perry gave a slight nod of his head, signaling he'd heard enough.

"I tend to agree that the Commonwealth might have been able to better vet those in Dr. Radcliffe's immediate circle to see if they knew where these items were," the judge said. "But the fact of the matter is that this evidence appears to have gone missing as a result of the defendant's actions. This court is not going to make a ruling that rewards such conduct. I will grant a two-month continuance in this matter to allow the items to be processed. But this trial will start on the twelfth of August, barring an act of God."

# CHAPTER 25

*Monday, August 12, 2019*
*9:43 a.m.*

Robert Phillips looked at the floor as he walked to the lectern, a slight smile coming to the corner of his mouth in a rehearsed aw-shucks manner. He set a stack of notes on the mahogany surface and rested his large hands on the sides, nodding to the judge for permission to begin his opening statement.

"May it please the court. Counsel," Phillips said, giving Melissa Cooper an amiable smile. He turned and faced the jury. "Ladies and gentlemen, I don't mean to alarm you. But I'm sorry to say what I've got to tell you is quite shocking. This isn't simply a case of child abuse or even murder. This is a case about broken promises, violated trust and, most of all, greed. Not greed for money, but the greed of a man who would do whatever it took to get what he wanted — no matter who paid the price.

"By day, Dr. Marvin Radcliffe was a seemingly respected psychiatrist who worked closely with troubled youth in our community. You're going to hear about the children he helped and the volunteer work he's done. You'll find out that he serves on the boards of several prominent organizations in our community. You're even going to hear that he has previously testified for the prosecution — my office — in criminal cases where we needed psychological assessments.

"Well, he fooled us all, myself included. Because you're also going to hear about Dr. Radcliffe's dark side. The secret life he lived and concealed from us all. You're going to hear that Dr. Radcliffe bore witness to horrific crimes against the four victims — Justin Gonzalez, Kimberly Foster, Emma Nguyen, and David Kowalski. All of them were teenagers. Still children. And they were sexually abused, forced to perform unspeakable acts in front of a camera for the entertainment of depraved men," Phillips said.

Here, Phillips paused for effect, pretending to scribble a note on his papers as he let the jurors think over his turn of the phrase. A couple of them fidgeted in their seats, rubbing their hands over their mouths. Phillips could hardly have been more pleased.

"All of those children are now dead. And I would like you to remember that they're dead because they saw that side, that secret side, of Dr. Radcliffe. Ladies and gentlemen, the testimony you are going to hear will prove beyond a reasonable doubt that Dr. Radcliffe conspired with another individual — a substitute teacher named Vincent Gillespie, who himself was involved in this child pornography ring — to kill these children. The children were incriminating evidence, and Dr. Radcliffe made a calculated decision to get rid of them, no different than a robber might throw away a gun after a stick-up.

"But what is different about this case is the depths of the depravity Dr. Radcliffe and Mr. Gillespie showed in disposing of their trash. They didn't simply put a bullet in the heads of these children. They didn't slit their throats and kill them quickly. No, what they did was much more insidious and sadistic.

"These men created a white-noise app for these kids to install on their cellphones. The app was purportedly meant to help them sleep. What the children didn't know was that behind the static, Dr. Radcliffe had hidden a subliminal message — a recording of Vincent Gillespie's voice. The message said, 'They're watching me always. Nothing can make it stop. End it now. Before they find out.'

"Now, I don't know what the defense is going to argue, but I submit that there's only one way to interpret that message. And on top of that, Dr. Radcliffe was continuing to see these children in therapy sessions. You will hear that he and Mr. Gillespie were doing everything in their power to make these kids feel desperate and hopeless. They used them and decided to throw them out like household trash, so they used these kids' own shame against them in a twisted plot to avoid detection. It was psychological warfare. Dr. Radcliffe and Mr. Gillespie tormented and bullied these kids until they were utterly broken. These kids had no one to turn to because the people they were supposed to trust — their psychiatrist and their teacher — were conspiring against them to end their lives.

"Ladies and gentlemen, there is only one common-sense ending to this story. Dr. Marvin Radcliffe did everything he could to ensure those kids died and couldn't testify against him. He employed duress and deception in using the subliminal messages to get in their heads. That is the crime of causing suicide. He engaged in grossly negligent conduct in counseling these children and encouraging them to take their own lives. That's involuntary manslaughter. And the evidence will clearly show he was involved in a criminal conspiracy with Mr. Gillespie.

"In the end, I trust you will find Dr. Radcliffe guilty as charged. Thank you."

Phillips slowly gathered up his notes and stepped away from the lectern, resuming his seat at the prosecution table. Judge Perry looked to the defense.

"Ms. Cooper?"

"Thank you, your honor," Cooper said.

As she stood up, her chair slid back across the tiled floor, sending the echo of wood scraping through the courtroom. She walked to the lectern briskly. Although the gallery was full of spectators, the sound of her heels clicking on the floor was the only break in the courtroom silence.

Cooper laid several pages of notes on the lectern, but she didn't have a prepared speech. She preferred to speak directly to the jurors. She also found prepared speeches made it difficult to improvise and respond to what opposing counsel had said. Altering a prepared speech on the fly always seemed to her to result in a disorganized rebuttal, which the jury could take as a sign of being unprepared.

Looking up from her notes, Cooper scanned the jury for several moments, looking at each member before she spoke.

"Ladies and gentlemen, we are a nation of laws. These laws are the core of our beliefs, and they say that the prosecution has the burden of proving Dr. Radcliffe's guilt beyond a reasonable doubt. I submit they won't be able to do that. They can't do that, because our laws also say Dr. Radcliffe has the right to a fair trial. He has the right to confront his accuser. As you're going to hear, the only person who ever accused Dr. Radcliffe of wrongdoing is dead. And Dr. Radcliffe isn't accused of killing him. The police did that.

"So instead you're going to hear from people who spoke to Mr. Gillespie. You're going to see a note Mr. Gillespie allegedly wrote. But we're not going to have the ability to question Mr. Gillespie's statement. And that's very important in this case. Because I urge you to think about the final days of Mr. Gillespie's life. Think about his situation.

"When the police first showed up at his house, Mr. Gillespie was their prime suspect. They searched his house and seized his computer, camera equipment, and external hard drives. We now know that those items contained irrefutable evidence that Mr. Gillespie molested the children in this case."

Here Cooper paused, letting the jury think on that and hopefully begin seeing Gillespie as the real villain.

"He was a child pornographer who was caught. He knew he was going down. So he did what criminals do when they get caught: he tried to cut a deal. He gave police information about a legitimate business partner he had — Dr. Marvin Radcliffe — in a desperate attempt to shave some time off the decades-long prison sentence he knew he was facing.

"Well, the police swallowed the story hook, line, and sinker. But I'm hoping you'll be smarter than that. I'd urge you to use your common sense and to look at the evidence. Because what you don't hear is just as important as what you do. You are not going to see any recordings of Dr. Radcliffe molesting children. You are not going to hear anyone accusing him of committing such vile acts. In fact, Dr. Radcliffe is not even charged with sexually abusing the children or with anything related to child pornography. He's not charged with that because the Commonwealth knows it doesn't have the evidence to prove it.

"They found his computer. They searched his computer. They didn't find anything on it.

"And if he wasn't involved in Mr. Gillespie's child pornography operation, I would ask you to consider why Dr. Radcliffe would work with him to hurt these children. He had no dog in this fight. Of course he wanted to help his patient, Mr. Gillespie, but he wasn't going to kill for him.

"Now, we don't dispute that Dr. Radcliffe was a business partner with Mr. Gillespie. Mr. Gillespie was a troubled man and had been seeing Dr. Radcliffe for years. When Mr. Gillespie needed some help creating a white-noise app he wanted to market, Dr. Radcliffe offered to help him get the business started. He was trying to help Mr. Gillespie, who he knew was a troubled soul. But Dr. Radcliffe had no knowledge of any subliminal messages that Mr. Gillespie put in the app, and he certainly never counseled these kids to harm themselves.

"Dr. Radcliffe is a respected member of this community who has spent a lifetime helping people. Now the Commonwealth is asking you to throw all his good work away solely on the word of a caught pedophile. I urge you to use your common sense and ask yourselves who is more believable. Ask yourselves if the Commonwealth has proved Dr. Radcliffe guilty beyond a reasonable doubt. I think when you do that, the only logical answer is that he is not guilty."

Cooper's heels clicked across the tile floor as she made her way back to the defense table. Judge Perry nodded.

"Thank you, Ms. Cooper," he said, using an index finger to push up his glasses. "The prosecution may call its first witness."

◆ ◆ ◆

The prosecution's case was entirely circumstantial. A forensic analysis of Dr. Radcliffe's computer and drives determined they were so mangled the data was unrecoverable. There was no evidence of him possessing child pornography, so Phillips' hope of re-filing that charge was dashed. But the police had gotten to Gillespie first, and they still had his computer. It contained numerous emails exchanges between Dr. Radcliffe and Gillespie. The tone of the messages was cryptic, but to Phillips that was almost as good as an outright admission. This way he could argue they were intentionally being vague in their discussions to avoid creating a paper trail documenting the conspiracy.

Phillips also had the paper records from Dr. Radcliffe's office, which he had not had time to destroy. The records proved Dr. Radcliffe had been treating all four of the victims. Even better, they also showed he had instructed every one of them to use Soma. But to Phillips, the fatal blow was brief annotations in the records Dr. Radcliffe had scribbled as reminders. In Justin Gonzalez's file, there was a handwritten note in the margin saying, "JG in good spirits. Bring up secret." The page containing the note was dated two weeks before his death. Emma Nguyen's file contained a similar note, showing Dr. Radcliffe planned to talk to her about what would happen if her father found out about the baby.

After running through his police and forensic expert witnesses, Phillips called Daly to the stand, hoping the jury would see his encounter with Dr. Radcliffe as a tacit admission of guilt.

Hearing his name, Daly slowly began walking to the witness stand, aware that the creaking of his leather shoes was now the focus of everyone in the courtroom. He reached the stand and turned to the clerk, raising his right hand to be sworn in before taking the witness chair.

"Good morning," Phillips began. "Can you state your name for the record?"

"I'm Erik Daly."

"How old are you?"

"I'm forty-four."

"How are you employed?"

"I'm a reporter for the Wilkes-Barre Observer."

"Were you involved in the Observer's coverage of the deaths of Justin Gonzalez, Kimberly Foster, Emma Nguyen, and David Kowalski?" Phillips asked.

"I was. It was my story for the first few weeks," Daly said.

"Why were you removed from the story?"

"My editor, John Richardson, became concerned that I could have a conflict of interest."

"And why was that?"

Daly shifted his weight in the chair, taking a moment to think about where to begin.

"Through my reporting, I discovered that the victims were all using an app called Soma," Daly said. "It was a white-noise app that was supposed to help people sleep. At first, when I listened to it, I just heard static. But one day I got distracted with work and left it running for a while. When I came back to it, I could hear something in the background. Something other than static.

"I called a friend, George Timmons, who has some high-tech stereo equipment. He was able to isolate the sound, and we discovered it was a voice," Daly said.

"What was it saying?"

"They're watching me always. Nothing can make it stop. End it now. Before they find out," Daly said.

"So why was that a conflict for you?" Phillips asked.

"Well, that alone wasn't," Daly said. "But through my reporting, I also discovered that the app was being sold by a company called Sleep Song, LLC, which lists Dr. Radcliffe as the president and Mr. Gillespie as the vice president. When I discovered that, I brought it to the attention of the police. John Richardson felt that at that point I could potentially be called as a prosecution witness, so he wanted to ensure the Observer's coverage could not be perceived as biased."

"I see," Phillips said, putting on a thoughtful expression. "During the course of this reporting, did anything unusual happen? Did anyone contact you about the story?"

"Probably about a week after I started researching the story I got an anonymous note," Daly said.

Phillips gestured to an assistant to flip on a projector to display the note for the jury to see: "MR. DALY: YOU KNOW WHAT HAPPENED TO THE CURIOUS CAT, DON'T YOU? BE VERY CAREFUL."

"Is this the note?" he asked.

"It is."

"Did anything about this message stick out to you at the time?"

"At the time, no," Daly said. "But about a week and a half after I got the note, I went to Dr. Radcliffe's office to ask him about Soma. That's when he threatened me."

Cooper leaped from her seat like she'd been stung by a hornet.

"Objection to the characterization, your honor," she said.

"Sustained," Perry said, turning to Daly. "Please just describe specifically what happened, Mr. Daly."

"Yes, your honor," Daly said.

"What did Dr. Radcliffe say to you?" Phillips asked.

"He reminded me that I have a daughter and said I should be more careful," Daly said. "He warned — said — that I could never know when someone might throw a firebomb through our window. He said, 'Curiosity killed the cat.'"

"And did the mention of a firebomb have any special significance to you?"

"About a week and a half before that conversation, my house was destroyed in a fire. Someone threw a Molotov cocktail through the front window," Daly said.

Phillips nodded his head and turned to his notes, pausing for a moment to let the jury absorb the testimony.

"I see. And were you still working on the story on April 9,

2018?" Phillips asked presently.

"That was after I was taken off it," Daly said.

"But you were involved in an incident on that date, correct?"

"I was," Daly said.

"What happened on that day?"

"I received a tip that Dr. Radcliffe and Mr. Gillespie were going to be arrested in connection with the cluster of teen suicides," Daly said.

"And what did you do?" Phillips asked.

"Well, since I was off the story, another reporter, Joe Reed, was assigned to go to Magistrate Brian Holland's office to cover the perp walk," Daly said. "I decided to go and watch simply because I had been on the story so long I wanted to see it through."

"Did you go to the arraignment?" Phillips asked.

"No. As I was leaving, I realized I might be able to get video of Mr. Gillespie's arrest because I already knew where he lived," Daly said. "So I headed up to his house in Pittston."

"What happened there?"

"Well, apparently Mr. Gillespie knew something was going down, and he spotted me out on the street in my car. He pulled a gun on me and forced me into his house," Daly said.

"Was anyone else there?"

"Not inside the house. But as he was forcing me inside the police showed up to make the arrest. They saw I was being held hostage and surrounded the house."

"What happened during the standoff?"

"Mr. Gillespie was panicking and volatile. Like a trapped animal. At first, he didn't say much. But I was able to get him talking and he eventually told me about the operation he and Dr. Radcliffe were running."

"Objection, your honor," Cooper shot out of her seat. "Mr.

Gillespie never testified about this alleged conspiracy. Allowing someone else to provide hearsay testimony without the defense having the ability to cross-examine Mr. Gillespie violates the Confrontation Clause."

"Sustained," Judge Perry said.

Phillips skimmed his notes for a moment and then picked them up, tapping the edge of the papers on the lectern.

"Thank you. No further questions," he said.

The district attorney marched back to the prosecution table. Cooper was already rising from her seat when Judge Perry turned the cross-examination over to her.

"Good morning," she smiled at Daly. To the jury, her face was the picture of cordiality. It bore no hint of malice. Nothing about her pleasant smile belied what was really happening in the courtroom at that moment.

"Good morning," Daly replied.

"Do we know each other?"

"Yes, we do," Daly said.

"How is that?"

"I've interviewed you in the past. For the Observer."

"So just so the jury understands, how would you characterize our relationship?" Cooper asked.

"I would say we are professionally acquainted," Daly said. "We know each other through work."

"So we're not friends?" she asked, flashing a feigned look of hurt at the jury.

"Well, I think we are on Facebook," Daly smiled back.

"Fair enough. So now, Mr. Daly, if we could back up a bit to your earlier testimony, did you say that you learned about the arrests of Dr. Radcliffe and Mr. Gillespie from a tip?" Cooper asked.

"That's correct," Daly said.

"And what was the source of this tip?"

"I'm afraid that's confidential," Daly said, adjusting in his seat.

"It was a confidential source who provided you with this information?" Cooper asked.

"It was," Daly said.

"Well, let's try it this way then. Was it a representative of the Luzerne County District Attorney's Office?"

"Objection, your honor," Phillips shot out of his seat, trying his best to wear a look of indignation on his face. "There has been no testimony to suggest there was a leak from my office, and I think the implication is inappropriate. It's an obvious ploy to garner sympathy from the jury. Furthermore, I'm sure Ms. Cooper is well aware that journalists cannot be compelled to reveal confidential sources under the Pennsylvania shield law."

Judge Perry gave both attorneys a look that warned them to cut back on the theatrics.

"Sustained," he said. "Move along, counselor."

"Yes, your honor," Cooper said.

She'd lost the argument, but she knew she would. More important to her was the jury hearing that the prosecution could be up to some underhanded tactics.

"Okay, Mr. Daly. So you began reporting on this case after Kimberly Foster's death on March 22, 2018, is that correct?" Cooper asked.

"That's right."

"But you said you were removed after making the discovery about Soma?"

"Yes. John Richardson wanted to make sure there wasn't the appearance of a conflict of interest," Daly said.

"But isn't it true that you were aware of a potential conflict of interest even before learning about the message in Soma?"

"Well, there was some concern about that because of an earlier incident. But that was never definitively linked to this case, so I was able to stay on the story."

"That 'incident' as you describe it was actually the fire you previously testified took place at your house, isn't that correct?" Cooper asked.

"That's right," Daly said. "Someone firebombed my house."

"Objection," Cooper turned to the judge. "I ask that answer be stricken as unresponsive."

"You asked the question, Ms. Cooper," Judge Perry said, his mouth curling into a wry smile.

"Yes, your honor," she said, facing back to Daly. "In fact, you and your daughter barely escaped with your lives, correct?"

"Yes."

"And isn't it true that was because you were too drunk to hear the smoke alarm?" Cooper asked, her soft voice not betraying the slightest hint of animosity.

"What? No. I ... uh ... I mean, I had a few drinks that night. But I heard the ... whatever you want to call it — the device — come through the window. I heard the smoke alarm going off," Daly stammered out his answer, caught off guard by the shift in questioning.

"Were you aware the fire department recovered at least ten opened beer bottles from the area of your kitchen table?" Cooper asked.

"I ... no, I wasn't."

"Did you drink all those beers by yourself?"

"I guess I must have."

"Now, March 29, 2018, was a Thursday, was it not?"

"I believe it was," Daly said, trying to contain his growing anger.

"Is it commonplace for you to drink nearly a twelve pack of beer on a weeknight?" Cooper asked.

"I don't know if I would say it's 'commonplace,' but I guess it does happen," Daly said. "Penn State was playing Utah that night in the NIT Championship."

"Fair to say you're a heavy drinker, are you not?"

"I guess you could say that."

"The kind of guy who throws back at least ten beers and then has no trouble waking up at 1:30 a.m.?"

"It would seem so," Daly said.

"So let me ask you, Mr. Daly, do you ever drink at work?" Cooper asked.

"Never. What I do on my personal time is my business. But when I'm at work, I am fully at work," Daly said.

"I see. And what about the afternoon of April 9, 2018 — the day of the arrests. Had you been drinking that day?" Cooper asked.

"No. I was at work all day before going to Mr. Gillespie's house. I remember what he said."

"Is that right?" she said, eyes narrowing. "You were admitted to Geisinger Wyoming Valley Medical Center to be treated for a gunshot wound after this incident, correct?"

"Yes. I was shot in the stomach during the police raid."

"And isn't it true that you were diagnosed at the hospital with transient global amnesia?"

"That's right," Daly said. He was finding it harder with each question to conceal his rage.

"In fact, you told Dr. Maria Torres that you couldn't remember how you came to be in the hospital, right?" Cooper asked.

"At the time, I could not. But my memory came back. Quickly," Daly added, sheepishly.

Halpin

"But you admit that you didn't record this interview you supposedly conducted with Dr. Radcliffe, correct?"

"I wouldn't describe it as an interview so much as a brief conversation, but no, I didn't record it," Daly said.

"And you didn't take any notes?"

"No."

"Well, then I guess we'll just have to take your word for what happened," Cooper said. "No further questions."

# CHAPTER 26

*Friday, August 16, 2019*
*4:37 p.m.*

The exodus was over. As the end of the workday drew near, the county employees had filed out of their cubicles and offices in droves, heading for the time clocks downstairs. Their march was perfectly synchronized so that each employee hit the clocks at the precise moment. Two minutes after closing time, the upstairs corridors of the cavernous courthouse were desolate.

Daly sat alone in a padded mahogany chair outside the courtroom, resting his head against the wall with eyes closed. After five days of trial, the lawyers had finished delivering their impassioned closing arguments. Now, twelve men and women sat at a long table in a cramped deliberation room discussing the fate of Dr. Radcliffe. They had been in there since lunchtime, sustained by delivered pizza and frequent smoke breaks, but the few questions they brought back to Judge Perry did little to reveal which way they were leaning.

It had been an exhausting week for Daly, sitting through the trial he could not cover. He had been accused of subverting the case and then learned the prosecution most likely would never pursue an arson case against Radcliffe.

Robert Phillips had broken the news to Daly after the first day of trial. Investigators had gotten search warrants for Radcliffe's phone records, but they just showed his phone was at home the entire night of the firebombing. Radcliffe, of course, refused to speak to them about it. The only useful evidence the police found was a grainy surveillance video from a gas station a few blocks from Daly's house that showed a car entering the neighborhood shortly before the fire and then speeding away moments later.

The video was so bad that the police themselves were torn about whether the car was a black Lexus LS like the one Radcliffe drove or a black Toyota Avalon. Phillips delivered the bad news with apologies, but there had been no sincerity in his eyes.

On top of all that, Daly had been ripped apart and publicly humiliated by Melissa Cooper. Daly had made a point of not reading the papers the day after the episode on the witness stand. But it was clear that just about everybody else had. His acquaintances were their normal pleasant selves, but he could feel their eyes following him as he moved through the courthouse. He'd gotten a few text messages of support from friends, and John Richardson had even called him into his office just to say he could take whatever time he needed if he had to deal with any issues. What issues, specifically, he didn't say.

But it absolutely broke his heart when Lauren called him up from her new dorm room in Stanford, California. She had never been much for following the local news, but the article had popped up in her Facebook news feed. She had read all about how her father was torn apart on the stand, made to look like an incoherent alcoholic.

"Daddy, you know that's not true," she had said. "People who know you know that's not who you are. I know what happened at the fire, and I know that Mr. Gillespie said all those things, because you heard it."

Daly held his head in his hands as he thanked her. Inside, he felt the hatred festering. It was a self-loathing he'd held onto for years, since the day Jessica was killed. He felt brooding animosity at himself knowing that he could have prevented her death if he'd just been a little more patient or a little more apologetic. If only he'd had enough self-control to turn down a bottle of Cabernet Sauvignon, the whole thing would probably have ended much differently.

The irony didn't escape Daly that the root of his torment — the bottle — was now the crutch he relied on to dull his pain. He knew it was a problem.

But. Always but.

Putting the brakes on the booze was never a problem, at least in the short term. But on days Daly thought about Jessica, it was the only thing that numbed him enough to stop blaming himself.

At least until morning.

Drinking brought Daly restless, dreamless sleep, and that was just what he wanted most nights. So what had been the occasional beer or glass of wine before Jessica's death had turned into a nearly nightly habit. He'd take a deep, long pull on his beer and quickly feel the weight lifting. With each sip of the cool, bitter liquid, Daly could feel the boozy warmth rising inside him. His problems faded and his weariness receded. His normally taciturn behavior vanished like Dr. Jekyll. But he was no Hyde. No matter how his head swooned, or how the room began twisting in the darkness of night, Daly kept control. For to him, the only thing more important than the bottle slept just down the hallway in the next bedroom. He knew how fragile it was and how easily he could lose it with the simplest of mistakes. So he never got behind the wheel after more than a drink or two. He never let on that he was slowly drinking himself to death.

Which was, it seemed, his eventual goal.

So to Daly, it was never a problem. He continued getting up

on time in the mornings, getting Lauren to school and showing up at work on time. Hell, some mornings he might start the day still feeling fine from the night before, but he was always on point. He did his job and he did it well, and no one ever questioned him about the glazed weariness in his eyes.

His secret habit being aired out in open court had been a reality check for Daly.

When he heard his daughter try to defend it, the thought of putting the business end of a .38 Special to his temple flashed through Daly's mind.

Just like Jessica.

He shook away the thought and turned his attention back to Lauren.

"Listen, don't worry about that. It's just what lawyers do. They have to try and discredit anyone who testifies against their client," Daly said. "Anyway, that's going to be your job someday, isn't it?"

"I know, Daddy," Lauren said. "But I'm not going to be so miserable about it."

"She's just doing her job," Daly said. "Anyway, how are things with you? You just about finished being a freshman yet?"

"Almost. I've got finals in two weeks."

"Have you decided what you're doing for the summer?"

"I still don't know. I really like it out here: The weather, the energy, the people ... I was kind of thinking about staying here," Lauren said.

"What's his name?" Daly said.

"What?"

"What's the guy's name?"

"Daddy, it's not like that."

"So you're not seeing anyone then?"

"Well, not exactly ..."

"I knew it! So who is this man who makes you want to miss seeing your own father?" Daly asked.

"His name's Josh," Lauren said, laughing. "He's just a guy I met in history class. You'd like him. He's a writer at The Stanford Daily."

"Well, now I know he's not going to be able to pay down whatever student loans he's taking," Daly said. "Anyway, I wish you would come back here. I miss you. I haven't seen you since Christmas break."

"I know. I was thinking I'd come visit at some point. I just wasn't planning to stay the whole summer."

"Okay. We can talk later. I love you."

"I love you too, Daddy," Lauren said.

Sitting alone on the third floor of the courthouse, Daly played the conversation back in his mind. He was glad that she was settled in and was happy, but he felt nothing but guilt that she felt the need to defend him — and his habits. *A good father would never do that to his daughter*, he thought. *None of this would ever have happened to a good father ...*

"Erik?"

A voice pulled Daly out of his tailspin. It was Emily Hayes, an attorney with the Public Defender's Office. Daly had interviewed her a few years earlier for a story about how staffing shortages were affecting the caseload. They had struck up a rapport and remained friendly, mostly gossiping about other people's cases when they bumped into each other at the courthouse.

"Hey," Daly said. "What are you doing up here?"

"I just came to check this out. The jury still out?"

"Yeah. They've been deliberating about five hours so far. No end in sight," Daly said.

"Could be a late one."

"Looks that way."

"Are you okay? You look a little ... gloomy," Emily said.

"Yeah. I'm fine," Daly said. "I was just thinking about my daughter. And this whole goddamned week."

"I saw the articles," Emily said. "It was pretty brutal."

"The worst part is my daughter saw the articles too. I just ... I don't know. I feel terrible," Daly said, rubbing his temples.

"How about I buy you a cup of coffee when this is over?" Emily asked. "It would probably help to have someone to talk to."

Daly turned and looked at her, surprised by the invite. They frequently spoke in the corridors of the courthouse and Daly had always viewed her as a potential source. Now, he saw her just a little differently, like the moment a glint of sunlight reveals a hidden coin.

Was she asking him on a date? Or just trying to be kind?

Daly had been out of the game for so long that he'd nearly forgotten how to play.

There was no denying Emily was an attractive woman. She was a few years younger than Daly and had flaming red hair, parted in the middle, that flowed in waves to her shoulders. Her sharp hazel eyes seemed to smile perpetually at the world, and her lips were always painted deep red, a stark contrast to her pale skin. She was beautiful, but also a smart attorney who kept Daly guessing. She seemed to be a walking contradiction — she was a defense attorney who supported the death penalty and a gun rights advocate who supported abortion. Conversations with her were always interesting because Daly was never quite sure where she would go next.

The thought of getting to know her better sounded quite intriguing.

"Coffee sounds great," Daly said.

◆ ◆ ◆

After more than six hours behind closed doors, the jury forewoman hit a buzzer and signaled a verdict with a bell that echoed through the cavernous courthouse. Deliberations had gone on for too long for the prosecution to feel at ease, but not long enough for the defense to get overly optimistic.

During the deliberations, the jury had asked several questions and had sought clarification on the difference between murder and manslaughter. The prosecution took that as a good sign because it meant the jury had not ruled out criminal culpability entirely, even if the jurors were still divided.

Jurors had also requested to see some of the evidence again, particularly a note Gillespie had left on his desk prior to taking Daly hostage and several emails recovered from his computer.

To Daly, neither item seemed fatal to Radcliffe's case. The note Gillespie left showed he planned to die, and that his chosen method was suicide by cop. But it was a rambling mess conceived by a panicked man who was not thinking clearly. In the note, Gillespie apologized for what he described as "hurting the children" and said he should have known better because of "things that were done to me." The note was full of euphemisms and passive language, leaving it to anyone's guess who he felt was to blame.

His emails were not much better. There were a number of exchanges with Radcliffe, but it was apparent from the tone that they were speaking about much more than was being written in the messages. They were clearly being careful and never mentioned anything about children or pornographic videos.

Only one exchange seemed, to Daly at least, to implicate Radcliffe in something more nefarious than making a harmless white-noise app. It came after they had been discussing the plan to form Sleep Song, LLC, while they were talking about designing the actual app.

"We're going to need to be able to overlay several tracks for this," Radcliffe had written. "Do some research and figure out what software can do that."

It was far from a smoking gun. But it did demonstrate two things: That Radcliffe was in charge of the operation, and that he wanted to have multiple sounds playing at the same time.

It wasn't much, but Daly hoped that combined with his testimony it could be enough to put Radcliffe away. He had looked into Radcliffe's eyes that day outside his practice and had seen the desperation. The look of a wild animal caught in a trap. The look of a man who was capable of anything. The look of a guilty man.

If Radcliffe walked, Daly didn't know how he would be able to live with himself. He knew Radcliffe was guilty — and guilty of much more than simply the crimes alleged in this trial. This was a dangerous man who needed to be locked up in prison.

Daly sat outside the courtroom full of anxiety as he watched the parties file in to learn the verdict. Some people were making small talk or whispering their thoughts about the case, but most observers were solemn. When the last of the attorneys had entered the courtroom doors, Daly got up and followed them inside, taking a seat on the pew at the back of the courtroom. The room was eerily quiet and filled with electricity.

Radcliffe sat at the defense table, wildly bouncing his knee up and down. This moment was, by far, the most important moment of his life. He knew he had everything to lose. The chances of winning an appeal are remote. A conviction here could mean dying in prison.

This was it. This was Radcliffe's judgment day.

Presently, Judge Perry's assistant opened the chamber door and escorted the judge out, crying out for all in the courtroom to rise. When he reached the bench, Judge Perry took his seat, simultaneously telling those in the courtroom to be seated.

"I understand the jury has reached a verdict," Judge Perry told the attorneys before turning to his tipstaff. "Let's bring in the jury."

The courtroom doors swung open and the jury began filing in, most members taking a keen interest in the floor tiles as they made their way between the tables where Radcliffe and Robert Phillips waited.

Everyone in the room watched the jurors intently, looking for any sign of the decision they had reached. The jury was opaque.

When the jurors had taken their seats, Judge Perry asked the forewoman to stand.

"Madam forewoman, has the jury reached a verdict?" he asked.

"We have, your honor," said the forewoman, an overweight middle-aged woman wearing a lumpy sweater and thick-rimmed glasses.

"You may publish it to the court," Judge Perry said.

The woman cleared her throat before reading.

"In the matter of the Commonwealth of Pennsylvania vs. Marvin Radcliffe, we, the jury, find the defendant not guilty of causing suicide as criminal homicide."

From the gallery came an audible gasp as family members with gaping mouths and raised eyebrows absorbed the news with disbelief. Radcliffe bowed his head slightly, closing his eyes and squeezing his fists in a slight expression of victory.

Radcliffe's eyes lit up and he nodded his approval to Melissa Cooper as the forewoman continued to say he was also not guilty on the criminal conspiracy charges.

But his hopeful expression quickly faded as the forewoman finished reading the verdict slip, convicting him on four counts of involuntary manslaughter.

With those words, the courtroom erupted in chaos. Radcliffe, deluded into expecting a victory, nearly jumped out of his seat, prompting the sheriff's deputies standing guard over him to grab him by the shoulders and slam him back down into the chair. Women sitting with the victim's families began sobbing uncontrollably, while a man — Daly thought it might have been Jack Foster — shouted into the courtroom.

"This isn't over!" the voice shouted. "May God have mercy on your soul!"

Judge Perry began banging his gavel and demanding order in the courtroom, to little effect. Deputies raised their arms, palms out, ordering audience members to stay seated and quiet. At the prosecution table, Robert Phillips brought a hand to his temple and closed his eyes, rubbing his head as though a terrible headache was approaching.

Another voice shouted something incomprehensible from the crowd of dozens of victims' relatives seated in the gallery, and Judge Perry again hammered his gavel down on the mahogany sounding block.

Then, without warning, Emma Nguyen's father Vu leaped to his feet, vaulted the banister separating the gallery from the front of the courtroom and lunged at Radcliffe. A tuft of black hair hung over his forehead, obscuring from most observers a look of wild, murderous rage in his eyes. He nearly had a hand on the back of Radcliffe's neck by the time the first deputy was able to grab him and halt his advance.

Vu Nguyen collapsed to the courtroom floor as the deputies piled on top to restrain him. Screaming and thrashing violently, he struggled against their weight in a futile effort to break free and exact revenge upon his daughter's killer. When his screaming subsided, it was replaced by the sound of fevered panting, then gasping.

Those closest to the fray could faintly hear the sound of Vu Nguyen sobbing uncontrollably.

# CHAPTER 27

*Saturday, August 17, 2019*
*12:15 p.m.*

Daly sat at a small table outside a coffee shop in the warm afternoon sunshine along the main drag in Wilkes-Barre, sipping a black French roast. A light breeze fluttered napkins on the tables and sent wisps of the waitress' hair into her face as she tried scribbling drink orders onto a small worn pad. A few clouds slowly drifted across the deep blue sky, occasionally casting light shadows over the streets as they passed. It was the kind of welcoming summer day that brimmed with possibility. Parents brought their children to the parks. Teenagers cruised the strip in freshly polished borrowed cars. Hustlers in grimy tee-shirts roamed Public Square, looking to score some dope or some drama.

Down the street, Emily Hayes was making her way toward Daly, giving him a smile and a wave as she neared.

"Hey!" she called out.

"How's it going?" Daly said, rising to greet her. "What are you having?"

"Umm ... I'll take a latte," she said to the approaching waitress.

The woman scribbled the order into her tiny notepad and turned away without a word.

Emily pulled a metal chair out from under the table and looped the strap from her purse over the back before taking a seat.

"So," she said.

"So," Daly said, awkwardly. "That was crazy, what happened last night."

"Oh my God. It was absolutely bananas. Did you see the look on Judge Perry's face when Emma's father jumped the rail?" Emily said, breaking into a laugh. "I've never seen anything like that."

"I thought he was going to lose it," Daly said, laughing along.

"I mean, I can't say that I blame him. Can you imagine your daughter's killer almost getting off?"

"I'd go nuts," Daly said, turning serious. "It was a crazy verdict. I thought it would be all or nothing. It seemed like if he was guilty of some of it, he should have been guilty of the rest."

"Well, the manslaughter charge means they believed he was acting negligently during his counseling sessions," Emily said. "I guess they just didn't think the evidence was there to tie him to Gillespie. Either that or they just compromised so they could go home."

"So what's he looking at anyway? Dr. Radcliffe, I mean," Daly said.

"Involuntary manslaughter is a misdemeanor. Maximum of five years on each count."

"Holy shit. So he's looking at an absolute max of twenty years in prison?" Daly said.

"That's the worst he could get."

Daly shook his head, trying to make sense of it all. All this death. All this suffering. And now, the man behind it all could foreseeably get out of prison one day — possibly after serving only a few years behind bars. Up to this point, Daly had been adamant that he'd done nothing wrong in confronting Radcliffe. He was a reporter doing what good reporters do: researching and fact-checking and trying to get both sides of the story. But for the first time, he really began questioning his decision. He couldn't escape the fact that his actions could have helped Radcliffe get off easy.

Emily could see the worry in Daly's face and gave him a slight smile, pulling a strand of red hair from her cheek.

"That's not your fault," she said. "It's the DA's job to get the conviction, regardless of what obstacles come with the case. Don't let him dump this on you."

"I know," Daly said, unconvincingly.

"Just think, without your research in this case they might never have linked Dr. Radcliffe at all. He could still be out there preying on kids," she said.

Emily reached across the table and wrapped her delicate hands around Daly's interlocked fingers. She smiled the kind of smile Daly hadn't seen in years. Not since Jessica died. Emily's gaze was warm and inviting. It frightened Daly. For years, he had been left alone to look after Lauren, and he had nearly forgotten the feel of a woman's gentle touch. Inside, he longed for the companionship. But he also knew he was damaged goods, an overweight, middle-aged, low-paid journalist. He was struggling as a single parent to put his daughter through a school he could not afford. And he drank too much because he was haunted — still and likely always — by the memory of Jessica.

Daly pulled his hands free from Emily's grasp and leaned back in his chair.

"Emily, I like you. I really do," Daly said.

"Erik, you don't have to ..."

"Hold on," Daly said. "I just want to get this out, before this goes any further. You know I have a daughter, right?"

"Yeah, Lauren," Emily said. "I've seen her picture on Facebook."

"Well, did you know that I was married to her mother?" Daly asked.

"I figured you might have been. That doesn't matter to me," Emily said.

"No, it's not that. It's how things ended for us. We didn't get divorced. She was killed," Daly said.

"I'm ... sorry. I didn't realize."

Daly paused a moment, looking into Emily's eyes. He could feel a bond growing between them and decided he wanted to level with her. If Emily was getting involved, she had a right to know what she was buying into.

◆ ◆ ◆

Daly first met Ken Duncan on January 23, 2004. It had been a Friday in the dead of winter, a cold night with an icy mist drifting down from pink-tinted clouds above. Daly had just been promoted from being a clerk at the Observer, a job he landed to get his foot in the door right after college, to general assignment reporter — a gig he had aspired to for years. With a wife and young daughter at home, Daly needed a job that paid better than a clerk's salary. But more importantly, it would let Daly report the news and get a byline in a professional newspaper. He felt like he'd hit the big time.

That meant it was time to celebrate. When Daly got home from work that evening, Jessica had surprised him by wearing a tight black dress with her hair made up. She met Daly at the door and wrapped her arms around his shoulders, pressing herself against his chest as she whispered that Lauren was at the sitter's.

"We've got the place to ourselves," she had said.

Daly dropped his computer bag near the door and smiled as he embraced Jessica, letting his hands drift south.

"Not so fast," Jessica said. "I didn't get all made up so you could ruin it the second you walked in the door. We're going out."

Daly put on a blazer and a tie, and they headed out for a night on the town.

For dinner, they went to Daly's favorite spot for a night out, Mackenzie's Steak and Seafood. The drinks were exorbitant and the food even more so, but for a special occasion they could justify a dinner at the best restaurant around.

Jessica got the roast chicken and a glass of water. Daly ordered the prime rib, medium-rare, and a bottle of Cabernet Sauvignon.

"We don't need the bottle," Jessica had said. "I'm not drinking."

"What? We're celebrating," Daly said, turning to the waiter. "We'll take the bottle."

They talked about the new job and Lauren and their plans for the summer. Jessica had always dreamed of going to Iceland to see the glaciers and fjords, and Daly began talking about how it finally might be a possibility. He had expected Jessica to jump out of her seat with excitement. Instead, he was disappointed when she put the brakes on the trip. The timing didn't seem right, she said.

"If it's the money, don't worry about it," Daly said. "I know it's not that big of a raise, but we can make it work."

"It's not the money," Jessica said. "I'm pregnant."

For a moment, Daly tried to comprehend the abrupt shift in the conversation. Thoughts of sipping champagne in a hot tub under the shimmering aurora borealis were replaced by those of dirty diapers and sleepless nights. The look of shock on Daly's face was enough to draw the waiter's attention.

"Is everything all right, sir?" he asked.

For Daly, everything was, in fact, fine. The news startled him. They hadn't been trying for another child, but they hadn't exactly not been trying either. They both wanted more children at some point and had felt it would happen when the time was right. It seemed that now the time had come.

"Everything is perfect," Daly said, smiling.

They spent the rest of the meal talking about baby names and layout decisions for the nursery. They left the restaurant in each other's arms.

"Are you okay to drive?" Jessica asked when they got to the car. "You've had a few."

"I'm fine," Daly said. "I only had three drinks."

They slid into the car and headed for home. The road to the Back Mountain had been clear coming down, but during dinner the icy mist had turned to a steady snow. The road was now blanketed in a thin layer of white, sliced by tires to reveal the black pavement below. Wind caused the snow to whip across the road, and as Daly hit the wipers to clear off the melted flakes on the windshield, the frigid air froze a trail of moisture in their wake.

Daly tapped his brakes to gauge the road's slickness. The car immediately slowed, showing no sign of slipping. Again he hit the gas and continued climbing the mountain. At a sharp bend in the highway, they came up behind an eighteen-wheeled tractor trailer lumbering up the road with its flashers on, going well below the speed limit. After a few moments spent riding in the disorienting wake of spray the truck kicked up, Daly moved over to the passing lane to get around it. The right lane was more traveled and thus more clear, but the left lane still seemed passable.

Daly hit the accelerator as he tried to clear the water the truck's massive wheels were throwing off to the back and sides. As the car crept alongside the truck, its massive wheels belted out one last burst of spray, blurring Daly's windshield. It lasted only a second, until the next tick of the windshield wiper blades, but when the view cleared Daly saw he was closing in fast on a dark pickup truck.

The pickup had also been passing the tractor-trailer, but much more slowly.

Daly heard Jessica shout, "Look out!" and had time to jerk

the wheel to the left in a futile attempt to avoid a collision. The front right corner of the car clipped the back left of the pickup before both vehicles lost their grip on the slick road. Daly's car spun to the left, continuing the trajectory of the turn until it had completed a one-hundred-eighty degree rotation and slammed into the Jersey barrier in the median of the highway.

Having been tapped from the left side, the pickup began a clockwise spin and rotated forty-five degrees before the tractor-trailer made contact with the passenger door. The impact sent the sound of shattering glass and crunching metal into the night sky.

The tractor-trailer driver hit the brakes and brought the rig to a stop with its load jackknifing across most of the highway. The passenger side of the pickup appeared to be in the engine compartment of the rig. It was impossible to tell where one vehicle ended and the other began.

For a moment, the road was eerily silent as soft-falling snow began laying an icy blanket over the vehicles' tracks. Then, the sound of a man shrieking rose into the night, a guttural, agonized cry from a man brought to the breaking point by pain.

The tractor-trailer driver popped open the door to the cab and stuck his head out, tossing the remains of a Camel cigarette to the ice below. He slowly stepped down to the highway, looking at the gnarled mess of a pickup that was now embedded in his livelihood.

A moment later, the severity of the crash registered, and the truck driver ran forward to assess the injuries in the pickup. He came around to the driver's side door, which had a shattered window and crumpled frame.

Peering inside, he saw that the driver had slid over to the passenger's side and was clutching the bloody head of a young girl, perhaps twelve years old. The child was limp. Blood was spattered across the interior of the truck's cab.

The man looked out to the truck driver, tears streaming down his face as he held Kelly Duncan like a rag doll, her open eyes staring upward but seeing nothing.

"Oh my God," the wide-eyed trucker whispered, reaching to his pocket to get his cellphone to call 911. He turned away from the carnage and ran his hand through his hair as he started relaying the location of the crash to a call-taker. Whether from the shock of the crash or being distracted by his conversation with emergency services, the trucker didn't seem to notice when the other driver kicked open the pickup's door with a jarring screech of metal.

With blood on his hands and a wild look in his eye, Ken Duncan pushed through the crunched, bent metal that had been the door to his pickup truck and stepped onto the icy pavement. For a moment he had stood there, looking confused. Then he saw Daly's car crumpled against the Jersey barrier and headed toward it.

Inside the car, Daly shook his head back and forth, trying to clear his mind after his temple had slammed into the window. He looked across to Jessica, who had a trickle of blood running down her cheek from a cut on her forehead.

"Are you okay?" Daly asked.

"I think so. I just bumped my head," Jessica said.

"Me too," Daly said. He reached for the door handle and pulled it, but there was no movement. He pulled the handle again and threw his shoulder into the motion. Finally, the door creaked open with a painful squeal.

Daly unfastened his seat belt and stepped out of the car. Down the hill, a growing line of cars shone bright white lights toward Daly's car, their brake lights bathing the trees along the highway in red. Up the hill, he could see the yellow hazard lights of the tractor-trailer flashing, highlighting the twisted remains of the pickup at regular intervals.

In the golden flashes, Daly could also see the silhouette of someone staggering toward him, slipping on the pavement as he made his way down the hill. When the man got closer, the headlights from the blocked cars revealed a man with a goatee and a leather jacket, his torn and faded jeans tucked into black biker boots. A tuft of long, greasy hair obscured the man's left eye, but as he approached Daly could see the man had blood on his hands.

He could also see that the man he would come to know as Ken Duncan was carrying a revolver.

"Is everyone okay?" Daly asked. "I'm so sorry. The road ..."

"You killed her," Duncan cut in, staring coldly at Daly.

The words hit Daly like an icy wave, knocking him back on his feet.

*I wasn't going that fast,* he thought. *Could someone really be dead?*

"Where is she?" Daly asked, pulling out his cellphone to call 911. "Let me see if I can help."

"You've done enough," Duncan said, raising the gun toward Daly.

"Hold on," Daly blurted out, panic rising in his voice. He raised his hands, palms out. "I didn't mean to hurt anyone. It was an accident."

"My baby is dead," Duncan said. "And I smell booze on your breath. It wasn't no accident."

"Let me get my wife," Daly said. "She's got some first-aid training. She might be able to help."

Duncan turned his attention to Daly's car, seeming to notice

248

it for the first time. Then he pushed past Daly, nearly knocking him to the ground, and bee-lined to the car where Jessica was still reeling from the crash. Duncan peered inside through the open door and met Jessica's gaze. As she looked at Duncan's hands and saw the blood and gun, her breathing quickened, sending short puffs of steam billowing from her lips in the cold air.

Daly ran toward Duncan, yelling for him to stop. Duncan raised his .38 Special. Jessica, trapped and with no way of blocking the shot, turned and looked toward Daly with tears in her eyes.

The shot exploded in the quiet of the night. Daly reached Duncan and grabbed his wrist, trying to turn the gun away. The men fell to the ground and started struggling for a brief moment, until their figures were bathed in flashing blue and red lights as a police car arrived on the scene. The cop got out, saw the gun, and drew his own.

"Freeze!" he yelled, aiming at the men brawling on the pavement.

Duncan dropped the gun and both men put their hands up, sitting on the ground.

"My wife!" Daly yelled. "She's been shot!"

From where he sat, Daly could only see Jessica's left arm draped across the center console and resting on the driver's seat. It was covered in blood.

And it wasn't moving.

Under his breath, quietly enough so the cop wouldn't hear, Duncan whispered to Daly the last words they would ever exchange.

"Now we're even," he said.

Jessica had been shot through the neck, a wound that tore through her jugular vein and ripped out her throat.

Blood spatter covered the windshield and dashboard, and the front of Jessica's black dress was soaked. Authorities later told Daly she had died within seconds of massive blood loss.

She hadn't suffered long, they assured him.

The police charged Duncan with murder. At trial, his lawyer had argued that Duncan was guilty, at most, of voluntary manslaughter because Duncan acted in a sudden and intense passion after his daughter had been killed in the crash. Prosecutors argued that Duncan's passion was the result of a perceived provocation by Daly, not Jessica, and that Duncan's decision to get even with Daly by killing his wife amounted to a cold-blooded execution. Jurors agreed and convicted Duncan of first-degree murder.

He got life in prison.

Daly got no solace.

For some time, Daly had lived under the threat of being charged as well. For weeks, as he struggled to cope with the loss of his wife, he had to live with the possibility that Lauren could also lose her father — for at least a little while. If the blood tests came back showing he had been over the limit, he would be charged with vehicular homicide. Then, in addition to losing his wife, Daly would risk losing his daughter and his career.

When the results came back from the laboratory, they showed Daly had been just under the limit to be considered a drunken driver. Daly was cited for careless driving, but the district attorney declined to press criminal charges in the case. Daly had been able to get back to the new normal of life, in the absence of Jessica.

Lauren had cried when Daly told her about Jessica, but she was only three. She clearly didn't grasp that she would never see mommy again. And she never mourned the sibling she almost had, because Daly had never been able to bring himself to tell her about it.

◆ ◆ ◆

Emily sat in stunned silence, at a rare loss for words. She brought her hand to cover her gaping mouth and tried to comprehend what Daly had been through that night.

"Ever since then, I've had this dream where she dies," Daly said. "Except, in the dream, it's not Ken Duncan who kills her. It's me. For months after, I went to a therapist about it, but the dream kept coming back. Eventually, I just started drinking it away. That worked, mostly. But the rest of the time, the guilt tears me up. I just can't stop thinking about Kelly's picture. And what Jessica looked like afterward ...

"Then when all the dying children started making headlines ... I guess I thought I might be able to help. Like, if I could make a difference ... I don't know. Maybe that I could somehow redeem myself. Maybe I could save someone or stop the abuse. Maybe then the dream would go away. Maybe this downward spiral that has consumed my life for the past fifteen years would turn around. And you know what? It kind of worked. I haven't had the dream since the day Radcliffe was caught. But then the case went to shit. Now I don't know where I stand," Daly said.

"Nothing's changed," Emily said, finding her voice again. "Radcliffe is still caught. He's still going to prison. That's because of your work. And you know something? None of this changes my opinion of you. You made a mistake, but you've atoned for it. You paid a price no one should have to pay. It's time for you to move on with your life."

Daly gulped down the last of his rapidly cooling coffee and

tried to shrug off his embarrassment.

"I know. The trial made me see things differently. I'm going to try to move on. And I'm going to try to stop drinking. For Lauren's sake," Daly said.

"So what do you like to do for fun?" he asked to change the subject.

"Roller derby."

Daly nearly snorted.

"What?" he asked, chuckling. "Are you serious?"

"Yeah. I've been doing it with my girlfriends since middle school. My skater name is Tress Passer."

"Wow. I had no idea. Are you guys any good?"

"We do pretty well. We've played together a long time so we make a good team. But mostly we just play for fun. Ever since we graduated from high school it's been hard getting everyone together for it. What about you? Do you skate?"

"Not at all. I'm more of a basketball kind of guy. The last time I strapped wheels to my feet, there was almost a mass-casualty incident at the skating rink."

"Maybe you should try it again sometime," Emily said, taking a sip of her coffee. "It's good exercise. And you might have some fun."

"I think I'm going to have to pass on that. For health reasons," Daly said.

"Well, you should probably know that I don't take kindly to rejection," Emily said. "If you pass the offer up now, you might not get another one."

"Oh, I'm not turning you down," Daly said. "Just the possibility of imminent death. The Pittston Tomato Festival is going on this weekend. How about we try that instead? We probably still have time to catch the tomato fight."

"Sure. Let's do it."

◆◆◆

Emily pulled her wilderness green Subaru Outback into a lot off Main Street in Pittston. The city had long been dubbed the "Quality Tomato Capital of the World" because of its climate and soil. At some point in the mid-1980s, someone got the idea to build a festival around it. Since then, tens of thousands of people flock to the event each year for the food and festivities.

By the time Daly and Emily arrived, the five-kilometer run and parade were already finished. Taking Emily by the hand, Daly led her down the crowded streets to the registration area for the tomato fight and slapped a twenty-dollar bill down on the table.

"Hold on ... I thought you meant you wanted to watch," Emily said. "I don't have any extra clothes."

"Neither do I," Daly said. "You're not scared, are you, Tress Passer?"

"Please. Give me those," Emily said, grabbing a pair of rubber goggles.

Emily strapped the black elastic strap over her flaming red hair and raised an eyebrow at Daly.

"Well? How do I look?"

"Like you're about to get splattered with rotten tomatoes."

"I nailed it."

They made their way through the throngs of people to take their starting positions. What once had been the black-topped parking lot of a popular seafood restaurant on this day had been transformed into a battlefield. Two columns of combatants faced each other like opposing forces in medieval combat, ready to unleash fury in the form of pelted tomatoes. To that end, boxes of the softening, overripe ammunition were lined up in front of each column. Daly and Emily took their places at the end of one group and waited.

Separated by only a couple of strips of police tape, the opposing forces marched forward when the air horn blared its battle cry, signaling the start of the conflict. The warriors advanced to the front lines and assumed the positions they would use to launch the smashed fruit into the air.

Some sought shelter behind the front lines, opting to launch their ammunition like artillery fire and take out the enemy from above.

The bravest of them, a selfless few, ran straight to the front lines, oblivious to their own safety as they tried to secure victory by attacking head-on.

Daly and Emily grabbed handfuls of tomatoes and let loose from the middle of the pack. But where there is sometimes safety in numbers, they quickly learned that maxim does not apply in the midst of an earnest tomato fight. No sooner had they released their first handfuls of fruit had they been splattered by the wares of the opposition.

Daly cursed.

Emily shrieked.

They both laughed.

The onslaught lasted only minutes. When it was over the tomatoes' casualties numbered in the hundreds and both sides were claiming victory. Daly took a deep breath, pulling the goggles from his eyes and wiping a gob of tomato juice from his cheek.

"That was fun," he said breathlessly. "I've always wanted to try it."

Emily smiled at him, pressing a handful of tomato guts from her shirt onto his.

"That was fun. But you owe me a shirt."

She leaned in and kissed him softly on the cheek, her soft lips pressing against the roughness of his five o'clock shadow. The kiss sent a shock wave through Daly's body that he hadn't felt in years. Not since Jessica died.

For a moment, a flash of guilt came over him. It almost felt like he was cheating on Jessica. But it had been years. He knew she would want him to be happy. Then Daly smiled back at Emily and took her by the hand.

"I guess I do," Daly said. "But it was worth it."

# CHAPTER 28

*Friday, August 30, 2019*
*10:33 a.m.*

The hard pews lining the courtroom gallery were packed. Reporters, the victims' family members, and curious onlookers occupied every available seat, anxious to learn Dr. Radcliffe's fate. A platoon-sized contingent of sheriff's deputies dressed in black shirts and green slacks surrounded the courtroom, eager to prevent another embarrassing outburst like the one Vu Nguyen had the last time he saw Radcliffe in court.

The doctor remained free on bail after his conviction and had come in early through a side door, hoping to avoid the media cameras. He had been seated alone at the defense table for well over an hour as dozens of hate-filled eyes stared at his back.

Melissa Cooper strode in and dropped her document bag on the floor next to her chair, then leaned in and whispered to Dr. Radcliffe. He handed her a sheet of paper that she began scanning, checking over the statement he planned to read to the court.

From his seat at the back of the courtroom, Daly could see Cooper's expression shift from mild curiosity to stunned amazement. She lifted her eyes off the paper and leaned close to Radcliffe's ear, suddenly impassioned. Radcliffe started shaking his head and Cooper slapped the paper down on the defense table, rubbing her brow in frustration.

She took her seat next to Radcliffe, who then shifted his eyes to the gallery. As he scanned the observers, Radcliffe lifted an eyebrow, apparently impressed by the level of turnout he'd drawn. Then his eyes settled on Daly. He stopped and stared hard at Daly for nearly a full minute. When the tipstaff came out of chambers and called for everyone to rise, Radcliffe gave Daly a smirk before facing front and rising from his seat.

Judge Perry ascended the bench and lifted the back of his robe slightly before taking his seat.

"Good morning, counsel," he said. "Are we ready to proceed?"

"We are," the attorneys answered.

"Very well. Please approach."

The attorneys rose from their seats and walked forward to stand in front of the bench. Radcliffe joined them, standing at Cooper's side as two sheriff's deputies moved into position behind him. Radcliffe almost certainly knew he was going to prison, but it wouldn't be the first time someone panicked and tried to run after learning his fate.

"Your honor," District Attorney Phillips said. "As you are aware, this is an atrocious case involving the homicides of four minors. These children did nothing wrong. But they were selected and groomed by Dr. Radcliffe along with his deceased co-defendant for their personal pleasure. Now, I understand that the Commonwealth did not pursue child pornography charges against Dr. Radcliffe. The jury was not able to hear the statements Mr. Gillespie made before his death, but this court has the Commonwealth's sentencing brief that outlines the statements he made to Wilkes-Barre Observer reporter Erik Daly. Those statements make clear that Dr. Radcliffe was not equally responsible for these deaths — he is the person who is most responsible.

"Dr. Radcliffe was the ringleader, if you will, of a criminal enterprise that used our most precious resource — our children — and then discarded them like so much trash. He was so desperate not to be caught that he devised a sadistic scheme to get rid of them. He didn't simply take a gun and kill them. His plan was much more devious. He counseled them and created an app with subliminal messages in an effort to make these poor children so ashamed of what happened to them that they would kill themselves. The level of cruelty inflicted on these children simply boggles the mind, your honor.

"It's true that Dr. Radcliffe has no prior criminal history, but the heinous nature of these crimes, I believe, justifies a consecutive prison sentence. Dr. Radcliffe is an extreme danger to our community and our children, and he needs to be held accountable for his actions. As a result, the Commonwealth requests this court to impose the maximum possible sentence for these offenses."

Phillips looked over his shoulder at the courtroom gallery and cleared his throat before continuing.

"Your honor, before we turn this over to the defense, we have a couple victim impact statements."

"Very well," Judge Perry said. "Bring them up."

Phillips gestured to the gallery and waved his hand for those who wanted to speak to come forward. Jack Foster and Celeste Gonzalez rose and walked to the front of the courtroom. When they got there, Jack extended his fingers, signaling for Celeste to go first.

In her trembling hands, she held a folded piece of paper. She slowly unfolded the sheet and slipped on a pair of reading glasses before addressing the judge.

"Your honor, I want you to know my son was a good boy,"

Celeste said. "He loved his family and his church. He did well in school. He had a bright future ahead of him. Everyone who knew him knew he was going to be successful at whatever he did. But because of this man — this monster — he'll never get to do any of it. This monster changed my son. He used to be a happy and outgoing boy. But because of what this man did, my son killed himself in the garage like some kind of outcast. Because of this monster, I had to walk into my garage and see my boy hanging there …"

Celeste began sobbing uncontrollably. Phillips put a hand on her shoulder and handed her a tissue from the box at the bench. After a moment, Celeste composed herself enough to continue.

"No mother should ever have to go through that," she said. "And what's worse is that I knew something was wrong. I knew my son was communicating with Vincent Gillespie. I tried to stop it, but it wasn't enough. Now I stay awake at night wondering how things would have turned out if I'd called the police. If only I had been brave enough to put aside my pride, my son might still be alive.

"This man will continue living with what he's done, but I urge this court to make him live with it in prison. What he did sickens me to my core, and I hope he dies in prison for it," Celeste said.

"Thank you, ma'am," Judge Perry said, turning to Jack Foster. "Sir, do you have a statement as well?"

"Yes, sir," Jack said, stepping forward to the bench. He didn't carry a speech and wrangled his hat in his hands for a moment before speaking.

"My daughter Kimberly was popular in school. She was a cheerleader. She was a good daughter who would do anything to help others. Because of this man's actions, nobody will ever remember any of that. She will always be the girl who killed herself on the Internet. She will always just be a crazy story and a punchline. People won't remember the real Kimberly Foster. This man made sure of that. He changed her legacy. And he ruined our lives," Jack said, turning to look directly at Radcliffe.

"Do you have any children?" he asked. "Can you imagine what it's like to hear a gunshot and walk into your daughter's room late at night to find her bleeding out on the floor? To see your wife clawing at the pieces of her head, trying to put it all back together?"

As he listened, Radcliffe was silent and still, acknowledging neither Jack's presence nor his words.

"Your honor," Jack said, turning back to Judge Perry. "I agree with Mrs. Gonzalez that this man is a monster. I can't even begin to comprehend how someone could do something so vile. He needs to be punished severely for what he did, and he needs to be locked away so that he can't hurt anybody else."

With that, Jack lowered his head and backed away from the bench. Judge Perry nodded and turned back to Phillips.

"Anything else from the Commonwealth?" he asked.

"No, your honor," Phillips said.

"The defense?"

"Thank you, your honor," Cooper said. "Let me start by thanking District Attorney Phillips for correctly noting that Dr. Radcliffe was not charged with producing child pornography. As much as the Commonwealth would like to paint Dr. Radcliffe with that brush, it simply doesn't stand up. They didn't think they had enough evidence to take that allegation to the jury, so they certainly can't turn around at this juncture and try to use it against Dr. Radcliffe.

"What the evidence in this case has shown is that Vincent Gillespie was a very disturbed man. He was producing child pornography with the victims in this case, and as a result, he clearly had a motivation to commit the homicides. The evidence presented to the jury did establish that Dr. Radcliffe helped Mr. Gillespie produce the Soma app that ultimately resulted in the deaths of four youths. It was an unfortunate mistake born of Dr. Radcliffe's helpful nature. He had known and worked with Vincent Gillespie for years, so when he needed help Dr. Radcliffe didn't hesitate. Had Dr. Radcliffe understood the full scope of what was transpiring, I think the situation would have turned out differently."

Cooper paused as a murmur broke out in the courtroom. Jack Foster and Celeste Gonzalez exchanged looks and began shaking their heads in disbelief.

"I would urge this court," Cooper continued, "not to throw away this man's life work over one mistake. Dr. Radcliffe has been a respected member of this community for many years and has done good work with the youth, including here in this courthouse. This is a man who has no criminal history and who has devoted his life to helping others. I would urge the court to impose a concurrent prison term to hold Dr. Radcliffe accountable for his role while also acknowledging the mark he has made — and can continue to make — upon this community."

"Thank you," Judge Perry said. "Is there anything else from the defense?"

"Your honor, I believe Dr. Radcliffe would like to make a statement," Cooper said. "I would like to note for the record that I have advised him against doing so, but Dr. Radcliffe has insisted."

"Oh? Is that correct, sir?" Judge Perry asked.

"Yes, your honor," Radcliffe said.

"Very well, proceed."

Radcliffe ran a hand through his salt-and-pepper hair and smoothed out the paper containing his speech. He scanned the parties standing at the front of the courtroom before beginning. As he spoke, the creases on his forehead rose and fell like ocean waves.

"I have spent a lifetime working to better the lives of those in this community," Radcliffe said. "It has been my life's honor to help those who are less fortunate than myself. In a great many cases, I have been able to markedly improve the lives of my patients. People with crippling psychological ailments have been able to turn their lives around and make something of themselves. Such instances are why I got into the field in the first place.

"Unfortunately, I have not been able to save everybody. One such unfortunate case was Vincent Gillespie. I worked with Vince for years, and on a few occasions, I thought we were close to making a breakthrough. But it seemed like every time we took a step forward he would slip back two steps. He was neurotic and had a case of impulse control disorder. I believe he had a sexual compulsion. He was compelled to act out his fantasies — particularly his homosexual fantasies — with gay people such as Justin Gonzalez."

Radcliffe paused for effect and smirked at Celeste Gonzalez. The color drained from her face and her jaw dropped. Celeste's eyes watered up and she groped at the tiny golden cross hanging around her neck. She had been so careful to protect Justin. She could have called the police and stopped the abuse. But she didn't because she was mortified about how it might affect him.

Now Radcliffe had outed Justin in front of a packed courtroom. The whole world would now know the secret Justin died to protect.

What was worse, Radcliffe seemed to be suggesting that Justin wanted it — that he wasn't a victim at all but a willing participant in a perverse pornographic operation.

Phillips immediately objected to the characterization, and Judge Perry warned Radcliffe against denigrating the victims.

But by that time, Celeste was already running down the marble stairs of the courthouse, dark streaks of mascara riding down teardrop streams flowing over her flushed cheeks.

◆ ◆ ◆

Radcliffe watched her go with a contemptuous sneer on his face that did not go unnoticed by Judge Perry. The judge pounded his gavel on the bench to restore order among the murmuring, gossiping onlookers, until at last the commotion had settled. He laid the gavel down next to the sounding block and turned his attention to Radcliffe.

"Sir, I will not tolerate that kind of behavior in my courtroom," Judge Perry said.

Radcliffe assumed a clinical air and offered his apologies.

"Your honor, I did not mean to offend anybody ..." he began.

"Save it," Judge Perry interjected. "I've been on this bench long enough to know passive-aggressive behavior when I see it. Try a stunt like that once more and I will hold you in contempt of court."

"Yes, your honor," Radcliffe said. "I apologize. May I please finish?"

"I think I've heard enough," Judge Perry said, turning to Cooper. "Does the defense have anything else to offer?"

Cooper turned and briefly consulted with Radcliffe, then looked to the gallery. A woman who looked to be in her sixties stood up in the front row and waved. Cooper gestured for her to approach, and the woman walked uncertainly to the front of the courtroom. She had graying brown hair and wore a Navy blue ankle skirt with a light blouse and a pearl necklace. Cooper put a hand on her shoulder and leaned close to one ear. After a moment, the woman nodded and then stepped forward to the bench.

"Can you please identify yourself for the record?" Cooper asked.

"My name is Elizabeth Radcliffe. I'm Dr. Radcliffe's wife."

"And do you have a statement you would like to make on his behalf?"

"I do," she said. "I have known Marvin for thirty-six years. During that time, he has been my partner, my travel companion, and my soulmate. We have visited far-off lands and had our ups and downs, as all couples do. He was always there for me. But not just me. He was also there for his community. Whether it was serving on the board of trustees for the community college or helping troubled youths here at the courthouse, he was always willing to invest his time to better this community. That's what everybody always thought. That's what I always thought."

For a brief instant, she stumbled for words. Radcliffe turned his head slightly, raising an eyebrow as if questioning where his wife was going with her statement. She continued on, ignoring her husband's gaze.

"Then one day, I went into his study looking for him," Elizabeth said. "He was gone, but his computer was still turned on. I went over to put it on sleep mode when something caught my eye. It was a file called 'Soma.' It just seemed unusual and got me thinking that I didn't really know all that much about what Marvin was working on. I knew he was working on this case or that one, but I didn't know what exactly he was up to all those long hours at work. So I opened the folder ..."

Her voice briefly trailed off and Radcliffe tried cutting her off.

"Not another word," Judge Perry said, stopping Radcliffe mid-syllable.

"I can't even describe what I saw," Elizabeth said. "It was awful. Like something out of a nightmare. The day I found it, I just couldn't stop thinking about those poor children. I was up all that night, crying and thinking about those poor children. But I'm ashamed to say I never said anything about what I saw. Not even to Marvin. I guess I thought if I just ignored it, things could continue like normal.

"The day Marvin was arrested, he came storming in around lunchtime, asking if a reporter had called the house," she said. "I told him no and he seemed relieved. He ran into the study and started collecting all of his computer stuff. I remember watching him and knowing right away what was going on. I didn't even have to ask. He told me to give him a ride, and he guided me to a spot up near Larksville Mountain. He took the stuff into the woods and came back to the car a little while later without it. He didn't say a word.

"I finally asked him what was going on to see what he would say. He mumbled something about his computer being a piece of you-know-what. He couldn't even look me in the eye when he said it."

People in the courtroom gallery sat in stunned silence for a moment as they digested the words. Radcliffe shifted his gaze from his wife to his loafers. His wife — his one remaining ally in life — had defected.

"Mrs. Radcliffe, am I to understand that you were the source of this tip regarding the location of the computer?" Judge Perry asked.

James Halpin

"I was," Elizabeth said, holding her head high despite her flushing cheeks. "For a long time, I struggled with reconciling the loving husband I knew with the monster who would keep such things on his computer. But sitting in court here today, I know now, for certain, that they are the same person. I have never before seen such a cold heart as the one I witnessed today. So before he is sentenced, I just wanted to let you know what kind of a person you're dealing with. He fooled me for thirty-six years."

# CHAPTER 29

*Monday, September 2, 2019*
*12:22 p.m.*

A light breeze lifted Daly's sandy brown hair as he squinted in the bright afternoon sunlight radiating from a deep blue sky. In his hands, he carried a bouquet of red roses wrapped in cellophane and a new photo of Lauren.

He gazed across the green cemetery hills and marveled at the neat rows of gravestones protruding from the earth and extending outward in every direction, seeming to go on forever. So much death.

Daly crouched down next to the grave in front of him, a stone placed on a slight downhill slope near a large oak tree that had stood for centuries. The stone read:

*Jessica Thompson Daly*
*Loving Wife and Mother*
*May 12, 1977 ~ Jan. 23, 2004*

Daly placed the roses at the base of the stone, then kissed the tips of his fingers and touched them to it. He stared at the granite slab for a long while in silence before rising to his feet.

"It's over, babe," Daly said. "Judge Perry gave Dr. Radcliffe the max, up to twenty years. He'll be in prison for most or all of the rest of his life."

He took a long pause, scanning the cemetery before continuing.

"I took a lot of shit over this case," he said. "The DA blamed me for tipping Dr. Radcliffe off. I didn't mean to, but I guess I did. I mean, I was just trying to report the story. I needed to learn the truth. I needed to find out what was happening to those kids. I needed ... redemption, I guess. I needed to make amends for what I've done. I know I can never make it up to you. I'm going to have to live with it for the rest of my life. But I just wanted you to know that I'm trying. I'm trying my best to live a good life."

Daly dropped his gaze to his hands. He clutched his knuckles with white-tipped fingers, unsure how to say what he had come to say. Instead, he changed directions.

"Lauren's doing really well. She finished her freshman year at Stanford, and I practically had to drag her back for a visit. She loves it out there, and she's met a guy she really likes. Josh. He writes for the school paper, but apparently, he's going to be an English teacher. Which is good news because I told Lauren she was forbidden to marry a journalist," Daly said, his somber expression giving way to a brief smile.

"She wants me to meet him. I told her maybe I would go out for a visit in the fall. Thanksgiving, maybe. Then I could meet this guy and see what all the fuss is about."

Daly again crouched down and reached out to touch the tombstone, feeling the cold, hard granite and getting no solace. For a moment he looked down and then looked back at the stone.

"I needed to tell you ... I ..." his voice trailed off. He slightly chuckled before continuing. "I don't know why this is so hard. It's been fifteen years. You'd think by now I would be able to get my shit together. I just wanted to tell you that I've met someone. A woman. Her name is Emily, and I like her. It's not too serious yet, but I felt like I needed to tell you before it got serious. I just felt ... weird, like I was cheating or something. I know you'd want me to be happy, but I just feel kind of guilty when I'm with her. So I felt like I needed to come clean and be honest with you. So there. The secret's out.

"Anyway," Daly continued, "I think you'd like her. She really reminds me of you, which is why I like her. And actually, Lauren's meeting her today. So I guess that will be the real test."

Daly reached for the bouquet of roses and pulled a single rose from the dozen, pricking his thumb on a thorn as he did so. He cursed and sucked at the pinhead-sized drop of blood on the tip of his thumb as he stood back up, feeling the blood rush through his numbing legs.

"I know you would understand," he said. "Lauren's been telling me for years that I need to get back in the game. I'm sure you would say the same thing. I just want to make sure you know it doesn't change the way I feel about you. I will always love you."

Daly wiped the hint of a tear from the corner of his eye and began walking. The breeze felt good in the warm afternoon, and he found himself enjoying the walk across the cemetery. He made his way up a path lined with mausoleums and oversize family tombstones, then continued through a sea of uniform rows of granite and marble markers. Midway through one of the rows, near the base of an old maple tree, Daly stopped. For a long minute, he stared at a white marble tombstone. It was his first time seeing it, and it was a hard sight for him to behold. His wary eyes welled up as he took a step forward and laid the single rose at the base of the grave:

*Kelly Duncan*
*Beloved Daughter*
*Taken Too Soon*
*Oct. 17, 1991 ~ Jan. 23, 2004*

"I'm so sorry. I never wanted any of this. I never wanted to hurt you," Daly said, beginning to sob. "I have never stopped thinking about how one stupid decision changed so many lives. It keeps me up nights, thinking about how things could have been different. If I had just not been drinking ... if I'd been a little more patient ... you would still be here. Jessica would still be here. Your father wouldn't be in prison. Both our families would still be families."

Daly took a step back, suddenly conscious of how he looked. He glanced around but saw no one. He wiped his eyes and cleared his throat before continuing.

"I don't know what I expected here," he said, suddenly feeling foolish. "I guess I just wanted to say sorry. I wanted to say I'm sorry for tearing your family apart. I'm sorry for being such a fuck up. I know your father never will, but I hope that wherever you are, you have been able to forgive me for what I did."

◆ ◆ ◆

Smoke from the barbecue rose into the sky in white curling spirals. The smell of grilling chicken filled the warm summer air. Daly stood at the grill, tending the chicken with oversize tongs as Robert Johnson's "Me and the Devil Blues" riffed on the Amazon Echo.

He took a sip from a sweaty glass of iced tea and realized that for the first time in a long while, he felt truly contented. With the trial over, he felt like he could finally move forward and put a dark chapter of his life behind him. Nobody was ever charged with setting the fire, but Daly knew the person to blame was behind bars — at least for the time being. And the insurance money had finally come through, so he'd been able to buy a new house not too far from where he lived before. The house wasn't as big as the one that burned, but with Lauren out of the house, Daly figured he could downsize a little.

Now, he looked across his yellow pine deck and was happy to see Lauren reclining on a lawn chair, engrossed in a conversation with Emily.

Daly had been nervous about their meeting. Lauren had been pushing for him to start dating again, but inside Daly always feared she would resent him for trying to replace her mother. That was a big part of why he never brought anyone else home, and it had taken a lot for him to get past his fear with Emily. But Daly could see that his fear had been misplaced. The two most important women in his life were becoming fast friends.

He turned back to the grill and used a brush to mop the chicken with thick, red barbecue sauce.

"Lauren, could you please grab me a plate?" Daly called out. "This is almost done."

"Sure," she said.

She got off the lounge chair, stepped inside for a minute and emerged with a large platter for the chicken. She carried it over to where Daly stood by the grill while Emily checked her phone.

"Not having a beer?" Lauren asked, handing Daly the platter.

"No. I'm giving it up," Daly said.

"Really?" Lauren said with surprise. "What happened?"

"I just realized I don't need it," he said. "Besides, I need to save the money to pay for your college."

"Ha ha. Well, I'm glad. I think it will be good for you," Lauren said.

"So what do you think about Emily?" Daly asked, his tone growing conspiratorial.

"She's really nice. She seems funny and smart. I like her a lot."

"I'm glad. You know I want you to be comfortable. I don't

want you to think ..."

"That you're replacing Mom?" Lauren cut in.

"Something like that."

"Dad, it's been fifteen years. I'm not a child anymore and I don't think you're trying to replace Mom. I think you're doing what you should be doing — and I know Mom would feel the same," Lauren said.

"Thank you. I'm glad to hear you say that," Daly said, wrapping an arm around her shoulders and giving her a kiss on the forehead.

"Erik?" Emily called from the other side of the deck. She sat forward in her chair and lifted her sunglasses as she squinted to get a better look at her cellphone screen. "You're going to want to see this. Apparently Marvin Radcliffe is dead."

"What?" Daly put the tongs down next to his tea and walked with Lauren over to Emily.

"Jennifer Talmadge just posted a story to the Observer's website," Emily said, handing Daly her phone.

Daly put an arm around Lauren and held the phone between them so they could read the article.

> WILKES-BARRE — The Kingston psychiatrist billed as the "suicide doctor" after being convicted of pressuring four teens to kill themselves was found dead at the Luzerne County Correctional Facility on Monday morning.
>
> Marvin G. Radcliffe, 57, was found hanging in his cell around 4:30 a.m., Warden Tim Watson said.
>
> "Correctional officers cut him down and attempted to perform life-saving measures," Watson said. "Unfortunately, they were unable to revive him."
>
> Radcliffe was pronounced dead at Wilkes-Barre

*General Hospital at 5:23 a.m., he said.*

*The psychiatrist had been alone in his cell at the time of his death and no foul play is suspected, Watson said.*

*Radcliffe was convicted at trial last month of involuntary manslaughter over the deaths of four teens who killed themselves last year. On Friday, he was sentenced to serve up to 20 years in prison for the crimes.*

*Prosecutors say he and substitute teacher Vincent P. Gillespie, 28, were using the teens to produce child pornography and that they then convinced them to commit suicide to avoid detection.*

*That effort involved counseling sessions by Radcliffe as well as the creation of a white-noise app called Soma that contained subliminal messages, prosecutors say.*

*Gillespie was killed in a shootout with police in April 2018.*

*The case came to light in part because of the high-profile death of 15-year-old cheerleader Kimberly Foster, who shot herself in a live web video that went viral.*

*Reached for comment Monday morning, her father, Hanover Twp. resident Jack Foster, noted the irony of Radcliffe taking his own life.*

*"I hope that at the end he was going through as much pain and suffering as he put my daughter through," Foster said. "He's a monster, in my book. Anyone who could do what he did to those children deserves a terrible death. I hope it hurt a lot, and now he can rot in hell."*

— 30 —

# ACKNOWLEDGMENTS

As I came to find out, writing a novel in between working and taking care of the kids and walking the dogs and maintaining a house can be a daunting task. This novel took me countless hours spread out over a year and a half, and without my loving wife Jamie I never would have been able to finish it. So I have to express my profound thanks to her for distracting our sons at intervals and helping me find the time to make this happen. Being an author has been a dream of mine forever, and I absolutely could not have done it without her.

Throughout this process, I learned that writing a work of fiction is fraught with pitfalls. Without having reality as a guide, it's all too easy to muddle the story. So I would also like to thank all the people who helped me find and fix issues ranging from plot inconsistencies and story organization to word choice and minor typos.

My mother and father, Janette and James P. Halpin Jr., were instrumental in helping with the formidable task of editing my manuscript. Of course, their help goes back a few decades and I would be remiss not to say how appreciative of all the love and support they've given me over the years, despite me often being a major pain in the ass.

I'd also like to thank my Gram, otherwise known as Roberta Holmes, for her support through the years and for helping me polish up this book. I'm so grateful she was able to give this novel a read and help to catch my many typos — especially knowing it was a bit gruesome for her tastes.

My wife's good friend Kendra Diehl Koontz was also an enormous help and provided many valuable insights during the editing process. She helped me realize that even the slightest roll of the eyes can make a difference.

Finally, I'd like to thank veteran homicide prosecutor Jarrett J. Ferentino, a man who knows something about putting away real-life bad guys. Over the years, he's worked to put away some of Luzerne County's most notorious killers, so I feel extremely grateful that he was able to take the time to help me with the legal details in this book. Any errors in the legal aspects of this story are mine and mine alone.

# ABOUT THE AUTHOR

James Halpin is an author and reporter who has worked as a journalist for more than a decade. He is a graduate of the University of Alaska Anchorage and has worked at several daily newspapers, mostly covering crime and courts. Prior to becoming a journalist, Halpin served in the U.S. Marine Corps in Okinawa, Japan, and at Camp Lejeune, N.C. He resides in Mountain Top, Pa., with his wife and two children.

.

52112718R00170

Made in the USA
Middletown, DE
07 July 2019